PAUL CONNOLLY was born and
and his first memory is hearing
age of five. After studying Biolog
he worked for many years as a te
puter industry, the foundation of

Paul sings bass with award-winning a cappella group
The Royal Harmonics, which provided the inspiration for
his debut novel, *The Fifth Voice*. He lives in Berkshire, visits
Lundy Island as often as possible, supports Everton FC, and
has a grown-up daughter.

For more information, or to get in touch with Paul,
please visit www.paulconnollyauthor.com.

The Fifth Voice

PAUL CONNOLLY

SilverWood

Published in 2014 by SilverWood Books

SilverWood Books
30 Queen Charlotte Street, Bristol, BS1 4HJ
www.silverwoodbooks.co.uk

ISBN 978-1-78132-119-5 (paperback)
ISBN 978-1-78132-147-8 (ebook)

British Library Cataloguing in Publication Data
A CIP catalogue record for this book is available from the British Library

Set in ITC New Baskerville by SilverWood Books
Printed on responsibly sourced paper

For George and Teresa
in loving memory

Acknowledgements

Many thanks to Paul Jones, Heather Adams, and Martin Ouvry for their invaluable reviews at various draft stages of the book. Also Sara Taylor, the first person to read my early efforts.

Singing with The Royal Harmonics, and being part of the British barbershop and a cappella community, inspired me to write the book, for which I am most grateful.

I also drew much inspiration from my beloved Lundy Island, where I wrote the book. The island also provides the location for two of the chapters.

Love and thanks to friends and family for their continued interest and encouragement, and in particular my daughter, Georgina.

Part One

The Road to Birmingham

One

Vince felt the sweat on his back cool momentarily as the airstream from the rickety floor-standing fan passed by, and he plucked at the thin cotton fabric of his shirt to detach it from his skin. At the same time, a darting pain ran the length of his left leg, causing him to get up from his desk and walk unsteadily to the nearest open window. Two questions crossed his mind. Would this first hot day of late spring, like so many in recent years, prove to be an impostor? And how long would it be before he was confined to a wheelchair?

For some reason he found himself caring more about the prospect of a decent spell of weather than about the recent tell-tale decline in his physical condition, but both thoughts served as a distraction from the tedium of compiling yet another management report for the board of Bowman-Lamy. These days, working in Human Resources was much more about reporting upstairs than helping the employees, and it was beginning to get him down.

If it wasn't for recruitment – the part of the job that still had some soul – Vince suspected that he'd have cashed in his chips by now. However, he enjoyed the opportunity to vet new blood, and he prided himself on always being able to sift out the best candidates: give him a haystack and he'd find the needle. And so it was with Danny Brennan.

In the latest round of recruitment, Vince had seen over fifty applications for the role of Senior Systems Analyst before Danny's CV emerged from the stack, saying *hire me*. He had all the key ingredients – solid academics, and an impressive achievement record with several blue chips

– but what clinched it was the second interview, when the trick was to find out more about the person behind the CV. It was immediately evident that Danny was the most eloquent and socially adept candidate so far, and discovering that he didn't speak in technobabble, unlike most of the others, counted in spades. However, it was his response to the *tell me more about yourself* question that sealed the deal for Vince. Danny spoke about his love of, and eclectic taste in, music with a passion that matched his own. Here was a kindred spirit. All it needed was a final conference with the IT Director and that was that. Danny got the job.

Vince saw Danny several times during his first couple of weeks with Bowman-Lamy, as they worked through the formalities of Danny's induction to the firm. And today, the hottest day of the year, during which the office air-conditioning system had breathed its last, Vince suggested a drink after work. It was about time he found a decent drinking buddy.

Vince's favourite pub was unusually busy, as builders in vest tops and cut-off jeans quenched their thirsts alongside office workers, ties loosened and sleeves rolled up. The common topic of conversation was the upturn in the weather.

It seemed to Danny that Vince knew everyone. As they walked through the bar, he stopped to shake hands with, or embrace, several people, saving his warmest greetings for the female drinkers, all of whom seemed delighted to see him.

'Bit of a ladies' man, I see?' said Danny, as they sat down with their pints.

'East Berkshire's answer to George Clooney, that's me,' said Vince. 'It's the chiselled good looks and the easy charm that do it.' Only the twinkle in his eye told Danny that Vince was being just a little facetious.

In turn, Vince found himself weighing up Danny. He

looked more like a distance runner than someone who enjoyed a few beers, he thought (medium height, toned and lean, and with a hungry look in his eye). *Could he handle a few beers?*

They started chatting and, after ten minutes of work talk, Vince steered the conversation towards music (he'd been looking forward to this). Before long they were discussing the guitar technique of Frank Zappa, the lyrics of Ray Davies, and their favourite albums of all time. And an hour and three pints later, the conversation started to lose a little of its intellectual sparkle, descending into a game of musical *Top Trumps*.

'I don't care how many bloody copies it sold,' said Vince, getting agitated, 'there's no way that *Sgt. Pepper* is a better album than *Astral Weeks!* You really believe that a pile of over-contrived, trippy nonsense is more worthy than one of the most breathtakingly beautiful albums ever made? Oh, please, just get the beers in...and while you're at the bar, consider your answer to the big one very carefully. What's *the* best album ever made and why?'

Danny smiled, picked up two empty pint glasses, then grimaced as he struggled to extricate his legs from between a bench seat and a battered wooden table.

'You're not getting away with that ridiculous Beatles slur. And remind me, why did we have to come to this dump?'

Vince sighed.

'It's called a proper pub. Look around. Original wood panelling...the ceiling still beautifully nicotine coloured years after the smoking ban...old Eddie in the corner has been there since his wife died in 1983...and the barmaid is built like...well, like a barmaid should. Not to mention seven real ales. Seven!'

'Same again, Vince? Pint of lager? Seven real ales, my arse.'

'Ah, you're a breath of fresh air. Honestly, the other

sods in the office are no fun at all. If you can get them to the pub after work, it's half a shandy, bring back hanging, and the demise of index-linked pensions.'

'Honestly, you're wasted in HR,' said Danny.

'Funny you should say that,' said Vince, gesticulating to the barmaid as Danny approached the bar. He had intended to introduce Danny to Angie properly, but the pub was far too busy just now, and it could wait for another time.

When he returned with fresh pints, Danny let a packet of crisps and a packet of peanuts drop from his mouth on to the table.

'That was quicker than I thought. I'm sure there were two blokes in front of me.'

'It must be your animal magnetism. I don't think Angie could resist serving you first,' said Vince.

'Very funny. I'm a married man. Happily married.'

'Are you? You kept that quiet.'

'No I didn't. It's on my CV – under *Personal Details*.'
Vince felt a twinge of embarrassment as he quickly ran though Danny's CV in his head, summoning up extracts from *Work Experience, Education,* and *Interests,* but drawing a blank on *Personal Details.*

'Well, blow me. I really must be losing the plot,' said Vince, evidently flustered. 'Anyway, we'll come back to that. So, what's the best album of all time and why?'

'The Beach Boys' *Pet Sounds,* no question. Brian Wilson's creative peak. The sound of a generation. Incredible instrumentation. But most of all, the harmonies. Just wonderful.' Danny's answer was rapid and concise.

'Interesting. Did you know that Paul McCartney cites *Pet Sounds* as the inspiration for *Sgt. Pepper*?' asked Vince, searching for a gap in Danny's knowledge.

'Yes, and as I was saying earlier, *Sgt. Pepper* is, in my opinion, the second best album of all time. So that makes perfect sense, don't you think? Those two albums between them shaped the whole of the rest of pop music. When *Sgt. Pepper* was released, Kenneth Tynan in *The Times* said it was a decisive moment in the history of Western civilization. QED surely,' said Danny, taking a self-congratulatory slug from his pint.

'QED bollocks.'

'And they say the art of debate is dead.'

Vince flashed a bright white smile, and ran a finger along the bristly underside of his square chin.

'So, tell me about your new wife.'

Danny spluttered into his pint.

'You crack me up, you really do. She may be new to you, but Hannah and I have been together nine years, married for five. Ben, our son, is two and a bit.'

'Tell me more,' said Vince.

Danny spoke with pride about Hannah, an ex-equestrian professional, about how she had been one of the top British eventers, and how she would have competed at the London Olympics if it hadn't been for a serious neck and shoulder injury that ended her career. And about Ben, whose vocabulary was growing by the day, who goes to sleep cuddling an old Everton scarf, and who made his heart melt when he first said the words "Love you, Daddy".

Vince latched on to the word "love", steering the conversation back to music.

'Do you know that the word "love" appears sixty-seven times in The Beatles' *All You Need Is Love?*'

'God, you're a mine of useless musical information,' said Danny, amused by Vince's habit of changing topics at the drop of a hat.

'Music is my first love, and it will be my last…' said Vince.

'John Miles, 1976?'

'Damn it, you're good,' said Vince.

'Not quite on a par with you. And what else do you get up to when you're not immersing yourself in music trivia?

Married? Kids? I'm sorry, but I don't have the benefit of having seen your CV,' said Danny.

Vince had to give Danny that one, and he swiped the air with an index finger, as though chalking up another point for his friend.

'No, no. I prefer not to get too attached,' said Vince, shooting a furtive glance towards the bar. 'I'm all for the simple life. The pub, music, and singing occupy most of my social time. Do you sing by any chance, Dan?'

The rapid change of subject again. Danny sipped his pint and thought for a moment.

'Well, I love singing in my own company, but I've never sung to an audience, if that's what you mean. Growing up I always wanted to sing for people, but I never quite conquered the shyness. And it annoys Hannah, funnily enough. She thinks I've got a great voice, and that I'm wasting some sort of talent. And what am I supposed to do about it? Queue up outside the O2 Arena with ten thousand other *X Factor* wannabes? I don't think so. Anyway, tell me about your own singing exploits…'

'Well, I sing tenor with an a cappella chorus. Oh, and you'll love this…up until recently I sang in a barbershop quartet with three other fellas from the chorus.'

Danny laughed.

'*Barbershop?* What, you mean stripy jackets and straw hats?'

'That's *old* hat, mate. Barbershop quartets are cooler than you think these days. Glen, our lead, is a session musician working with loads of top bands. Henry, the bass, is some bigwig in the City, and Neil, the baritone, is fresh out of a music degree at uni. Not a straw hat between us.'

'What happened to the quartet?' asked Danny.

'Glen went off on a world tour with some folk rock outfit and that was that. *C'est la vie.*'

'Still…why barbershop?' said Danny.

'Because the harmonies are the best you'll hear. And you can't knock it if you're a Beach Boys fan. Brian Wilson attributes the success of their early sound to the barbershop harmonies of The Four Freshmen. Come along to chorus rehearsal next week – we've got a few quartets singing, and you'll see for yourself what it's all about. I'll send you an email to remind you.'

'I don't know about that, Vince. Anyway, I must be on my way. *Bloody hell*, is that the time? Must dash, otherwise I'll miss Ben's bedtime,' said Danny, noticing the clock above the bar.

A mobile phone went off, and Vince pointed towards the coat rack.

'I'm guessing that's yours. Who else would have *Sloop John B* as their ring tone, I wonder?'

Danny quickly got to his feet, collected his jacket, fumbled in an inside pocket for his phone, and gave Vince a thumbs-up as he walked towards the door and out into the cool of the evening.

'Hell-o?'

'Hello, is that Danny Brennan?'

'Yes, that's me.'

'This is Emma Grant. Listen, there's no easy way of saying this. But I believe that your wife is having an affair with my husband.'

Henry sat awkwardly, his large frame and long legs engulfing one end of the tiny café table. The place was crammed with City types grabbing takeaway lunches at the counter, or huddling around tables to discuss the morning's business over coffee. Motorcycle couriers flitted in and out, adding a dash of hi-vis colour and a crackle of walkie-talkie static to the general hubbub. Jeffrey sat opposite Henry, his rather smaller frame neatly contained within the available space, his manicured hands joined together in front of him, as though in prayer. Henry had started to explain how he had been let go by his firm earlier that morning, but had paused for a moment. Jeffrey's bright blue eyes were alive with anticipation.

At last, Henry pointed to a Japanese restaurant across the street, in the shadow of the Gherkin (which he always thought looked much more like a fir cone).

'You know, only last Thursday I was sat in that window over there planning my exit strategy – my last three years with the firm. Ha! I did the numbers on the back of a napkin, over a plate of sushi and a glass of sake. I reckoned three more years of this and I'd be able to retire to the yacht in Puerto Banus with enough put by to keep Jenny in Botox and bubbly for the rest of her life.'

'You haven't touched your bacon sandwich,' said Jeffrey. 'Do you mind if I...'

'Be my guest,' said Henry. He planted his elbows on the narrow table and looked momentarily into the palms of his hands before allowing his spindly fingers to cradle the smooth shining dome of his head in a *where did it all go wrong?* kind of gesture. As he did so, the words of Monty Python's *Galaxy Song* whirled around in his head – the bit about feeling very small and insecure.

'So, how did it happen exactly?' asked Jeffrey, his mouth full of soft white bread and sweet greasy bacon.

'A hastily convened and swiftly despatched meeting with the Head of Commodities Trading,' Henry muttered, his hands still cradling his head.

'Come out of there and speak up, will you, Henry?' said Jeffrey, brushing a crumb from the lapel of his expensive designer suit.

Henry brought his hands down to his face, rubbed both eyes with his index fingers, and blinked a few times before focusing on the vision of smugness before him. What was it with Jeffrey? Henry couldn't think of anyone else who enjoyed hearing about other people's misfortunes quite so much.

'Well, the first I heard was on the radio news at six o'clock this morning. The US holding company went into administration overnight. I got to the office at a quarter to eight, and by half past it was all over. A team of security guards arrived on the trading floor, and all of a sudden the biggest commodity around was cardboard boxes...within minutes, everyone was heading for the exit, ferrying their possessions in cardboard boxes.'

'So, where does that leave your *grand* plan then?' asked Jeffrey, with a little too much *schadenfreude* even by his own standards. Henry couldn't help smiling at Jeffrey's insensitivity, which was starting to seem almost comical.

'Well, it's not the end of the world, is it? It's not like I'm headed for skid row just because I've lost my job. It's just the shock. It's never happened to me before. Oh, and thanks for being *so* supportive,' said Henry.

'What do you mean by that?' said Jeffrey, detecting a hint of sarcasm.

'Do you know *Galaxy Song* by Monty Python?' asked Henry, deciding to wrong-foot his friend and wind him up just a little.

'What sort of a question is that? What's that got to do with—'

'Well, I'm learning the song at the moment, and there's this bit about praying that there's intelligent life somewhere out in space because there's bugger all on Earth. It just struck me, listening to you, that there's more than a hint of truth in that,' said Henry, brightening as Jeffrey's expression changed from one of confusion to mild indignation.

'I was only trying to help,' said Jeffrey, getting up from the table, adjusting the half-Windsor knot of his tie in a gesture that seemed to say *whatever*, and turning on his heels. 'Give my regards to Jenny.'

Henry smiled graciously at his friend as he reached into his jacket pocket to pull out a flattish circular object, shiny chrome on one side, black plastic on the other. He held the object black side up and revolved it in his fingers until the symbol *Bb* appeared at the twelve o'clock position. Putting the object to his lips and blowing very gently, Henry hummed in harmony with the emitted note, then started to sing *Galaxy Song* quietly to himself as he got up from the table, nodded to the swarthy guy in the white apron behind the counter, and headed for the bright sunlight of Leadenhall Street.

Neil glanced at the time in the corner of the computer screen, and was amazed to find it was almost seven in the evening. He had been in his room since mid-morning, working on a harmony chart, and he had stopped just twice, once for a quick snack, the other for the bathroom. Time seemed to evaporate when he was arranging. He leant back in his chair, took off his glasses, and squinted at the screen, which was a blur of grey squiggles on a bright white background. Twenty-three with the eyesight of a seventy-three year-old, he thought.

The screen blacked out as the computer went into hibernation, and Neil found himself looking at his own reflection. Had he put on a few pounds since university? He put his glasses back on to check. It looked like a few months of decent eating back at home might have taken its toll.

He glanced up at a framed photo of himself with his brother Robert on the wall above his desk and felt a familiar sadness. How similar they were. Two heads of unkempt black hair, and the signature family features: the sharpness of the nose, the fullness of the lips, and, of course, those big brown eyes. Neil's thoughts started to drift back to another time.

'Neil…dinner's ready, darling,' came his mother's voice

from the foot of the stairs, causing him to return from his daydream.

'Okay, okay…' Neil shouted back with a little irritation.

The next voice was his father's. 'We're waiting!' he boomed.

Neil got up and closed the lid of the laptop.

Downstairs in the dining room, Margaret was placing several bone china serving dishes on to a pristinely dressed table: crisp white cloth, shining silver, crystal glass, and a vase of freshly cut flowers at its centre. She moved with a nimbleness and grace that defied her years.

George was deep-mining the *Financial Times* for the umpteenth time that day, with a gin and tonic for company. He glanced over the top of his half-rimmed glasses as Neil entered the room and breathed a sigh that betrayed a combination of exasperation and distain.

'Busy day, Neil?'

Neil knew what was coming, and decided to get his retaliation in first.

'Quite busy, thanks. I had Obama's people on the phone this morning, badgering me about the Middle East crisis again. Jacket potato for lunch, then a spot of open heart surgery in the afternoon. You?' Neil sat down, and waited for the return volley.

'Oh, the usual, you know. Doing an honest day's work, keeping the wheels of industry turning…keeping a roof over *your* head.'

It had been a few days since his father had been quite so boringly confrontational, so Neil decided not to back down.

'Not to mention visiting your accountant Mr Coral and draining Balls Brothers of vintage Merlot at lunchtime, eh, Father?'

Margaret reappeared from the kitchen.

'Will you two give it a rest for just five minutes!' she snapped, as she slammed a steaming bowl of new potatoes on to the table. 'All you two ever do is snipe at each other. Now can we have some peace while we eat?'

George folded his newspaper, drained his gin glass, and reached for the open bottle of red in front of him.

'You partaking, dear? Calm the nerves?' he asked as he dispensed a small measure for Margaret and a rather larger one for himself. He then tipped the neck of the bottle in Neil's direction, raising his eyebrows in truce as he did so.

'Not for me, thanks. I'm not drinking at the moment,' said Neil.

'Keeping your strength up for some young lady, eh?' said George.

'Nope. Just keeping my voice in good nick. There's a scratch quartet session at rehearsals on Wednesday evening.'

'Barbershop, I might have guessed. And what, prey, is a *scratch* quartet?'

'What it says. A quartet – *four singers?* – put together from scratch. They may never have sung together before. That's the fun of it.'

'Ah, and there was I thinking it meant the same as a scratch golfer – you know, someone who's actually good at something.'

'*Have you ever even heard me sing in quartet?*' Neil fired back sharply.

'No, and I don't think I've ever seen you do a decent day's work either. Pass the French beans would you, dear?' said George.

Two

Hannah pressed the tip of her nose against the window pane, slid her hands into the back pockets of her skin-tight jeans, and raised her heels so that she could just see over the top of the privet hedge on tip-toe. If Danny had caught his usual train she'd be able to spot him in the distance by now.

'Daddy home!' came Ben's voice from behind her.

'Not yet, darling.'

It had been an average kind of day. Dropping Ben at nursery, half a day at the library, coffee with her mum in town, picking up the things for dinner, and then back for Ben. No, not average, come to think of it. Someone at the library had taken out a book on show jumping that had a picture of Hannah with *Buena Vista*, her best horse, in full flight on the cover. Not that the customer recognised her, and Hannah couldn't quite bring herself to point out the lady's oversight. Hannah wondered what else she could tell Danny about over dinner. Ben's latest creation, a car made out of an egg carton, was in pride of place in the centre of the dining table, and he could see that for himself when they sat down. Where was he?

'Come on, matey,' said Hannah, prising Ben away from *Scooby Doo*. 'Time for your bath, then into your jim-jams before Daddy's home.'

'I want Daddy,' said Ben. As luck would have it, the cartoon credits started to roll, and Ben gave in to Hannah's bath-time request with a minimum of fuss. He was starting to yawn.

An hour later, and still no Danny. Not even a phone call.

Hannah had placated Ben by reading his favourite bedtime story twice, and he had dropped off just before the giraffe made friends with the hippopotamus for the second time that evening. *Where the hell is he? This is so unlike him.* Hannah tied back her long blonde hair tight against her head – usually a sign that she was getting anxious about something – and took off her make-up. She was in no mood for staying made-up if he didn't have the decency to call and explain himself.

Half an hour later, she heard rapid footsteps come to a halt outside, then the front door open and close quietly. Seconds passed by. Hannah went into the hallway to find Danny standing with his back to the wall, breathing heavily.

'My God, what's wrong with you? What's happened, Danny? Where have you been? Ben's asleep. He's been asking for you, but he was too tired. *Danny! Will you just say something…*'

Danny brushed past his wife, his thin face pallid, his eyes glazed and unseeing, a line of sweat visible across his top lip.

'You're scaring me, Danny. You look awful. *Are you alrig*—' said Hannah, her voice cracking slightly.

'I've been running. And throwing up. I need to see Ben.'

'Don't disturb him. He's…'

Hannah's voice tailed off as Danny's eyes suddenly came alive with a fiery glint. He started slowly climbing the stairs, Hannah following nervously behind him.

Ben's bedroom door was ajar, a yellowish nightlight glow seeping out on to the landing. Danny gently pushed at the door, took a step inside, and listened for his son's somnolent breathing pattern. He stepped towards the bed without making a sound, and crouched so that his head was level with his son's. The frayed edge of a blue-and-white scarf wafted gently in rhythm as Ben breathed peacefully, deep in sleep. Danny tucked the edge of the scarf beneath the pillow, kissed Ben softly on the forehead, and retreated, Hannah backing out ahead of him.

'*What's wrong, Danny?*' said Hannah as they descended the stairs, her voice reduced to an anxious whisper.

They entered the living room. Danny closed the door behind them and turned to Hannah.

'How many times have I missed Ben's bedtime, do you suppose?'

'I don't know...not often. That's why I'm worried. And *look* at you...'

'Well, this is the fifth time in two years. There was the time of the train strike, the two nights I had to be at a conference in Brussels, and the stag party I couldn't say no to, seeing as I was the best man.'

'And now this evening. Danny, what's happened...are you ill?'

'*Sick* would be the better word. Sick to the core.'

Hannah reached out her arms towards Danny, whose eyes had glazed over again, his gaze fixed on a point somewhere beyond Hannah's right shoulder.

'*Please tell me what's wrong, love,*' she said at last.

Danny flinched at the warmth in Hannah's voice, then switched his gaze directly into his wife's eyes for the first time.

'I had a phone call from a woman who said you are having an affair with her husband.' His voice was weak but he pronounced each word carefully.

Hannah's arms fell to her sides and her mouth fell open without a sound. A single tear welled in Danny's right eye and slowly ran the length of his cheek.

Hannah's eyes returned to Danny's.

'*Listen to me.* This can only be a cruel practical joke. Who *is* this woman who called you? Who put her up to this? Is this one of your silly mates getting his own back for something? Or is it some crazy infatuated bitch who's trying to come between us? What type of person would do such a thing, Dan—'

'It was Emma Grant. She found a birthday card in Ian's briefcase, which she assures me is from you.'

'What! She finds a birthday card to her husband from a friend and that somehow means they're having an affair? *Don't be so ridic*—'

'Save it, Hannah. She insisted on reading me the message inside the card. I can remember it word-for-word if you'd like me to repeat it. But I can't promise I won't be sick again.'

'Sweeeet!'

Henry purred as he followed the line of his ball, soaring arrow straight down the middle of the sun-dappled fairway, then started singing the bass line to *On a Wonderful Day Like Today*.

Jeffrey shuffled unconvincingly to the tee, stooping to place his ball.

'You're certainly chipper for a man who's just lost the goose that laid the golden egg,' he said.

'It's a beautiful day, Jeffrey. And what's all this guff about geese and golden eggs? I take it you're referring to me losing my job?'

'Well, yes, I was,' said Jeffrey, a bit sheepishly.

'You make it sound like I haven't *earned* my living! I've put my neck on the line for that firm day-in, day-out for more years than I care to remember. I've earned every penny, matey. Unlike some part-timers I could mention. Oh, bad luck…'

Jeffrey's ball came to rest in a clump of trees to the right of the fairway.

'So, how did Jenny take the news?' asked Jeffrey.

'She was out most of the day being pampered at the spa. *Pampered?* What's all that about? Anyway, her phone had been switched off, so she hadn't picked up my messages, and was oblivious to the whole thing until she saw me in the evening. I have to say her initial reaction was interesting.'

'How so?'

'A sort of inability to take it on board. No real feeling for the gravity of the situation. No feeling at all really. No "poor darling" or "we'll get through this" or anything even approaching sympathy or concern. It was like she'd been pampered into an emotional coma. And her face seemed fixed in an inane grin, but then I realised it was just a fresh batch of Botox. Her first words were "but this doesn't affect you of course, does it?" I didn't know whether to laugh or cry. I had to sit her down and explain it to her like you would a small child. *Lost – my – job. Out – of – work. Bank – ing – Cri – sis.*'

'She's not normally slow on the uptake, old Jen,' said Jeffrey.

'Don't let her hear you say *old* Jen, or she'll have your guts for garters. But you're right, an unusual reaction to say the least. I think maybe she just didn't want to hear what I was telling her and blanked it.'

Henry stopped three yards from his ball, propped his bag on the fairway, took out a nine iron, and assumed the position.

'It took her a couple of hours and most of a bottle of Cristal for it to sink in, and then there it was. A rather unpalatable mixture of anger and self-pity. A bit of an eye-opener, I have to say.'

Henry took a delicate swing at the ball, which arced high into the pale blue, cloudless sky, landing on the edge of the green. Jeffrey set off towards the clump of trees.

Two shots later Jeffrey caught up with Henry, who was speaking into his mobile phone. He finished the call and turned to his friend.

'That's a pity. There was a rumour that a Japanese bank

was keen to soak up our redundant staff, but turns out that's all it was. A rumour. Never mind. Time for a lesson in the short game, I think, Jeffrey. Observe.'

'You shouldn't be using your mobile on the course, you know. I hope it was on silent at the very least, and it's a good job there's no one around to report us,' said Jeffrey.

'Well, not quite no one. I did spot José Maria Olazabal over by that bush a moment ago. I think he's checking me out for a Ryder Cup place, but I've probably blown it now on the grounds of poor etiquette,' said Henry, his twenty-yard putt stopping eighteen inches from the hole.

'Ha bloody ha. So, you say Jenny was all angry and self-pitying?' said Jeffrey.

'Well, all she could do was think about the impact on herself. Not *us*, the marital partnership so to speak, but herself. I'm sure something will turn up soon, so I'm hoping we won't take a financial hit, but to listen to Jenny you'd think we were one step away from the poor house. "But I've just ordered my new SLK," she says. "I'm not giving up my weekend breaks at the Abbey," she says. "What will Laura and Clive think?" she says. *Holy shit*, I say.'

Henry's ball stopped agonisingly close to the hole.

'Tap it in, would you Henry? I fancy my chances of levelling this one,' said Jeffrey.

Jeffrey addressed his ball with a flourish and holed out from twenty-five yards.

'Now *that*, my friend, is a lesson in the short game.'

Margaret had been meaning to take Neil shopping for new clothes for some time, but she knew that he'd rail against the idea. However, she couldn't allow him to continue slouching around in the same jeans and T-shirts for much longer, and so she disguised the purpose of the trip as an opportunity for them to catch up (it had been a while since they had talked properly) while Margaret shopped for new leotards and tights. She ran a senior citizens' ballet class in the village, and exercised every day, and it was surprising how quickly fitness gear started to look tired. In any case, Margaret knew that once they were amongst the shops, Neil would relent and try on a few new things, if only to please her.

After two hours' walking in and out of department stores and sports shops, and with mission accomplished, Margaret called a halt to the shopping.

'There's nothing like a bit of retail therapy, but I think we're just about done. Thanks for carrying the bags, darling. Let's stop in here and have a coffee.'

Margaret steered her son by the arm towards the entrance of a small Italian restaurant, gathered the shopping bags from him and made for the empty table in the window.

'Large cappuccino darling, would you? Lots of chocolate on top. And a couple of amaretti. Lovely.'

When Neil returned carrying a loaded tray, Margaret was reaching beneath the table massaging her stockinged feet.

'My bunions are playing up,' she said.

Neil unloaded the tray.

'One cappuccino, lots of chocolate on top. Two amaretti. One espresso grande, one bottle of acqua frizzante, one slice of Torta di Ricotta. *Voilà!*'

'I think that should be *Ecco!*, don't you darling? I mean, this is an Italian establishment, not French.'

'Ever the pedant, Mother.'

Margaret smiled.

'Do you remember that time your father accused you of being a pedant over some musical reference or other, and what he actually called you was a *pendant!* How I laughed!'

'I can't remember finding it too funny at the time. Pathetic, more like.'

'No, well, you two don't exactly share a sense of humour these days. And, honestly darling, I'm growing tired of the constant bickering between you. More than that, I'm saddened by the way your relationship with your father has deteriorated these last few years.'

'You say that as if I can do something about it,' said Neil, taking a sip of espresso and wincing slightly.

'Well, you *can* do your bit, darling. Don't rise to his bait, and don't goad him so.'

'Mother, I have had nothing but grief from Father since…well, since…Robert…'

Margaret turned her head to look out through the window, and lowered her voice.

'Grief is exactly what it is, darling. Lord knows I have grieved. When a mother loses a child, it's not something you ever get over. Losing Robert was devastating for us all, but we all react differently. Your father has become…'

'Bitter? Yes, well, he's turned his bitterness on me – the son he still has, whose inadequacies constantly remind him of the brilliance of the son he lost.'

'Now darling, that's harsh – on both of you. What inadequacies? What reminders?'

'Oh Mother, it's obvious. Nothing I ever do is good enough. When I graduated last year he hardly said a word. Why? Because in his eyes a 2:1 in music from Manchester is an insult compared to a first in medicine from Caius Cambridge. And you'd think I'm the only graduate not to be able to get a job the way he goes on. He makes out like I'm some sort of blood-sucking leech.'

'Tautology, darling. Isn't that what leeches do? No need for the compound adjective really,' said Margaret.

'Mother! How can you take this so lightly? You… *pedant*!'

They laughed together, and Margaret placed her hand affectionately on top of her son's.

'Look, darling, I'm not taking it lightly at all. It's just that your father needs...'

Neil withdrew his hand.

'There you go again! You keep seeing this from his point of view. But how do you think I feel? How do you think *I've* coped since Robert died? I looked up to him, and I wanted to be just like him all my life. I realise that you can't be exactly like someone else, you can only be yourself. But Father has never seen it that way, and me not living up to Robert's achievements is just one huge, unforgiveable disappointment. And his complete refusal to acknowledge that I'm gay just takes the biscuit.'

Margaret was gazing absently into the middle distance.

'Oh sure, take one,' she said faintly, pushing the plate of amaretti in Neil's direction.

Three

'On the risers, gentlemen! Quickly, please. We've a lot to get through this evening!'

Vince waved his arms in a shooing motion as forty-five men of various shapes, sizes and ages assembled slowly on to a set of stage steps arranged along one side of a cosy, red plush function room.

'Colin, Barry...if you could just put your pints down and join us? Thank you. Can someone put the bar shutters up please? There'll be plenty of time for that later. Thank you, gentlemen, and welcome to Maidenhead A Cappella's regular Wednesday night rehearsal. But this is no ordinary rehearsal night. Oh no! Because in the second half we'll be having a scratch quartet session, so all you budding quartet singers can show us what you've got,' said Vince.

Someone on the risers made a crude comment, raising a few laughs.

'Excuse me, I do the jokes around here,' said Vince. 'Now, where was I? Ah yes...for the scratch quartet session, we're delighted to be joined by no less than six guests this evening. So, please welcome John, Vic and Allan from the Wycombe Barbershop Club...our old friend Joe Jevons, who sang baritone in the 2002 silver-medal quartet The Allegro Joes...Jimmy Stevens over there, who we booted out last year but keeps turning up like a bad penny...and, all the way from the US of A...the only Berkshire boy ever to win an international quartet gold medal, the legendary Mr Cliff "Tonsils" Thompson!'

Vince's introductions were greeted with rapturous

applause, then he noticed someone else quietly entering the room. He gestured towards the door.

'Come in, come in...gentlemen, will you also please welcome my friend Danny Brennan...take a seat, fantastic you could make it. Danny's come along to find out what barbershop is all about. Okay, on with the show, and the best of order for your very own chorus director...Mr James Pinter!'

James Pinter, an imposing figure at six foot four and nineteen stone, stepped forward as Vince took his place on the risers.

'Thank you, Mr Chairman. Good evening, chaps. What a great turn-out – even Ken's here, everybody! Now, try to keep focused, Ken. No doing the crossword while the rest of us are trying to sing, okay? So, how about a little vocal warm-up? Blow a G please, and give me an *ah* vowel at the threshold of sound...no glottal attacks, no restriction in the throat, big open space in the mouth, keep it all relaxed, breathe, and...'

'Danny, good to see you! I didn't think you'd be able to make it...did you get a pass from the missus?' said Vince.

Danny managed a thin smile.

'Kind of, kind of. I needed to get out for an evening, and your email yesterday reminded me...'

'So, what do you think of it so far?'

'Well, for a start, you didn't tell me you were the club chairman,' said Danny, his smile widening.

'No matter, no matter...what about the singing?' said Vince.

'Well, I'm a bit gobsmacked if I'm honest. I didn't know what to expect when I walked in, but when you guys started to sing I was, well, blown away. The harmonies are just incredible, really.'

'Great stuff! So you've had your first taste of a barbershop chorus in action, and after the break you'll get to hear some quartets. That's really the heart of it – four blokes harmonising, no hiding place. Fancy having a go?'

'What? You must be joking! How could I possibly, Vin—'

'You can do it, mate, trust me. I had a dig around for a Beach Boys arrangement we used to sing in my old quartet. You know *In My Room*, don't you?'

'Well, yes, but—'

'Great. Just hang on a minute while I find Neil and Henry…'

'Hold on, let's not get carried away here…Vince…!'

Danny watched as Vince got up stiffly from his chair and walked between huddles of men, stopping here and there to speak briefly to some of them. Danny noticed that Vince was walking with a distinct limp and was wondering what it might be when he felt a sudden gentle tapping on his upper arm. He turned round to see the soft, welcoming face of a white-haired lady in her late sixties.

'Hello, Danny is it? My name's Lizzy. I help out around here. Taking photos, organising this and that. Would you like to sign our visitors' book?'

Lizzy passed Danny a faux leather album and a pen.

'Sure. So are you kind of a barbershop groupie, then?' said Danny, raising an impish eyebrow.

'Oh definitely! And you wouldn't believe how wild it can get around here. At least two of the guys have had to have pacemakers fitted. Thanks, Danny. Ah, here comes young Vincent…see you later.'

'You've met Lizzy then, I see. Good stuff. Now, let me introduce you…Guys, meet Danny…Danny, this is Henry, bass, and this is Neil, baritone. We're all set for *In My Room* – we've just had a look at the sheet music again and we're fine with the harmony parts; there's nothing complicated about the arrangement. Let's find a space somewhere for a quick run-through.'

Vince took Danny by the arm and led the group of four

through the exit door of the function room, through the members' bar, and out into the entrance lobby.

'This stairwell will do just fine,' said Vince.

'Vince, listen, I—'

Danny made a feeble attempt to bring a halt to proceedings, but Vince was in full flow.

'Dan, you'll thank me for this later. Now, Neil, can you blow a B please? So, Danny, just take your time and start singing the melody in that key, okay? Just as you would if you were singing along to the Beach Boys. This tempo... *There's a world where I can go...*'

Danny closed his eyes, took a deep breath, and started singing. He felt Vince, Henry and Neil move in closer as they started singing the harmony parts. Danny's eyes opened wide with surprise as he heard his voice blending with theirs, and he felt Vince place a reassuring hand on his right shoulder.

James Pinter rose to his feet, applauding.

'Thank you, lads. Another big hand for Vic, Joe, Colin, and of course Cliff...tremendous. And now for our final quartet of the evening...a scratch quartet with a difference. Henry, Vince and Neil are singing with one of our guests – Vince's friend Danny – who, I am reliably informed, has never sung in public before, let alone in a quartet. He's a big Beach Boys fan, and knows all their songs, which is not much good to him this evening, as the lads have chosen a song by Billy Joel. No, seriously, let's hear it for the lads, and especially Danny on lead, singing an old Beach Boys favourite, *In My Room...*'

The four singers got up from their chairs, Neil giving Vince a helping hand, and they walked towards the far wall of the function room, which was draped from ceiling to floor with shimmering silver strips. Vince gave a closed-fist gesture to Danny, and pointed to a spot on the floor where he should stand. The others then gathered around, forming a close semi-circle, and Vince nodded towards Neil, who blew the pitch pipe.

'In your own time, Dan,' Vince whispered, and Danny once again closed his eyes and prepared to sing.

At the end of the song there was silence. Just a second or two, but enough for Danny to wonder just how much of a fool he'd made of himself. Then came the most thunderous applause he'd ever heard. He opened his eyes and was met by a sea of enraptured faces, people standing up, shouting and whooping, and clapping their hands for all they were worth. Vince smiled knowingly at Henry and Neil, and slapped Danny firmly on the back.

'Beautiful, Dan. Just beautiful,' said Vince.

James stepped forward and shook hands with all four singers, then gave a sweeping theatrical wave towards the audience.

'Ladies and gentlemen, how about that? I do believe we've just heard something quite special, don't you? Lizzy, is that a tear in your eye? And Ken, did I see you look up from your crossword halfway through that performance? What an absolute delight. I give you Henry, Vince, Neil, and – how about it – Danny! Well done, lads!'

'That was a fantastic vocal, Danny. And the four of you sounded so good together – a really great blend.'

James Pinter sat down next to Danny, who was sipping at a glass of water.

'You know, it would be seriously remiss of me not to try and recruit you for the chorus. You'll make a great addition to the lead section and, well, I'm sure I'm not the only one who can't wait to hear you four guys sing together again.'

'It certainly was a tight, well-matched sound,' Neil added.

'The best buzz I've ever had singing in quartet,' said Henry.

Danny looked like he was in shock.

'Thanks, thanks a lot. I'm still shaking with nerves. I can't believe I just did that. And thanks so much for making me welcome this evening…but as far as joining the chorus is concerned, I'm really not sure about that,' said Danny.

'Assuming you pass your audition, that is!' said Vince. 'But, honestly, mate…if you felt anywhere near as good as I did just then, you've got some serious thinking to do! It's a drug, this harmony singing lark, and you've just had your first fix.'

Danny looked up at Vince, and placed his water on the table in front of him.

'Actually, can I have a quiet word, Vince?' he said, nodding towards the door. 'Excuse us for a moment would you, gents…'

Danny led Vince out towards the street. His sense of shock was giving way to renewed anxiety as he anticipated telling Vince his news. As he pushed open the main door, he felt a cool breeze drift across his face, and words started tumbling out.

'Fresh air. That's better, that's much better. I thought I was going to faint in there for a while. Listen, Vince, this has all been a bit of a whirlwind. I hardly know you, but I feel I've known you for ages, so what I'm about to tell you may seem strange, as it's a bit, well…personal.'

'No problem. Shoot.'

'It's just that something happened since I last saw you. Something serious. In fact, it was that phone call as I was leaving the pub the other night. Look, without going into detail, Hannah and I have hit a bit of a crisis, and I'm not sure how it's going to pan out. The way things are right now, chances are we'll be separating…I only just told you how wonderful everything was at home, and now…well, we're in the shit, and my mind's a mess, and the only reason

I came here tonight was to get away from the atmosphere in the house. I didn't know I'd end up singing and being signed up by Simon Cowell in there…'

Vince allowed a moment's pause.

'James knows a good'un when he hears one, Dan. Listen, mate, I'm really sorry about whatever's happened. And surprised. From what you said last time, you two lovebirds seem like a match made in heaven. I really hope you can work this out, and let me know if there's anything I can do to help. I mean, the last thing our quartet needs is a suicidal lead on its hands.'

'Please, be serious for a minute, will you,' said Danny.

'I am being serious. If there's anything I can do to help on the personal front, just shout. And do I think we should form a quartet with Henry and Neil? Absolutely. Danny, trust me. I've got a feeling this could be very good for all of us.'

Just then, the door to the social club swung open and a huge figure appeared, dressed in a bright orange Hawaiian shirt, enormous khaki shorts, calf-length socks, and the whitest of tennis shoes. Cliff "Tonsils" Thompson walked towards Danny and Vince and placed a fat, sun-tanned arm around each of their shoulders.

'I've just been sayin' to the other two fellas in there that you guys are dynamite together! Have y'all thought of entering the British championships? I do believe the qualifiers are in November. Take my advice and go for it, fellas. You'll knock 'em dead! See ya next time!'

And with that, Cliff "Tonsils" Thompson turned and waddled off in the direction of the setting sun.

'You'd never guess he comes from Slough originally, would you?' said Vince.

Four

Jenny pushed the recline button and closed her eyes as the passenger seat eased gently backwards. She needed to gather her thoughts.

Though she could make sense of Henry's redundancy, she felt uneasy and vulnerable. The economy was in free-fall, the banks were in chaos, and there seemed to be a crisis around every corner. Even Henry wasn't immune to what was happening in the City. And yet he was one of the top traders out there, and ordinarily she would expect him to bounce back quickly. Except that Henry was behaving oddly. Probably a natural reaction to being on the sidelines for the first time in decades, but odd nonetheless.

She felt the Bentley's smooth acceleration as Henry put it into top gear, and she opened and closed her eyes quickly, just enough to see that they were on an open stretch of road with dense banks of deciduous woodland on either side. Henry cleared his throat, and she wished she had kept her eyes shut.

'How about we get away to Spain for a couple of weeks, darling? I think we need to relax, take stock of things, and decide what next. A bit of a break will do us the world of good. What do you say?'

'I was just closing my eyes,' said Jenny, pulling up the collar of her jacket to signify her intentions further. But then an uneasy thought occurred to her and she sat up. She tried to keep her tone as non-confrontational as possible.

'If you ask me, this isn't the time to be getting away. Shouldn't you be putting yourself out there, working your contacts, and showing the big guns in the City what they're missing? That's *my* Henry!'

Jenny flipped down the sun visor and checked her newly-styled hair in the vanity mirror. She sensed that Henry wasn't in the mood for flattery.

'Jen, *your* Henry is someone who's worked his proverbials off for years, someone who's barely stopped for breath and, if I may say so, I think we've done all right,' he said, looking around at the interior of the car as though it were their world in microcosm. 'A few weeks away isn't going to make much difference to anything. Come on, darling!'

Jenny teased a few loose strands of hair into place. She wasn't in the mood for backing down.

'It's a *few* weeks now, is it? What happened to a couple? Oh, it's just...you know how I get anxious about these things, Henry. If you're out of the loop, you might miss out on a big move, and I just think now's not the time.'

'Good Lord, we're in the second decade of the twenty-first century. All I need is a mobile phone and an internet connection, and I'm as in touch in Puerto Banus – or Timbuktu or the Kalahari Desert for that matter – as I am in Ascot. And Jeffrey's got his ear to the ground for me. If anything crops up, I'm sure to know about it within minutes. *But, you know what...?*'

Here we go, Jenny thought, as she began rifling through a large make-up bag on her lap.

'Mmm. What's that?' she said finally.

'The thing is...I'm not sure I want to be on the end of a mobile phone or an internet connection all the time. I'm beginning to think there's got to be more to life than chasing the next deal, making money for the sake of making money. If I didn't work again, we'd be all right financially. More than all right, I'd say. There's just got to be a better alternative to the rat race...'

So that's what's been going on in his head. Jenny snapped.

'What are you suggesting, Henry? That we sell up and adopt some sort of alternative lifestyle? Tom and Barbara Good, is that it? I hope you're joking, Henry, because that's certainly not my vision of the future!'

That was it. The gloves were off.

'Good God, woman! Did I say anything about an alternative lifestyle? Talk about a vivid imagination! Are you so scared to think about a better way of living that all you can do is ridicule and pour scorn? And what exactly have you been doing these last few years since you left work to pursue a life of luxury? I'm not sure that being *pampered* all day and having your face pumped full of neurotoxins is actually such a great contribution to our financial well-being!'

Henry punched the car ceiling with his fist.

'Shit, I'm sorry…that was over the top…look, let's stop there,' he said.

'I think you should have stopped before that last comment, Henry. Okay, you work, I don't. That was what we agreed after my last operation. How does it help to bring that up now?'

Jenny opened the glove compartment and pulled a paper tissue from a concealed box.

'I said I'm sorry. It's just that…well, you make me feel that unless I'm some high-flyer in the City then I'm nothing…that *we're* nothing. But that's crazy. Making deals leaves me cold these days. Buying and selling commodities is a soulless business, Jenny, and I'm not sure I want any more of it. It's a young man's game. And do you know what got me thinking this way?'

'Surprise me.'

'The other evening, Vince, Neil and I sang in quartet with a new guy who came along to rehearsal for the first time. And it was amazing. Something clicked. We all felt a buzz…a connection. We sounded so good together, and the response we got from everyone at the club made me feel completely alive. It was like I'd discovered something very special.'

Not sure that she could believe what she was hearing, Jenny let out a derisive laugh.

'Oh, no, it's worse than I thought. Let me get this straight. You sing with a few of your pals on a Wednesday night, and something happens that makes you want to change the course of your life. And what's the plan from here? Busking in Covent Garden? *Britain's Got Talent?* This is a serious mid-life crisis, Henry. You should get help, and quickly.'

'There's no crisis. I'm just seeing the bigger picture, other possibilities. Look, say yes to Spain. Let's get away and put all this into perspective. Let me explain things better, when we're both more relaxed.'

Jenny was defiant.

'I don't think so, Henry. I've got things on over the next few weeks. A check-up at St Luke's, a weekend at the Abbey with Laura, and the charity ball at the golf club.'

'That's a pity,' said Henry. 'But I still need to get away. Perhaps not Puerto Banus, not on my own. I don't think I could stand the marina crowd now I come to think of it. In fact, maybe I'll go somewhere…remote.'

Neil smacked the side of the vending machine with the flat of his hand and cursed to himself.

'Frigging thing! Coffee probably tastes like arse gravy, anyway.'

He gave the machine a final defiant smack before backing away and almost colliding with a uniformed nurse who was walking briskly along the corridor behind him. Muttering apologies, he walked over to the nearest window to stare out at a bleak grey building site beneath a bleak grey sky. His thoughts turned to a similar scene on a similar day a few years earlier.

Minutes must have passed before Neil became aware of his friend standing alongside him.

'A penny for them?' asked Vince. 'Come on, let's get out of here. I could murder a pint.'

'Sorry, Vincent, I was miles away...how did it go?'

'Later, later. Let's go. And will you stop with the "Vincent"? Only three people have ever called me Vincent – you, Lizzy at the club, and my mother!'

'Sorry, Vince. Which way did we come, anyway? Is it back towards Paediatrics, Haematology and Obstetrics & Gynaecology, or down there towards Occupational Therapy, Endocrinology and X-ray Unit? These places are such a maze.'

'How about we follow that sign there...the green one that says *Exit?*'

Neil rolled his eyes and pushed his tongue out at Vince as they headed for the exit, Neil walking more slowly than he would normally, but letting Vince set the pace.

'Thanks for driving me here and for hanging around. I could have got a taxi, you know,' said Vince.

'I told you, I'm more than happy to...I wasn't busy today, and it gives us a chance to chat about our quartet performance last week. And well, I do *know* what you're going through, don't I?'

'Yeah, of course, thanks. Now, take us to The Ship, driver!' Vince said as they reached the main entrance of the hospital. 'What a grey day,' he added, looking dejectedly at the gloom outside.

'The catch phrase of deceased camp comedian Larry Grayson, I believe,' said Neil.

'Actually, I was thinking of the song by Madness. You know, the one where the guy says his arms and legs and body ache, while the sky outside is wet and grey. Apt, don't you think?'

'You're not going to turn all self-pitying on me now,

are you Vincent?' said Neil, deliberately emphasising both syllables of his friend's name.

'Oh, bugger off and get the car will you. For every occasion a song, Neil – that's my motto. You should know by now.'

A heavy rain shower started. Neil turned up his jacket collar, and dashed towards the car park. When he returned with the car, Vince got into the passenger seat and wound down the side window to clear a haze of steam rising from Neil's upper body.

'You look like a Labrador who's been for a swim,' said Vince, 'and that tweed jacket of yours smells like one too. Take a right at the T-junction.'

Vince directed Neil to the pub, and the rain stopped just as they turned into the car park. Rays of sunlight started to appear as gaps in the cloud cover opened up.

'I have a song in mind. Think you can guess it?' said Vince.

'I'm not a mind reader. Give me a clue at least.'

'Well, if I said that I can see clearly now the rain has gone, what would you say?'

'It's going to be a bright sunshiny day?'

'Exactly! Johnny Nash,' said Vince. They smiled at each other and started singing in harmony as they got out of the car and walked to the rear entrance of the pub.

The barroom was empty except for an old man in one corner and a young couple who looked like they had only called in to avoid the rain. On the table in front of them were two small Cokes and an Ordinance Survey map.

'Neil – you know Angie, don't you? The best barmaid in Berkshire!' said Vince, approaching the bar.

'Of course. Nice to see you again. Excuse me while I sort myself out,' said Neil, making his way to the toilet. Vince leant over the bar and kissed Angie on the lips.

'You all right, babe?'

Angie looked both surprised and pleased to see Vince. 'What are you doing here on a weekday afternoon?'

'Just been for a hospital appointment, and Neil offered to drive. I thought I'd drop by and see you.'

'Gagging for a pint, more like. How did it go?' said Angie.

'Well, you know. The usual. Do the honours would you, babe?'

Angie poured a pint of lager and passed it to Vince, who drank half the glass in three enormous gulps, then wiped his mouth with the back of his hand.

Neil returned, ordered a lemonade and lime, and asked to see the lunch menu. They sat at the bar chatting with Angie, Neil sipping his soft drink and eating sandwiches and crisps, while Vince only drank.

With an exchange of knowing glances, Neil and Angie conspired to take the rise out of Vince, who was clearly content to lose himself in the beer.

'So, why is it, Angie, that Vince always introduces you as the best barmaid in Berkshire rather than "my beautiful girlfriend the former glamour model" or something similar?' asked Neil. 'Don't you find it ever so demeaning?'

'I'm used to it,' said Angie. 'He can't help being a chauvinist pig. But he doesn't know how lucky he is to have me.'

Angie busied herself behind the bar, serving a slow trickle of customers, stocking shelves, and keeping the place orderly, returning every few minutes to continue the banter. At five foot six, with a slim and busty figure, feline eyes and high cheekbones, Angie looked like she belonged in front of a camera instead of behind a bar. But those days were in the past. She was elegant and poised, and completely comfortable with herself wherever she was.

'Why didn't you introduce me to that good-looking chap you were with the other evening, Vince?' Angie asked, continuing the routine.

'Good looking? Really? That was Danny. New guy at work. Anyway, the place was packed. You had your hands full,' said Vince, taking the bait.

'And he's a great singer,' said Neil. 'We sang with him a few nights ago at the club.'

'Good looking *and* a great singer, huh? Watch out, Vince!' said Angie, with a huge smile. 'Right, that's it. I'm off shift now, so I'll leave you to it. See that he gets home safely, will you, Neil?'

Angie gave Vince a quick peck on the cheek, and went on her way. Vince and Neil returned to discussing the scratch quartet evening, and talked excitedly for another half hour.

'It would be a shame not to get together with Danny again and see if we can make some plans as a proper quartet. I'm really excited, and I know Henry is too,' said Neil.

Vince suddenly became more lively, less focused on his beer.

'That makes three of us, but it all depends on Danny. He's the new boy to all this. He's not sure if he can commit to anything, and he's going through a bad patch in his personal life just now.'

'Tell me who isn't.'

'Sure, we've all got things we have to deal with, but this has all come at once for Dan, and the timing might just be wrong. For me, it's clear – I've been plugging away at barbershop for years, searching for that elusive quartet sound that'll make the difference between solid B-level performers and championship hopefuls. I told Danny straight that I'd love us to enter for the nationals next year, but he said himself that it all seems like a bit of a whirlwind at the moment and he can't quite take it all in.'

'I can't say I blame him,' said Neil.

'And yet I know he'd love it every bit as much as we would. He's got music in his soul, just like you and me. One thing's for sure, I'm doing my very best to persuade him. If we don't grab this opportunity, who knows if we'll ever get the chance again? I very much doubt that I will, in any case,' said Vince.

'Meaning what, exactly?' said Neil, looking at Vince suspiciously.

'You know what.'

'Are you being melodramatic, Vincent, or is there something I should know? What did the doctor say earlier?'

'What I thought he would. It's gone from relapsing-remitting to progressive. They can't be sure how it will play out, but it's not going to get any better, is it? You saw the same thing with Robert.'

'Dear God,' said Neil.

Danny looked around the modern waiting room with its light oak floors, leather and chrome retro chairs, and abstract art prints. Sunlight flooded through elegant stained-glass windows, throwing kaleidoscopic shapes on to the pristine white walls and ceiling. A tall potted palm stood in one corner.

Hannah flicked through a lifestyle magazine on the glass table in front of her, too fast to see the pictures, let alone read the words. She kept her head low, avoiding the possibility of eye contact with her husband.

A door opened, and a small, slim, well-dressed woman in her early fifties entered.

'Hannah and Danny? I'm Denise. Would you like to come this way?'

Hannah got to her feet quickly, and made towards the door, her hand outstretched. Danny followed, smiling and nodding, as they walked through a narrow connecting corridor to another large, well-lit room containing little more than a rectangular beech coffee table with a water jug and three glasses on it, a three-seat red leather sofa and a matching armchair.

Denise walked towards the armchair, and gestured towards the sofa. Danny and Hannah sat down, each taking an end seat. Denise picked up an A5 notebook from the table, crossed her legs, and sat back.

'I understand this is the first time you've been to a relationship counsellor, yes? So, it's a brave thing you're doing, and you'll probably be feeling anxious and apprehensive right now. Well, try to relax while you're here. My job is to allow you the space and time to tell your story and air your differences in an unbiased environment. I'm here to listen, provide input when I can, and allow you to see your problems from each other's perspective. Everything that's said here is entirely confidential, so you can talk freely. But, of course, there are no guarantees as to how things will work out. We just have to find our way as we go. So, let me start with you, Danny. Can you tell me your story please?'

Danny moved uneasily in his seat, took a slight sideways glance towards Hannah, then started to speak. Five minutes went by without interruption before Danny concluded.

'I was in a blind panic when I presented Hannah with the evidence. There it was in black and white, a very intimate message to a lover, leaving nothing to the imagination. Hannah's own handwriting. The same handwriting I'd seen a hundred times before, expressing messages of love... but to me. And we're both stood there looking at this ugly photocopy sent to me by a woman I hardly know, who's probably hurting every bit as much as I am, but I don't care about her. I'm staring at this piece of paper, incapable of believing what I'm seeing, but with a cold, sick feeling in my gut that's telling me it's true. And I look at Hannah for some sign that it's a joke or a dream, or something... but nothing. No words, just silence. We have barely spoken since then, other than to agree to get help. I have a million questions I need answers to, but we can't even speak to each other, it's too painful...'

Danny's voice tailed off and he raised a hand to signal that he was finished.

'Thank you, Danny. Hannah, can you tell me your story please?'

Hannah took a sip of water and composed herself.

'Danny arrived home in a state one evening, saying he'd had a phone call from a woman accusing me of having an affair with her husband. I denied it. Then this photocopy of a birthday card arrived in the post, and Danny confronted me with it, and I was dumbstruck. I couldn't find any words that made sense of anything or that would help in any way. The fact is that when I say I'm not having an affair, I'm telling the truth.'

'How the hell can you sit there and say that? Why are you lying?' said Danny.

'Danny, please, let Hannah continue,' said Denise.

'I am not *having* an affair. What I had was a...a *fling*... a long time ago. That birthday card is years old. I can't even remember writing it. It was never an affair, it was just a fling. I have regretted it ever since it happened. It was a mistake, a mistake I have tried to move on from, and have vowed to myself I'll never make again. But it's caught up with me. I'm really sorry, Danny.'

'How long ago was this?' asked Denise.

Hannah started to sob uncontrollably.

'Take your time.'

'No, don't take your time! Bloody well spit it out, will you! How long ago was it, Hannah?' said Danny, his voice now full of anger.

'Danny, please, let Hannah respond in her own way.'

'Three years ago,' Hannah said at last. 'It was three years ago.'

Five

'We've got the place to ourselves,' said Neil, removing layers of cling film from several plates of sandwiches. 'Mother's out for the day, but she's made us a bite to eat. There's cake and fruit over there as well.'

'A great spread it is too,' said Vince, piling sandwiches onto a side plate.

'Do start, Vince,' said Neil, looking edgily at his wristwatch. 'It's three-thirty now, so if we finish about five, that should give us a decent amount of clearance before my father gets back from golf.'

'Not a fan of harmony singing, your father, then, Neil?' said Henry, an egg-and-cress sandwich poised at his lips.

'Let's just say it's best we finish by five. Now, where shall we start?'

Vince sat forward in his chair.

'Well, some proper introductions for Danny's sake would be good. Then we can discuss plans and expectations, and think about songs.'

'Sounds good to me, Vince. You'd make an excellent secretary. Will you be taking minutes?' said Henry, popping a cherry tomato into his mouth.

'Thank you for that. Perhaps you'd like to start by telling Danny a bit about yourself, Mr Gekko?' said Vince, smirking as he piled more sandwiches on to his plate.

'Okay. I'm Henry Warrington, the old man of the group. I've been singing barbershop on and off for nine years, and I've been with the Maidenhead chorus for close to four years. I've done a fair bit of quartetting, but I've never quite found a foursome that's really clicked. Until now, I hope. Vince likes to call me Gordon Gekko, a rather lame and dated reference to the fact that I work in the City as a senior commodities trader – or, at least I did until a few weeks ago. A victim of Meltdown Monday, I'm afraid. Right now I'm unemployed, and in the process of re-assessing my life.'

'What, really? I had absolutely no idea,' said Neil, staring wide-eyed at Henry.

'My wife prefers to call it a mid-life crisis,' said Henry. 'Tomorrow I'm off to spend two weeks alone on a small island to work out what next – but one thing I know is that when I get back I intend to make creative pursuits a much higher priority. I realise that singing is the one thing that enriches my life more than anything, but up to now I've just been dabbling. When we sang together that first time, I felt something…something special, and I want more of it. Hence being here now.'

'Well, bugger me,' said Vince.

'An interesting suggestion, but no time for that now, Vince,' said Neil. 'Well, perhaps I should say a few words for Danny's benefit…I'm Neil Taylor, the baby of the group by the look of it! I graduated from Manchester University last year, since when I've been living back at home. Music has always been a big part of my life. I play piano to grade eight, and I've sung in various school and church choirs. I got the bug for harmony singing at uni, where I joined an a cappella society – a bit like the collegiate harmony clubs in America. So, when I returned home, I looked around for a decent a cappella group and found the Maidenhead chorus. I also do a bit of composition, and I've been arranging four-part harmony charts for a couple of years now. That's me, pretty much.'

'Thanks, guys. So, maybe I should tell you a bit more about me then?' said Danny. 'As you know, I recently joined the same company as Vince. We hit it off straight away, gassing about our favourite albums and bands, the way you do.

Then Vince said he was a barbershop singer, which made me laugh at first, but then I've always loved harmonies, so I found myself getting interested and I came along to the scratch quartet evening. The rest is history, I guess.'

'Thanks, Danny. It must seem quite strange being here…it's all happened so quickly for you. I hope you don't feel press-ganged,' said Neil.

'No, I've given it a lot of thought. I've got lots on my plate at the moment, and my first reaction was that I wouldn't be able to find the time. But I'm seriously flattered that you guys want me to join you, and I'm staggered by your confidence in me, a complete novice. I've decided I want to give it a go. I need something like this just now, and in a way I'll be fulfilling a promise I made to myself years ago. Just… thanks for the opportunity.'

'That's the bloody spirit, Danny Boy,' said Vince. 'So, we're all in then?'

Henry stretched his arms upwards, interlaced his fingers, and brought his palms to rest on the crown of his head.

'Absolutely. But I'm still not sure what the plan is. How exactly do we take this forward, chaps?'

'Well, here are my initial thoughts,' said Vince. 'There's the fun bit, and then there's the slightly more serious bit. The fun bit is that we start rehearsing regularly, start developing our own sound, our own unique identity as a quartet. We build a repertoire of songs and then, when we feel confident enough, we start touting ourselves for private parties, corporate dos, charity gigs, that kind of thing. That's how we really build our confidence – getting out there and singing for people who are expecting to be entertained.'

'Now I'm really scared,' said Danny.

'No, we'll have an absolute blast, I promise you,' Vince continued. 'But then there's the more serious bit. Competition. I think you know my thoughts on this…I'd love us to have a crack at the British championships in Harrogate next May, but before that there's the small matter of the preliminary qualifying round in Birmingham at the end of November. That's less than five months away. So, if you're asking me for a plan, there it is. The fun bit and the serious bit. And if we do it right, it'll all be...serious fun.'

Henry stood up, picked up a butter knife from the tea trolley, and raised it to his mouth as though he were smoking a cigar.

'I would say to the House, as I said to those who have joined this quartet...I have nothing to offer but blood, toil, tears and sweat!'

'Winston Churchill to the House of Commons, June 1940, I do believe,' said Vince.

'Close, but no cigar! It was May 1940 that Winnie uttered those famous words – apart from the bit about the quartet, obviously. Damn it, Vince, that's got my juices flowing, I can tell you. That's a bloody great plan...what do you think chaps?' said Henry.

'Sounds good to me,' said Neil.

'My head's spinning,' said Danny. 'Can I ask a silly question? Before we go any further, can someone explain to me the basics of this style of singing? I mean, there's clearly a lot more to it than meets the eye...or the ear, I should say. What do I have to know to be able to get up to speed?'

Vince got up gingerly from his chair.

'Not a silly question at all. We were in danger of getting ahead of ourselves there. Neil, you're the technical man. Would you like to explain the basics to Danny? Excuse me while I pay a visit...' said Vince, walking towards the door.

Neil started to pace slowly across the conservatory floor.

'Well, barbershop is a style of a cappella, or unaccompanied vocal music, characterized by consonant four -part chords for every melody note in a predominantly homophonic texture...'

Henry threw a crumpled up napkin at Neil.

'No, no, no. Cut the mumbo jumbo and let's have the layman's version, hey?'

'Sorry...well, each of the four parts has its own role. Generally, the lead sings the melody, the tenor harmonises above the melody, the bass sings the lowest harmonising notes, and the baritone completes the chord, usually below the lead. Ideally, the four voices match very closely so that every chord throughout a song rings, which means that overtones are created. You know when you hear it, as the sound becomes a lot bigger, which is why it's often referred to as *expanded sound*. It's the effect that sometimes gives people goose bumps when they hear close harmony. Was that good enough, Henry?'

Henry picked up his napkin from the floor.

'Splendid, professor. So, Danny, as the lead, you sing the tune and we fill in around you. You get the easy ride when it comes to learning, as the melody is what people are familiar with, but when it comes to performing it's your job to tell the story of the song, so you need to be lyrical, articulate and compelling on stage. Piece of cake, really,' said Henry, biting into a piece of cake.

Vince reappeared at the doorway.

'So, now that you've scared him shitless, shall we think about songs?'

They talked about what songs they might enjoy singing as a quartet, and three-quarters of an hour later Neil attempted to summarise the discussion.

'So, we can add *California Girls* and *I Get Around* to *In My Room*, which gives us three Beach Boys songs. Then we thought we could do *The Longest Time, Country Roads,* and *Witchcraft* – all of which is fine and dandy, but we're missing something pretty important here, guys. Not one of those songs is competition material.'

'Run that by me again,' said Vince, scratching his head.

'Well, if the first part of your master plan is that we enter prelims in November, we need to pick two songs that meet contest rules. None of the songs we've talked about so far are strictly barbershop arrangements, are they?' said Neil.

Vince's face was a picture of incomprehension.

'Good God, Vince! How long have you been singing barbershop? You should know that there are strict guidelines for competition songs, the main one being that at least a third of a song's duration should consist of harmonic sevenths. I'm afraid none of the songs we've picked so far come even close. So, I suggest we put all those songs on the back burner for now, and pick a couple we can compete with. We've got less than five months, remember?'

'A good point, well made. And thanks for the refresher course in musical theory. I say we delegate you to pick two songs that meet the brief, and that aren't too complicated to learn. Have a think while Henry's away, dig out the arrangements, and bring them along to our next session. How does that sound?' said Vince.

Henry nodded in agreement.

'Sure,' said Danny, shrugging his shoulders.

'Time's marching on,' said Neil, looking at his watch. 'Is there any other business we need to discuss?'

'The small matter of a name? What shall we call ourselves?' asked Henry.

'Good question, Henry. Whatever we do, let's avoid anything too cheesy,' said Neil.

'You mean like…The Roque-Four?' said Vince, delighted with his pun.

'You just can't help yourself, can you?' said Neil, throwing a banana skin into Vince's lap for the hell of it.

Vince held the banana skin aloft. 'Okay, okay…then what about…what about…The…The Four Skins?' he said, starting to giggle, and throwing the banana skin back at Neil.

Henry and Danny looked at each other and burst into laughter simultaneously. Neil's resistance lasted only a few seconds longer before he too cracked, and they all laughed helplessly for several minutes.

Eventually, a voice cut through the cacophony.

'Good evening, gentlemen. Neil, won't you introduce me to your friends,' said Neil's father.

Before Neil could gather his composure, Henry jumped up from his chair.

'Good grief…George! How the devil are you? So, you're Neil's father? Well, well, well…'

Six

After a turbulent crossing of two hours, the ferry eased alongside the narrow wooden jetty stretching out from the slate and granite mass of the island. The three-mile expanse of rock looked magnificent and indomitable as it rose out of the soupy green sea to a height of four hundred feet, its upper reaches shrouded in a thin swirling bank of mist. Henry could see a rough-hewn road winding its way steeply up the side of the island, and high above he could just make out the shapes of ancient castle walls, a square church tower, and a simple wooden chalet perched on the side of a cliff.

He walked down the galvanised metal gangplank, along the wooden boards of the jetty, and past a green timber hut, to one side of which were gas cylinders, coils of rope and a pile of wicker lobster pots. The road hugged near-vertical slate cliffs, which were pinned and secured against weather erosion at regular intervals by giant rusting steel bolts.

Turning sharply right then left, the road climbed quickly above sea level. Henry stopped to look down upon a rocky beach some thirty feet below and a scattering of small boats moored in the bay beyond. Down on the jetty to the right of the bay, he could see a tractor trailer being loaded with cargo from the ferry, and beyond the jetty he noticed for the first time a smaller granite outcrop almost, but not quite, connected to the main landmass. Something moved on a cluster of rocks below. A large grey seal was basking in the warm sun, unconcerned by the straggle of people making its way slowly to the top of the island.

The road now became much steeper, and Henry put

his head down as he pushed on to the next bend. Here, the road turned sharply inwards towards a sparsely wooded valley, with the beach and the landing bay now out of sight. A freshwater stream gurgled somewhere off to the right, and Henry became aware of the sound of birdsong. Up ahead he could see, to his surprise, the cream-painted front elevation of a Georgian-style villa nestling in the crook of the valley. It looked out of place and right at home all at the same time, Henry thought. Having read a bit about the island, he knew that there was no shortage of curiosities to be discovered, and he felt a surge of excitement as he began to climb a set of natural stone steps leading to a higher path and what looked like a final steep ascent to the top of the island.

As his route march reached a plateau, Henry stopped to lean on a narrow five-barred gate that led on to a sprawling but well-kept expanse of grassland with a cluster of granite buildings beyond. This must be the village, he thought, if two or three buildings huddled into a space no more than fifty yards across could be called a village. Henry looked around him in all directions as though expertly surveying the landscape, while taking in huge lungfuls of air – really, really fresh air, he thought.

Dominating the skyline to the south of the village stood a huge, austere-looking Victorian church of familiar granite, and with a great square, castellated tower. The clock on the eastern face of the tower gave the time as three o'clock, causing Henry to check his wristwatch. Five past twelve. Excellent, he thought. With any luck, nobody cares about time too much around here.

To the north was farmland marked out by drystone walls, and with much of the usual paraphernalia of a working farm in evidence: silage dispensers, grain sacks, metal water troughs, and a tractor parked in the corner of one of the fields.

As Henry approached the main group of buildings he could see that the one on the far right must be the pub, as a couple of early drinkers were sat outside on a solitary bench seat tucked away in a shaded recess near a side entrance. He walked towards a black iron swing gate, which he guessed led to the front of the pub and gave access to whatever else the village had to offer. Guessing correctly, he found himself outside the main entrance of the pub, recognisable as such only by a simple painted sign board above the door; no colourful depictions of the pub's name or history, no crests, crowns, horseshoes, lions, stags, or anything else. Just the name of the place in white upper case lettering on a grey background.

A similar, but much smaller sign painted on to a stone slab on a nearby grass bank bore the word "SHOP" with a right-pointing arrow underneath. The plain elegance of the calligraphy reminded Henry of the village in the 1960s cult TV series *The Prisoner*.

Two further signs were visible next to the entrances of a simple stone outbuilding alongside the pub. With no roof to be seen, the sign marked "GENTS" appeared to lead to an open-air urinal. Henry recalled that the last time he'd used a *pissoir* was on a school trip to St Malo in Brittany when he was twelve. His mind was beginning to wander.

Snapping to, he remembered something about having to report to the island office upon arrival – he found it easily enough, as it was part of the pub building itself, just the next door along. There he was greeted by a pleasantly rotund lady in her late-fifties with fashionably cropped black hair and a rich south Wales accent. She directed him to his accommodation, which was south of the village, beyond the church and over a small hill towards the east coast cliffs. Henry hoped that this was the wooden chalet he had seen swathed in mist from the boat as it moored alongside the jetty.

He visited the shop to pick up some basic provisions: tea, milk, bread, butter, marmalade, eggs, bacon, biscuits. There he was greeted by a slightly-built man in his seventies, still fit-looking, with a full head of white hair, and a deep north Devon accent. He asked Henry where and how long he was staying and if he'd like to run a tab for his groceries, told him that the weather was set fair for the next forty-eight hours, and wished him a happy stay. Henry smiled to himself as he left the shop, and said aloud, though not too loud, 'I'm going to like this place.' His thoughts then turned to home, and Jenny, and he took out his mobile phone to let his wife know that he had arrived safely. He glanced down at the display. No signal.

As he wandered back through the village, he started singing *On a Wonderful Day Like Today*, with even more conviction than when he'd been playing golf with Jeffrey.

To Henry's delight, his accommodation was indeed the chalet he'd seen from the boat. The single-storey weather-boarded building sat in a sheltered dip on the eastern slopes of the island, with commanding views down upon the jetty and landing beach below, and out to sea towards the mainland, which was just visible as a faint bluish strip on the horizon. To the north, almost all of the island's three-mile stretch of east coast was visible, a series of steeply undulating slopes appearing like deep folds in the side of the island. Henry stood outside the cottage absorbing the views, breathing the air, and listening to the silence.

He spent the rest of the day exploring the southern part of the island, walking along winding paths cut into the sides of steep grassy banks, climbing over stiles, wading through bracken. He made his way along the lower west coast, observing how the character of the coastline changed from rolling slopes to sheer cliffs. At one point, he tested himself to see how close he could get to a cliff edge without the sensation of vertigo.

As he walked around, one landmark in particular seemed to dominate the skyline, drawing him closer. Standing implausibly some way inland, an old defunct lighthouse occupied the highest point of land, its one hundred-foot granite tower looming over everything. Henry wondered why anyone would think to build a lighthouse in such an unlikely place, and marked it down as another of the island's curiosities. He then reminded himself of the purpose of his enforced isolation: to sort out the curiosities in his own life. And with that thought in mind, suddenly feeling tired and in need of sustenance, he made his way back to the chalet to shower and change before heading to the village pub for dinner.

The next morning, Henry was awoken by the sun rising. He had left his bedroom curtains open by way of a natural alarm clock, and wasn't disappointed by the spectacle of first light shimmering and sparkling upon a calm green sea. He lay in bed staring at the sea and sky, his mind a complete blank. Then he remembered he hadn't called Jenny since his departure, and reached for his phone on the bedside table. He paused. Far too early to call her. Then he checked the display. No signal.

He got up, made tea, then returned to bed to make plans. *I'm here for two weeks. Two weeks in which to work out what I want to do next with my life. Have I overreacted to losing my job? Am I being petulant or unreasonable? Maybe Jenny's right. Maybe this is a mid-life crisis. Shit! What am I doing here alone on a remote island with barely any contact to the outside world? Am I playing silly buggers? Oh, Jen, what must you be thinking...?*

Henry, the hard-bitten commodities trader, having spent a professional lifetime making rapid-fire, high-risk decisions, suddenly felt not only indecisive, but helpless. He slipped from his upright position down between the sheets, pulled the blanket and counterpane up beneath his chin, and went back to sleep.

In that semi-conscious limbo state before fully waking, Henry dreamed that he was an island lighthouse keeper. One day, over a pint in the island pub, Patrick McGoohan, dressed in his *Prisoner* blazer complete with Number Six lapel badge, confided in him that the lighthouse was, in fact, a disguised rocket, and that it was his only remaining chance to escape the island. He told Henry, who was wearing a cream Aran sweater with a Number Four badge, that he had no choice but to help him, even if it meant incurring the wrath of the island authorities. On a midnight assignation, under a full moon, the duo met at the lighthouse to execute the escape. But in a last-minute hitch, Number Six failed to make it on board before the rocket, with Henry inside, launched high into the night sky before bursting into flames and exploding like an enormous firework.

Later that day Henry continued his exploration of the island, with very little human interaction except for the occasional greeting exchanged with fellow walkers. As he walked he questioned everything about his life. He thought about Jenny a lot. Why had she reacted so unsympathetically to his redundancy? Why, now that they could spend more time together, were they drifting apart instead? He suddenly felt anxious.

He tried and failed twice more to call Jenny on his mobile, before discovering that there was a coin-operated telephone in the back room of the pub. Armed with pound coins he called home, but the answering machine was on. He called Jenny's mobile, and after some difficulty feeding the machine with coins, managed to connect. He imagined the look on his wife's face as an unrecognised number came up on her phone display.

'Jenny Warrington. Who is this?'

'Jenny, it's me. How are you? Sorry I didn't ring yesterday. I'm here, but there's no mobile signal. I'm...'

'I thought the boat had sunk, Henry. This is a bloody awful line. I'm in the car just now.'

'On hands-free, though darling?'

'I'm not driving. It's my appointment at St Luke's at two-thirty. Jeffrey kindly offered to take me there and back.'

'Ah, good old Jeffrey. But you're all right, yes? Listen, I miss you, but you know I've got to think things through, don't you? You understand that I need to work things—'

'Sorry, Henry, I can barely hear a word. Look, must go. Later, okay?'

Henry felt deflated. With no reliable way of getting in touch, he wondered how long *later* might be. He felt butterflies in his stomach, but wasn't quite sure why. Jenny was seemingly fine. She knew that he was here to think and make important decisions about the future. He had explained it very clearly. This wasn't some sort of whim or jape. He was at a crossroads in his life, and he was taking it very seriously. It occurred to him that he should leave a message on their home answering machine, explaining all of this again. When she returned home, Jenny would play it back, hear the sincerity and purpose in his voice, begin to understand, begin to cut him some slack. However, in his mind's eye, he saw his wife pressing the delete button, taking a sip of Cristal, and returning to the sofa and *Sex and the City*. He decided against leaving a message.

On the basis that there wasn't much he could do to change things at home, Henry decided to go to the pub for lunch. He exchanged nods and smiles with a couple of familiar faces as he made his way to the bar, then he took his pint to a corner table from where he could observe the goings-on.

The barroom interior was mostly wooden-clad, with a flagstone floor. Counter-style tables and bench seating lined the far wall, with three windows facing east towards the valley leading down to the landing beach and the sea. An oblong table of perhaps nine feet in length dominated the centre of the room, and above it, hanging from the high ceiling was a gothic-looking chandelier. On the walls were numerous seafaring artefacts including life belts daubed with their ships' names, a salvaged brass bell, and several large ensigns draped from poles set high into the south-facing wall with its great bay window. Set into the north wall was a simple open fireplace and, up above, a minstrels' gallery with further tables and chairs. The serving area was a plain wooden hatch.

Henry sipped his beer and looked around the room. At the centre table was a group of what he took to be rock climbers, and elsewhere he detected small groups of divers and bird watchers. Family groups were scattered around, with children playing games of Jenga, dominoes and Scrabble. One or two young couples in the first flush of romance were clearly in evidence, and there were at least two other solos who, unlike himself, had their noses buried deep in a book, seemingly oblivious to the clamour going on around them.

On the table next to his, one of the solos, a slender woman in her mid-thirties with straggly shoulder-length hair, looked up from her book and caught Henry's eye. He smiled politely, wondering if he should say something, when the woman spoke.

'Any chance of a song then?'

Henry looked around to see if the question was intended for someone else, but the woman was looking straight at him, smiling, and had placed her open book page-side down on the table, as though waiting for a response.

'Sorry, a song? Are you sure you…?' said Henry.

'It's just that I've seen you walking around the island, blowing into a little mouth organ and then singing to yourself. Very nice too. Why not?'

'Pitch pipe. Ah, yes, well. I guess that must look quite strange. You see…'

'Please, you don't need to explain.'

'Well, no, quite. But just in case you think I've escaped from a sanatorium for the musically deranged or something…'

'And what if you have? We encourage and celebrate diversity around here.' The woman had a discernible twinkle in her eye.

'Sorry, I didn't catch your name.'

'I didn't say my name, but it's Cat.'

'Cat as in…'

'Cat.'

'I see. I'm Henry, pleased to meet you. So, if you don't mind me asking, what brings you to the island?'

Cat threw her head back and flicked her straggly hair behind her ears with the fingers of both hands as she did so. Henry could see her face properly for the first time. Her eyes were intense green, with large, slightly bulbous lids. Her skin was pale, uneven, and weather-worn, and her mouth was wide, with thin lips and slightly crooked teeth. She was not conventionally good-looking, but she was certainly attractive because she seemed to ooze some sort of life force.

'I live here. I'm the nature warden, so I look after the flora and fauna, you could say. My morning off, but I must get back to it. Excuse me for now, I need to check on the volunteers. We've got eight young offenders from the mainland being rehabilitated on the east side of the island. They're burning the rhododendron scrub. Let's hope that's all they're burning. See you around.'

Cat raised her eyebrows, her wide green eyes alive with humour. She then closed her book, stood up, and slipped away through the barroom throng.

Henry felt an instant warmth towards the nature warden, though she made him feel self-conscious. If she'd spotted him wandering around the island blowing his pitch pipe and singing to himself, he wondered how many other people had too. He had never stopped to think about it before, but he had to admit that it wasn't exactly everyday behaviour. Had the bird watchers already classified him? Did the kids point and stare at him as he marched by? Were the parents fearful that he might be some sort of Pied Piper, attempting to lure their children into the sea? The extent of his own vivid imagination surprised him, and he started to enjoy the idea that he might be playing his part in some sort of island Festival of the Eccentric.

Following his encounter with Cat, Henry found himself more relaxed, in a much lighter mood, and more able to think clearly. Over the next few days he explored every inch of the small island, from the automatic lighthouse at the southern-most point, to its sibling station at the northern tip. In between, he discovered an old castle with a cave beneath, disused quarries and the ruined cottages of the workers who mined them, the remains of an old battery point complete with rusting canons, fault lines left in the rock by an earthquake long ago, and an ancient graveyard.

Henry also found himself fascinated by the island wild-life. The cliffs of the west coast were alive with sea birds. Wild ponies, goats and sheep roamed the island. Deer proved elusive, but could sometimes be seen at twilight on the middle reaches of the east coast. Rabbits were abundant, and could often be seen in their scores, scurrying around on the steep grassy slopes. Grey seals were an easy spot at strategic points around the coast, and Henry even spotted (or so he thought) the fin of a basking shark in south-eastern waters. When he was in the chalet, he was visited by the same seagull at around eleven o'clock every morning, and if he was really lucky he would sometimes catch sight of a pygmy shrew darting between hiding places behind the skirting boards in the kitchen.

The days passed quickly and soon two weeks were nearly up. Henry had absorbed himself in the life of the island and, more than he could ever have imagined, discovered a different and richly fulfilling way of living. In two weeks he hadn't seen a motor car, watched a TV programme, or read a newspaper. He had been in bed before midnight every night, as that was when the island generator went off and everything was plunged into darkness.

Things that he had always taken for granted he now saw in a much more significant light. The elements, the wonder of natural light, the relentless force of the sea, the beauty and diversity of wildlife, the generosity of strangers, his health and strength, his ability to shape his own destiny.

His time on the island had allowed him to do the thinking he had promised himself, and he felt he was closer to knowing what he wanted when he returned home. However, he felt vulnerable and somehow in need of validation. How could he be certain that when he got back to the mainland his life wouldn't fall apart at the seams?

The night before his departure, Henry visited the village pub for the last time, to have dinner and to say farewell to a few friendly faces. As he entered the barroom, he heard a laugh he recognised, but couldn't quite place. As he waited at the bar, he traced the laugh to the far corner of the room. There, at the centre of a group of island locals, was Cat. He hadn't seen her since that first time, but of all the people he had met on the island, he felt he had most to thank her for. It had been her welcoming smile, her easy humour, and her genuine encouragement that had helped him get the most out of his stay, and he wanted to thank her for that.

Drink in hand, he walked across the barroom floor towards an empty table.

'Henry! Over here. Join us,' Cat called out, as though they were old friends.

Henry turned, adopted a look of surprise that wasn't

entirely genuine, and walked over to Cat's table.

'Hi, nice to see you! Look, I don't want to interrupt—'

'Don't be daft, music man. Pull up a chair. You know the guys, don't you? They all know you. We've just been talking about how you've become a bit of a landmark around here these last couple of weeks. *There goes the big fella with the lovely deep voice!*'

Cat laughed again, flicking her hair back behind her ears, and rocking in her chair.

Henry deflected the attention with a smile and a wave of his hand, sat on the edge of the group, and listened to the local gossip. Much of the talk was of who was dating whom, how many drinks so-and-so had last night, and who the most interesting summer visitors had been. To his embarrassment, Cat gave Henry the *Most Promising Newcomer* award. Cat seemed to be the creative centre of the banter, with the others joining in here and there. The ideas flowed, and her talents for behavioural observation, character analysis, and the art of the scathing put-down were admirable, at least in Henry's eyes, and he'd known a few banter merchants in his time.

After half an hour or so, the group started to disperse.

'Lightweights! So, you for another one, Henry?' said Cat, as the last of the locals left for home.

Henry stared at the half-inch of best bitter at the bottom of his glass.

'No, let me, please…' he said, getting to his feet. Then Cat gave him a look, and Henry sat down again.

When she returned with the drinks, the warden seemed somehow different. With the locals gone, she appeared much less larky, and any trace of insobriety had vanished.

'So, how's your holiday been?' she asked.

'Amazing. I'm not sure I know where to start, it's been such an eye-opener in so many ways.'

'But have you achieved what you set out to achieve? Are

you going home with a clear head and a clear heart?'

'Excuse me?'

'Henry, come on. This is a fantastic place to take a holiday, and it's an even better place to find yourself – or lose yourself, if you're of that mind. You came here to work something out if I'm not mistaken. Did you manage to do that?'

'Things are clearer, yes, but I'm still not entirely certain. Strangely enough, if you hadn't made me feel so welcome that first day, I don't think I would have been able to work anything out.'

'We all have things to work out, Henry. But it's all about deeds, not thoughts. Go home and do what you have to do. If your heart says fly, then fly. If your heart says sing, then sing. Now, give me your hand.'

Cat reached into a pocket and took out a small, slightly rough stone flecked with grey, white and orange crystalline patterns.

A little hesitantly, Henry offered Cat his open hand, and she placed the stone into his palm.

'What is it?' asked Henry.

'A little piece of the island. Keep it with you. It'll remind you of the place, and you never know, it might help you to work through the rest of your problems when you get home.'

'I'm not quite sure what to say,' said Henry.

'You don't need to say anything,' said Cat.

For reasons to do with prevailing winds, the boat's departure time had been brought forward by four hours. Henry's first reaction to the news was to feel slightly cheated of his last few precious hours on the island but, on reflection, he decided it was a good thing. An earlier get-away meant he would arrive home with plenty of Saturday evening left to enjoy with Jenny. Yes, much better, he thought. Catching up over a takeaway tandoori and a nice bottle of something was far preferable to arriving late in the evening with barely any time to catch up.

Henry sat at the side of the jetty, eyes closed, head pitched back slightly to catch the late morning sun full-face. He counted sounds. The sea lapping energetically against the steel pillars of the jetty, a gull screeching overhead, the stuttering of a nearby tractor motor, a child's laugh high above on the beach road, the mechanical whir and hum of the boat's loading crane. He then turned his attention to scents. Ozone, diesel, warm sun lotion. In his mind he ran a video reel of his time on the island, and he smiled to himself. All the while he turned a small grey stone in the fingers of his right hand.

The phrase *middle ground* summed things up nicely, he thought. He had spent two weeks in a place that had enabled him to strip everything back to bare essentials and, with a completely clear head, work out what he should do next. The conclusion was far from earth-shattering. He had reached a point where life in the fast lane had lost its appeal. He resented being defined by the thing he happened to do in order to earn money and sustain a certain standard of living. He wanted out of that. Jenny, on the other hand, was all for maintaining the high life, keeping up with the Joneses (or the Goldbergs, in their case), and flaunting it. Somewhere between the two there had to be a middle ground, and that would be where they would settle once he had explained things to Jenny with his new-found calm and clarity of vision.

The boat crossing was uneventful, the captain's decision to sail ahead of schedule presumably avoiding rough seas later in the day. Henry sat on the upper deck, his face to the wind, enjoying a final spell of weathering. His skin had turned an agreeable shade of tan these last two weeks, and his features had become somewhat craggier, he fancied. He felt very much like the handsome adventurer returning.

At first sight of the north Devon coast, Henry's heart simultaneously sank and flipped, if that was possible. He would miss the island solitude, and the simple magic of the place, but he knew he would return. At the same time, he looked forward to seeing Jenny, to a round of golf, and to singing with his new quartet.

The north Devon roads were free-flowing, and he didn't encounter any problems until the M5/M4 intersection south of Bristol, when the traffic (every other vehicle towing a caravan) slowed to a crawl for twenty minutes or so. After that it was full speed ahead and, an hour and a half later, Henry was turning into the driveway of his Ascot home.

He had decided to surprise Jenny with his early return, so had not called ahead to let her know. He imagined that she'd be just back from her regular Saturday afternoon four-ball, and would most likely be relaxing on the terrace with a gin and tonic.

Henry walked across the driveway, and felt the warm familiarity of home as he glanced across the expanse of pristine lawn with its neat borders displaying a riot of colour in the shape of begonias, petunias, pansies, fuchsia and marigolds. He squeezed the vivid blue head of a lavender flower between his thumb and forefinger, taking in the intoxicating scent. He stepped on to the porch, and guided the house key into the lock with a smooth, practised precision. As he closed the door gently and walked across the hallway, a breeze from the other side of the house greeted him, confirming that Jenny, as he suspected, was on the terrace. He walked through to the rear of the house, and called his wife's name as he approached the French windows of the garden room. He stepped out on to the terrace.

Jenny had been lying face-down on an upholstered garden recliner, but had sat up as she heard her name. She was wearing a tiny white bikini bottom, and was clutching the unfastened top half to her chest. Her mouth was open, but all she managed to say was the first syllable of her husband's name.

'Hen...'

Henry took in the scene before him.

'Hello, Jenny, I'm back. Hello, Jeffrey. Having a nice time, are we?'

Seven

Neil sat down on a lichen-speckled bench and closed his eyes.

I thought I'd bring you up to date with what's been happening lately. Father's still giving me a hard time about everything, and he gives me credit for nothing. He shows no interest in my activities or my aspirations. He refuses to believe that I'm trying to find a job, and he accuses me of freeloading. He picks fights all the time, and I fight back with sarcasm and cruelty sometimes. I know I shouldn't. Mother mostly takes his side, though I know she sees things from my point of view when she tries.

No special friendships at the moment...but there is someone I care for and worry about rather a lot. He reminds me of you in some ways. Of course, Father remains hopeful I'll bring a girl home some time, and maybe if I did he'd start treating me like a son again. But really, how blind can he be?

Music is really exciting at the moment. My quartet has found itself a new lead, and we blend really well. Spookily, for our very first performance we sang one of your favourite songs. Was that a sign? Anyway, the guys came round to our place to discuss rehearsal plans and so on – we even decided to try for the nationals next year! And just as we're about to wrap up, to my horror, Father arrives home early and catches us rolling around like kids, laughing at one of Vince's silly jokes. But get this...Henry, our bass, greets Father like a long lost friend. It turns out they know each other from the City and the Rotary Club. Can you believe it? So, for a bit of fun, Henry suggests that we sing for Father, and though the idea sent chills down my spine, I thought what the hell, let's give it a go. But then Father gives me a withering look and makes some excuse about having to make an important call, and disappears to his study. *He couldn't even be bothered to hear me sing. Or maybe he was just embarrassed by the whole episode. Either way, he managed to make me feel like a small, unloved child yet again.*

I shouldn't be saying all this to you, should I? I only wish you'd talk back to me for a change...

Neil got up from the bench, walked to the graveside, and placed a single white rose at the foot of the granite headstone.

'Happy Birthday, Robert. I miss you so much.'

It had happened before. Whenever Neil went to Robert's grave, especially on anniversaries and birthdays, he came away feeling desolate, friendless, and in need of love. This time, the last thing he could face was returning home to wallow in the shared but unspoken gloom of another birthday that Robert would never see. He could really do with a good sing right now, but there was no chance of getting the quartet together, with Vince resting up, Danny no doubt on family duty, and Henry away on his island retreat. He could call Vince and see if he needed cheering up; perhaps they could do some duetting. But on second thoughts, Vince had said he wanted some quiet time this weekend and, in any case, bari-tenor duets are hardly guaranteed to lift the spirits.

Neil left the graveyard and walked in the opposite direction to home, towards Maidenhead. That in itself did little to help his mood, as the pleasant leafy lanes and open spaces of Cookham gave way to the functional sprawl of Furze Platt, which in turn led to the faceless jumble of central Maidenhead. Neil made his way to the railway station and bought a day travel card to London.

The train into Paddington was full. Neil sat opposite a couple with their two young children, who were chattering excitedly about visiting the Natural History Museum and the London Eye. Across the aisle was a group of teenagers playing on mobile phones, rap music hissing out at high volume from beneath hoodies, feet up on the seats.

After exchanging a few words with the couple opposite, Neil plugged in his iPod, partly to escape the nearby rap pollution, partly to brush up on a couple of new repertoire songs the chorus was learning. He ran through the bari parts in his head, careful not to sing out loud or even mouth the words. He wished he could do what Henry did. If he were here now, he'd have those teenagers sitting upright, rap music off, listening attentively. Within twenty minutes he'd have them singing *My Wild Irish Rose* in four-part harmony, and they'd all be giving him high fives as they got off the train at Paddington. As it was, Neil felt it was wiser to learn his songs in silence for fear of being beaten up.

Two places were on his mind as the train pulled into the terminus: Soho and Brick Lane. Whenever he visited London, Neil made a beeline for the bright lights, cosmopolitan buzz, and unashamed seediness of Soho. And then, when he was hungry, his favourite place to go was the twenty-four-hour bagel shop in Brick Lane. Cream cheese followed by hot salt beef with mustard. Sublime.

He took the Bakerloo line from Paddington, getting off at Piccadilly Circus. Emerging from the underground and seeing the enormous neon signs always excited him (were they neon or is that old technology, he wondered? *The liquid crystal display lights of Piccadilly Circus* didn't sound quite so romantic, somehow). As always, he managed to emerge from the wrong exit, and had to weave his way across Piccadilly and Lower Regent Street towards Shaftesbury Avenue and the gateway to temptation.

Neil's sexuality had always been a bit of a struggle to him. As far as the family, and certainly his father, were concerned, it was not a subject for discussion. For as long as he'd had Robert to look up to, he had the epitome of masculinity and heterosexuality as a role model. He'd wanted to be everything that Robert was and, for a long time, if that included fancying girls, then that was what he would try to do. It wasn't until he was fifteen that Robert had told him, in the sweetest possible way, that he thought his little brother might be gay and that he should stop pretending. Neil's immediate reaction had been indignation, but Robert had simply smiled, put an arm around him, and told him he just had to be himself, and that they'd always be brothers no matter what.

After that, Neil had assumed that if Robert was onside, then the rest of the family would be too. He didn't feel the need to *come out* and, in any case, he had no interest in being actively homosexual at that time. The whole thing became a bit of a non-issue for a while. Only when Robert died had his family's ignorance, and in particular his father's tendency towards denial, become painfully evident.

Neil walked up Shaftesbury Avenue then turned left into Dean Street. As usual, he would wander around, more or less randomly, happening upon familiar places as he went. He had no sense of spatial orientation, and could never work out where any place was in relation to any other. With plenty of time on his hands and no particular agenda, that suited him just fine as he started to meander through the streets of Soho.

He loved walking past the stage doors of the West End theatres, imagining how many world-famous actors might be packed into just a few blocks on any given night of the week. The pubs he loved too, not that he cared to drink much, but because of the myth and legend associated with many of them. The French House, The Blue Posts, The Coach & Horses, De Hems – he appreciated them all for different reasons. He walked past The Groucho Club and wondered how cool it might be to be a member; and past Ronnie Scott's, where he had once been lucky enough to see the Stan Tracey Quintet.

He often stopped at the Vintage Magazine shop, where

you could find old copies of classic comics and film posters. He enjoyed nosing around the stalls in Soho market. In one of the nearby bric-a-brac shops he had once bought an enormous art deco mirror; it had been far too heavy and unwieldy to take on the train, and he'd had to take a black cab all the way home to Berkshire at considerable expense to his parents.

As he snaked through the back streets, he made a running count of the number of signs he could spot with the words "Model Upstairs" written in felt tip pen, and how many invitations he could solicit from the doorway seducers of rip-off erotic dancing clubs selling pretend champagne at £150 a bottle to unsuspecting tourists.

Eventually, he felt the inexorable pull of one of the many bookshops with an adult section downstairs. He descended the narrow creaking steps to a small, brightly-lit room with shelves of sex magazines from floor to ceiling. He browsed the straight section casually, before moving to the gay shelves and hovering uneasily. He flicked through one or two magazines, and then started to feel uncomfortable and just a little seedy. The room was hot and crowded, and suddenly he needed to get out of there. As he turned to leave, he felt someone's hand brush deftly against his crotch. He quickly pushed his way through the punters, ran back up the stairs and out into the welcoming fresh air.

What had he expected? He felt foolish.

He also felt hungry. He took a taxi to Brick Lane.

Neil arrived home at around nine in the evening, and while he could tell that his parents were at home, it was clear that they had both retired early, no doubt in order to put the day behind them as quickly as possible. He couldn't blame them.

On the train back from London he had questioned everything. Yes, his emotions were running high because of the significance of the day, but he just didn't seem to have a firm grip on his life at all. He was desperate to find a decent job, preferably in music. The chances of that were slim. So, the question was how long would it be before he ended up working behind a bar, or flipping burgers? He was a complete mess when it came to relationships, and wasn't entirely sure what he was looking for anyway. On the plus side, he was passionate about singing with the chorus, and wildly enthusiastic about the prospects of singing with the new quartet. But more than anything he wanted to hear Robert's voice one more time.

He opened the front door quietly, and made his way upstairs to Robert's old room. Though Robert had moved out of the family home long before he died, George and Margaret had made the room a shrine to their eldest son. Framed photographs lined the walls: Cambridge graduation; triumph in the varsity boat race; at his desk in Harley Street; astride his favourite motorbike; at a party with Imogen, his fianceé; the two young brothers playing football on holiday in north Wales nearly twenty years ago.

Neil sat on the edge of Robert's bed, closed his eyes and, in his mind, continued talking where he'd left off earlier in the day. He tried not to sound needy or hopeless. He just wanted to be in the same space as his brother, to tell him how he felt, and to see if he could…learn something.

Speak to me, Robert.

'What are you doing in here?'

His father's voice cut through the silence like an unexpected whip crack, breaking the mood, and making Neil feel instantly guilty of some crime.

'I'm talking to Robert, if that's okay with you,' Neil said softly and without any trace of confrontation in his voice.

'I see. His birthday, yes.'

'I visited the grave this morning.'

'Yes, the white rose. Your mother and I were there this afternoon.'

'Another year without him.'

There was an uneasy pause before George cleared his throat.

'Don't be long in here, will you?' he said.

Eight

Danny and Hannah walked between the living room, dining room, kitchen and utility room doing the usual round of Saturday morning chores: tidying up and cleaning surfaces, loading the washing machine for the umpteenth time, transferring bags of shopping from the car and unpacking them into kitchen cupboards.

They waltzed easily around each other like a couple of cleverly programmed household robots without exchanging a word, the genteel background chatter of Radio 4 taking the edge off the chill silence that had become the norm in recent days.

> 'Gillian Marshall-Jones is an ex-marriage guidance counsellor and the author of three best-selling self-help guides to modern living. Her latest book, The Infidelity Paradox, has caused something of a stir within the counselling profession with its uncompromisingly stark assessment of the role and effectiveness of modern day relationship counselling…'

Unaware that the dishwasher door was open, Danny walked into it, gashing his right shin. As he recoiled, swearing loudly, he collided with Hannah, who was transferring wine glasses to a wall cupboard. Two glasses fell from her hands on to the terracotta-tiled floor, shattering into tiny crystal shards that exploded in every direction.

For a moment they stood with their backs to each other as the swearing subsided. Danny reached to switch off the radio. Silence returned. Then, slowly, they turned to each other, not quite knowing what to expect.

'Sorry,' said Danny, gesturing towards the floor, then clutching his shin with both hands.

'This relationship counselling thing isn't working, is it?' said Hannah.

'Two hundred quid down the drain so far, if you ask me. Not that money's got much to do with it. What are we going to do?'

'Talk?'

'What time are you collecting Ben from your mum's?'

'One o'clock. We've got a couple of hours.'

'Cup of tea?'

'Dustpan and brush first, I think.'

After clearing up, Danny made a pot of tea and they went to sit in the living room.

'God, this is worse than the first time we went to see Denise. My heart's racing,' said Danny.

'Me too,' said Hannah.

'Why?'

'Why do you think?'

'No. Why...*did you cheat on me?*'

'I see. Will you let me speak without interrupting?'

'I'll do my best.'

Hannah breathed deeply.

'Okay. The first thing I want you to know is that I love you with all my heart, and that I wish it had never happened.'

'So, why...*why?* What did I do wrong? Why!'

Danny spat out the words impulsively, then quickly calmed himself.

'Sorry, carry on.'

'Look, I know you're still feeling anger and resentment, but you have to listen. Think back three or four years, and remember how things were. How I was. Well...how *were* things?'

'I can speak now, can I? Well, we hadn't long been married, and I seem to remember things were pretty blissful, weren't they?'

'No, Danny. No, they weren't for me. Yes, I was happy to be married, happy to be planning for the future, but I felt like I'd lost my identity. Look, this isn't new ground. I've said a lot of this in the sessions with Denise, but maybe I haven't explained things well enough. Let me try again…'

'Yes, please do. How exactly *did* marriage to me strip you of your identity? Enlighten me.'

'Sarcasm really isn't going to help, Danny. It wasn't marrying you that made me feel that way, you blockhead. Look, when I first met you I was Hannah the rising equestrian star, Hannah the next big thing in British show jumping… blah, blah. I was expected to have a glittering career, and I wanted it so badly it hurt. I was completely driven, totally focused on the dream. And that made me who I was. Then the accident. The months of agonising over whether I'd ever compete at the top level again. And then the bombshell, the gut-wrenching reality. The end of the dream. An overnight nobody. That's what happened, Danny…that's what happened.'

Danny said nothing and poured them both another cup of tea.

Hannah continued.

'The thing is, while I had my career, my life was full. I was a hard-working and successful sportswoman, and I enjoyed being recognised and admired for my talent. And I was lucky enough to be able to come home to a wonderful man who kept me sane, kept my feet on the ground. But then, when I couldn't ride any more, it was like part of me ceased to exist. Yes, you were always there for me, and I couldn't have asked for more from you. But suddenly I'd lost the thing that made other people think I was special.'

'So, I wasn't enough for you, is that what you're saying?

'No, it wasn't about you, or us together. I couldn't see it at the time, but I was desperately trying to fill a void. I was looking for something to make me feel special again. And then Ian came along, and he had this way about him. He admired me, I could tell. He talked about how talented I was, and then how intelligent I was, and then how beautiful I was. I fell for it. I gave in to him.'

'*Why the fuck...why?*'

Danny's voice fell to a whisper.

'How many times did you see him?'

'Just twice. The first time, I have to admit I felt exhilarated. Then afterwards, I felt nothing but guilt. I saw him a second time but by then I knew it was all wrong, and I knew it would never happen again. The love I felt for you came flooding back, and I wanted nothing more than to forget my mistake and build our future together.'

'What future is there now? I'm in turmoil. I can't sleep at night for agonising over everything...over one thing in particular.'

Danny paused, ran the palms of his hands down the sides of his face, and looked up to the ceiling.

'You know what I have to ask you, don't you?' he said.

'Yes.'

'Well...?'

'Well...the honest answer is that I can't be completely sure. All my instincts tell me that Ben is yours, but because of the timing I can't be a hundred per cent certain. I only know that you are Ben's dad in every sense that matters, and I can't imagine a closer father-son relationship than yours. You're wonderful together. It's not a question in my mind.'

'It's a question in *my* mind.'

'Do you want to find out for sure? And what if—'

'I don't know.'

'How do you feel about *us* right now, Danny?'

Danny placed his hands on his knees, dropped his head towards the floor, and spoke without looking up.

'Part of me wants to hold you and never let you go. Another part of me can't bear to be in the same room as you because I'm repulsed by your treachery. I'm so confused. It…it might be best if I move out for a while so I can get my head together.'

He looked up, suddenly more animated, and continued.

'But I want to see Ben every day, to keep things as normal as possible for him. If I'm here for half an hour every evening during the week, and pop over at weekends, he won't know the difference.'

Hannah looked at Danny with sadness written into her eyes.

'If that's what you want. But please let's work this out. I want us to get through this. And what you just said about Ben…well, it proves that you're the best dad he could possibly have.'

'Well, this is it. Welcome to Chez Vince.'

'Very nice. Very cosy,' said Danny.

'You mean desirable bijoux residence affording compact yet comfortable accommodation, ideal for town centre living? I had the estate agent's bullshit when I bought the place.'

'Cheers, mate. I really appreciate this. It won't be for long, I promise.'

'I told you. You can stay for as long as you need to get things sorted out…so long as you're out by Tuesday. Only kidding. Your room's over here. Throw your bags in, and I'll make a cuppa.'

Danny looked around the walls of the small living room while Vince busied himself in the kitchen.

'Bloody hell, I've never seen so many CDs. There's got to be, what, two thousand here? And you must have every music biography ever written.'

'Music is my first love, remember...the John Miles thing?' Vince shouted from the kitchen above the rising noise of a kettle coming to the boil.

When Vince reappeared carrying the tea things, Danny was reading the booklet from a CD case.

'Who are these guys, then?'

'Ah, The Gas House Gang. 1993 international quartet gold medallists. What a sound they made. Jim Henry, the bass, has recently won gold again with his latest quartet, Crossroads. And he's the director of The Ambassadors of Harmony too, multi-international chorus gold medallists. I saw them in Brighton a few years ago. A hundred and forty men on stage making the biggest, sweetest sound you ever heard.'

'How come I haven't heard of any of them, then?'

'Quite simple, barbershop isn't mainstream in this country. It's not even mainstream in the States, to be honest, but it's been around a lot longer over there. There's a big grass roots movement in the universities and colleges, the Barbershop Harmony Society in Nashville organises a network of local chapters across the States, and generally promotes the cause. Over here we've got the British Association of Barbershop Singers. They do a similar job, organising the annual convention, including the national championships, and providing support to choruses and quartets in terms of education, training, all that stuff.'

'I didn't realise there was so much to it.'

'You have a lot to learn, my son. And don't expect Jaffa Cakes with your tea every day of the week.'

'Seriously, this is a really neat place you've got here. Are you sure I won't be cramping your style? I mean, I don't want to be hanging around when you're thinking of bringing a lady friend back...'

'*Lady friend?* As it happens, I do have a lady friend, but we're cool with each other's space. In fact, I meant to introduce you to Angie…remember the barmaid at The Ship?'

'I seeee…I *thought* there might be a little something going on there!' said Danny, reaching for his third Jaffa Cake.

'Yeah, there's a little something going on all right, but not nearly enough going on for Angie's liking. She's a great girl, and she makes out like everything's cool with us only seeing each other now and then, but I'm getting the feeling she's angling for more. That's one of the bonuses of having you here for a little while – it helps to maintain the status quo, so to speak.'

'That's a bit naughty, isn't it, Vince?' said Danny, reaching for his fourth Jaffa Cake.

'Not at all. I'm helping out a friend in need. Now, why don't you get unpacked and settled in?'

'Yup, will do.'

Danny got up, walked towards his bedroom door, then stopped.

'Er, Vince, I couldn't help noticing a wheelchair in my room. Would you mind if I move it out of the way, so I can—'

'Bugger, yes, of course, I'll bung it in the corridor for now. Give me a mo…'

'The wheelchair belongs to…?'

'Me.'

'You have a wheelchair?'

'Yes, yes. I thought you knew. I do a Stephen Hawking tribute act in my spare time. Every first Thursday of the month at the British Legion.'

Vince continued, adopting a Dalek-like voice.

'*In a moment, I'll be explaining the correlation between the amount of entropy in a black hole and the size of its event horizon. But first, a song…*'

'No, seriously…?' said Danny.

'Well, I haven't needed the chair for a few years now.

But I'm not so sure I won't need it again. It's getting worse now, or so I'm told. Why are you looking so puzzled? Hasn't Neil mentioned it? I've got MS.'

'Shit, really? Oh fuck, Vince. I'm sorry. I mean, I thought *I* had problems…'

Vince smiled.

'You do, mate, you do. First of all, you've got to sort your bloody marriage out. Then somehow we've got to turn you into one of the top sixteen barbershop leads in Britain. The prelims are just over four months away. Only sixteen quartets qualify for the finals next year, and we're going to be amongst them, Danny Boy.'

Nine

Neil could barely contain his excitement as he paced around the conservatory floor.

'It's great to see you guys. I've been itching to get started with rehearsals. How was the island, Henry?'

'Ah, the island. Wonderful, too wonderful. I think I'm in love with the place. But back to the madness, I'm afraid. Life has a habit of belting you round the back of the head when you're not looking, doesn't it?'

As he spoke, Henry unconsciously rubbed the back of his tanned, high-gloss pate.

'Can you be just a little less cryptic, Henry?' asked Vince, looking puzzled.

'No, I'm afraid not, but I am sure glad to be here with you fellas. Can't wait to get singing…but I'm surprised you allowed us back here, Neil, after the scene with your father last time. I have to say I thought it was a hoot discovering that George is your old man, but he didn't seem to see the funny side.'

'I'm afraid that Father doesn't do funny these days, but there's no danger of a repeat performance today…he's away at a bridge piss-up – sorry, convention – in Scotland. He asked me to pass on his regards when I next see you, which I must say I hadn't expected.'

'Decent chap, George…and it's lovely to see Margaret again after all this time,' said Henry, pointing towards the kitchen where Margaret was busying herself. 'Right, shall we get started, then?'

'I have to be away by two. Picking up Ben,' said Danny.

'Oh, and just so you know, Hannah and I have, for the time being…well, anyway, I've moved in with Vince for a while.'

'Purely platonic,' said Vince.

'Thanks for the clarification, Vincent. Well, I hope it's not for long, Danny,' said Neil.

'Thanks. I just need some space at the moment.'

'Well you won't get much of that at Vince's flat, but I hope you and Hannah can sort things out—'

The doorbell rang.

'Ah, that'll be Ken…' said Neil, moving towards the doorway.

'Ken?' said Henry.

'*Ken?*' said Vince.

'Isn't he the bloke who does the crossword during chorus rehearsals?' asked Danny.

'Yes, that Ken. Look, sorry to spring this on you, but I asked him if he could lend an expert ear to proceedings… you know, get us started along the right lines…I only found out he could make it about an hour ago…he's a damn good coach…I'll just get the door.'

Neil skipped out of the conservatory into the house.

'What time did you say you have to be away, Danny?' asked Henry, scratching his head in a slightly agitated manner.

'Two.'

'Then we're doomed, because it'll be three before we get anywhere near singing. Ken likes to talk.'

'True, he does,' said Vince. 'But we'll have to keep him focused on the job. He's a barbershop guru, Dan. We can learn a lot from Ken.'

A moment later Neil returned with Ken in tow. A genial reddish face with a white pencil moustache, topped with a head of slicked-back white hair, appeared from behind Neil. Ken lit up the room as he entered, placed a briefcase and a folded copy of *The Times* on to the coffee table, and extended his hand first to Vince ('Mr Chairman'), then Henry ('Mr Warrington, my, what a suntan'), then Danny ('ah, the new kid on the block…sorry, I forget your name…'). Henry noticed that *The Times*' crossword was complete except for one clue.

Ken slumped into a rattan chair.

'Sorry I'm a bit late. I'm knackered after last night, coaching a ladies' quartet in Southampton. Didn't get home until one this morning. Comedy quartet called The Weightwatchers. Do you know them? Lovely ladies. The bass has a marvellous set of lungs on her, if you'll pardon the expression. The baritone needs a bit of work, though. And the tenor has a mouth on her like a merchant seaman.'

Henry glanced at the others as if to say *I told you so* as Ken continued without pausing for breath.

'Actually, I sang with a merchant seaman once – Bert Trapp his name was. Do you know him? Quartet silver medallist three times running in the late seventies with The Jive Jockies, Midnight Melody Makers, and The Four Pips. Never did get gold. Couldn't stay in one quartet for long enough. I told him it must be something to do with his seafaring days. Wanderlust, I believe they call it. Just couldn't stay put. Ah, dear old Von…that was his nickname…you know, Von Trapp, as in *The Sound of Music*? Talking of which, I picked up a rather lovely arrangement of *Edelweiss* the other day. Unusually, the baritone stays above the lead for quite a bit of the song. It works, though. I was thinking of suggesting it as a chorus song. Any chance of a cup of tea, Neil dear boy?'

As though summoned like a genie from a lamp, Margaret appeared at the doorway of the conservatory.

'Did I hear someone say tea? Here we are…oh, hello there…I don't believe we've met…'

For the next half hour, Margaret and Ken talked while the quartet feasted on chicken sandwiches, ham and tomato sandwiches, tea, Victoria sponge cake, and fruit.

Ken told Margaret that she reminded him of a rather beautiful lady tenor of his former acquaintance, who had sadly been hampered by a club foot since birth and had never quite developed the stage confidence to become the star performer her talent had promised. Margaret picked Ken up on aspects of his grammar and constructions of speech, and particularly delighted in spotting two oxymorons in the middle part of Ken's extended monologue on the subject of orthopaedic boots. The two got along like a house on fire.

Meanwhile, Neil found himself wondering whether they were destined to become a luncheon club or a debating society rather than a singing group. Eventually, out of frustration, he stood up and proclaimed loudly, 'Mother, Ken…can we please sing now?'

Margaret started to tidy up the tea things. Ken didn't bat an eyelid. He plucked a banana from the fruit bowl, peeled it, and then asked someone to pick a song.

'Okay, it'll have to be *In My Room*,' said Neil, waving his arms at the others to get them to line up in the middle of the conservatory. 'Ken, can you listen out for—'

'Wait. Just sing the song please,' said Ken, taking a large bite of banana. 'Off you go.'

After they had finished the song, Ken pursed his lips before delivering his verdict.

'You sang that rather well at the club recently. Not so well just then. I didn't hear many chords, and the melody faded here and there. Probably not your fault, Davey – sorry, *Danny* – I think the harmony parts drowned you out at times. Quite a sweet sound, though. Something there to work on. Now, start again from the edge…'

'Edge?' asked Danny.

'From the beginning,' Neil explained.

While they sang, Ken opened his briefcase and took out a ring binder stuffed with sheet music. He flipped through the alphabetical index cards to 'I', pulled out the score of *In My Room,* and waved it above his head.

'Thank you, stop there. Now, what do you suppose this song is all about?'

'A bloke in a room?' said Vince.

'I see. A bloke in a room. Well, that certainly explains things. From the way you sang just now, I'd guess that the room is painted entirely white. Featureless. And I'd say that the bloke in question is probably wearing a straightjacket, that the walls are padded, and that the door is heavily bolted from the outside. There, you've painted a picture for me. But do you think it's the one Brian Wilson had in mind when he wrote it? Mmm?'

'No. It's about finding sanctuary, somewhere where you can shut out the world's troubles and your own worries and, well, escape,' said Danny.

'Ah, that's more like it. Brian Wilson reportedly didn't have the happiest of childhoods, but he found refuge in his bedroom where he said he was never afraid. So, with that in mind, what sort of mood do you think you need to convey with this song?'

'Depressed?' said Vince, who quickly thought the better of it. 'No, probably not depressed.'

'Well, you certainly depressed me with your singing just now, but that probably isn't the best angle to come at it from, is it? How about contemplative, dreamy...hopeful even? So, once more with feeling, please...'

After three more run-throughs, Ken eventually conceded that the quartet was beginning to deliver the message of the song.

'That was ten times better than when you first sang it. You almost convinced me there. But let's move on and take a look at some technical things, starting with vocal production...'

For the best part of an hour Ken worked with each of

them, correcting posture, getting them to breathe properly, sing in a relaxed way, and produce reasonably matched vowel sounds. He digressed just once to tell the story of a quartet he once coached in Swindon, whose bass was an ex-circus dwarf undergoing gender reassignment therapy, and who sang standing on a tea chest.

At the end of the session, Neil told Ken that he'd given the quartet the best possible start, Henry thanked him for his brilliant insights, and Vince declared that he was 'completely cream crackered'. Danny checked his watch and announced that he had to leave in twenty minutes.

'Well, let's just catch our breath and summarise what we've learnt from Ken,' Neil suggested.

Ken raised a hand to stop Neil in his tracks.

'It's not rocket science, chaps. It's stuff you've heard from lots of people lots of times in chorus rehearsal. It's all about mastering basic vocal technique, and that comes with practise and repetition. You're aiming for well-supported, freely-produced, resonant sound, and close matching between the voice parts. In future, don't sing a note of any song unless you've warmed up with vocal exercises and you've worked on vowel matching. And when you do sing a song, make sure you know the story, have an interpretive plan, and can demonstrate the right emotions throughout. Tell the story, all of you, but particularly through the lead. Believe in what you're singing and the audience will believe in you. Now, can anyone help me with this last crossword clue?'

'Shout it out, then Ken,' said Henry.

'*Peripheral origin of eighties cinematic missive.* Three words. Four-three-four. First word – blank, R, blank, blank. Second word is almost certainly THE. Fourth word – E, blank, blank, E.'

Henry looked studious, Neil said he was hopeless at crosswords, and Vince started flicking through the sports pages. Danny's face suddenly cracked into a big, broad smile.

'From the edge,' he said emphatically.

'Sod it, I thought we'd finished singing for today,' said Vince.

'No, that's the answer. FROM THE EDGE. As in the eighties film *Postcard from the Edge*. Postcard is the missive, but that's not in the answer. '*Peripheral origin*' is what you're looking for, and that's FROM THE EDGE.'

Danny picked up the pen lying on the coffee table and passed it to Ken.

'Bloody Nora,' said Vince.

'We never did decide on a name for the quartet, did we?' said Henry. 'Well, I think we may just have found it.'

Ten

For the next two months, From The Edge met to rehearse every Saturday, either at Neil's house ('so long as Father isn't in residence'), or Henry's place ('while Jenny's playing golf or at the Abbey'), or just occasionally at Vince's flat ('*mi casa, su casa,* squeeze in where you can, and don't expect Jaffa Cakes every time'). They also met early on a Wednesday evening before chorus rehearsal, whenever Vince and Danny could get away early from work.

Despite his initial hesitation, Danny joined Maidenhead A Cappella and became a full member of the chorus as well as the quartet. This allowed the foursome to sing together more often, and to work on chorus songs as well as their own repertoire. Danny found that he could spend the time he wanted with Ben without much compromise, but he immersed himself in every chorus and quartet session, anaesthetising himself from the personal hurt that skewered him every other moment of his week. He hadn't told Hannah about it. Singing was his and his alone.

With advice from Ken, Neil picked two songs that he felt would be ideal for the quartet to sing at the prelims contest in November – a high-tempo number with an infectious rhythm, a rousing opening and an even more rousing finale; and a simple but moving ballad, technically not too complex, and easier than most ballads to deliver with something approaching genuine emotion rather than schmaltz. Neil saw this as *his* project. Song choices for contest were vitally important. Over-stretch and you can end up falling apart on stage, under-stretch and you might leave points on the table. He worked closely with Ken, who gave his time generously, on developing and honing the presentation plans for both songs.

Henry was exhilarated to be singing with From The Edge, which he proudly considered to be the most promising quartet he'd ever been part of, and surely the most warm, amusing and delightfully dysfunctional foursome he'd ever sung with. At home he and Jenny were avoiding difficult questions, agreeing to disagree, and spending less and less time together. Post-island reality wasn't what Henry had hoped it would be. In quiet moments he thought about the island a lot, all the time turning a small grey stone in the fingers of his right hand.

If Vince had felt proud when he was appointed chairman of Maidenhead A Cappella two years ago, he felt even more proud to be part of From The Edge. His pride, and his ambition to make an impact at national level, kept him going even when his limbs were close to failing him and when fatigue came in great waves, washing away all of his energy. He awoke feeling tired, went to bed feeling exhausted, and during the day he muddled by at work as best he could. Outside of rehearsals, when Danny was around, Vince encouraged him to sing lead-tenor duets, played CDs of past quartet champions, and pointed out specific vocal techniques, technical strengths, artistic qualities. *We can be that good, Danny Boy. We can be that good.*

One Saturday afternoon in late September, the quartet and Ken sat around on Henry's terrace enjoying the Indian summer, as sunlight percolated through the thinning tree canopy, throwing light and shade patchwork shapes on to the baize-smooth lawn. A faint smell of wood smoke reached them from somewhere.

'Time to take stock, I think, chaps. Two months to go to prelims. How do you think things are coming along?' asked Ken, as he fished out a slice of cucumber and a sprig of mint from his Pimm's, dropping them into a nearby plant pot.

'I could slice a banana into that if you'd prefer,' said Henry with a chuckle of affection.

'No, no, I'm fine. And the plant will be fine. All biodegradable, additional nutrients. So, who wants to start?'

'Well, we've learnt the two contest songs in pretty short order, and I think the presentation plans are coming together nicely?' said Neil.

'Okay, yes, yes. What else?'

Vince took a gulp of lager and cleared his throat.

'I think we've made progress being more sympathetic to the lead. We're singing through Danny, supporting him better, rather than swamping the melody like we used to.'

'Good, I'd agree with that. What else?'

'I think I'm setting the rhythm better in the up-tune,' said Henry.

'You are, it's true. All very nice. What do you think, Danny?'

Danny thought for a moment, started to speak, then hesitated.

'It's...it's like...well, what do I know, I've only been singing in quartet for five minutes, but...'

'Yes, carry on?'

'Well, it's a bit like we're painting by numbers at the moment. Learning words and notes, applying technique to order, doing the drills. But I think we're missing something...something needs to click, and I can't explain what it is...sorry...'

'Don't be sorry for putting your finger on the very nub of the issue, dear boy! You're spot on!' said Ken, becoming much more animated.

Vince gave Danny one of his *know it all* looks, followed by a wink.

Ken got up from his chair, looking suddenly like an evangelist about to deliver *the Word*.

'Where shall I start? What is harmony singing all about? Voices, four in this case, singing together – it could be homophony or polyphony, it doesn't matter – but four voices working together to make beautiful music, often quite complex music, an elaborate tapestry if you will. You each have to be devoted enough to learn your part perfectly before you even stand a chance of making music. All the right notes need to line up so that the chords have a chance of working. One wrong note from one of you and it sounds bad, doesn't it? Yes, but is getting a hundred per cent note and word accuracy all that this is about? My Aunt Fanny it is! Let me ask you this…how many voices should your audience hear when you sing?'

'Well, I'd hazard a guess at four,' said Vince with a cocky grin.

'Wrong answer, my friend. I'll accept One or Five.'

They looked around at each other with varying degrees of confusion, as Ken continued.

'You start out with four individual voices, but when those voices lock perfectly together, they become one voice, and that's what your audience should hear. One unified, harmonious voice. But then what happens when your individual voices lock and match perfectly?'

'You create harmonic overtones,' said Neil.

'Exactly. Listen to a top quartet ringing chords, and the room will fill with harmonic overtones. And at a purely physical level, you could say that those harmonic overtones are themselves an independent voice. A fifth voice, so to speak. But that's only part of the story. Any competent quartet can create *a* fifth voice, but very few find *The* Fifth Voice. That's something that goes beyond the physical. Something that comes from inside each of you. Something you have to search for.'

'Sorry, you've lost me, Ken,' said Vince.

'Then let me give you a clue. You guys have shown you

can learn fast and apply basic technique. Yes, you need to match vowels. And yes, you need to adopt a model sound and replicate it every time you sing. But it's much less about *here...*than it is about...*here!*'

As he spoke, Ken rapped his head and then his chest with a closed fist, allowed a brief dramatic pause, then carried on.

'It's all about empathy, unity, understanding. Wilsons, Everleys, Mills – all great harmony singers, but why? I'll tell you why...DNA. Siblings share similar vocal characteristics, they are wonderfully adept at mimicking each other, and they have a natural and instinctive understanding of each other's personalities. Okay, you're not brothers, but that's your challenge, chaps. Get to know each other a lot better than you do already. I can tell you all get along fine, and that's a great start. But, believe me, by becoming much closer as a group, the unity of sound will improve immeasurably. And who knows what else will improve too?'

'Well, Danny moving in with me has got to be a good thing, then. But, as I say, it's only platonic, Ken. Should we be looking to move the relationship on a bit, do you think?' said Vince.

No one laughed, and Vince felt foolish, his compulsion to crack gags getting the better of him yet again. After another brief pause, Ken continued.

'We're missing something – that was what Danny said. Now you know what it is, I suggest you go find it, gentlemen. Oh, and before I forget, I have a surprise for you...'

Ken leant to one side in his chair, reached into a back pocket and pulled out a folded sheet of paper, which he opened up slowly, then read:

Dear Ken,
I trust you and Bella are just fine. It's been ages hasn't it? We really, really need to meet up for dinner! But

forgive me, as this is a slightly less personal enquiry. Are you still singing with your barbershop quartet? I've got a bit of a luvvies' do coming up, and I thought of you guys as the ideal crew to greet guests as they arrive for drinks. It's a bit of an anniversary – forty years in the biz, can you believe it? – but I don't want any old duffers providing the background entertainment, and you guys are the best I know. All expenses paid, and a decent fee, goes without saying, but only two weeks' notice, I'm afraid! The do is at Television Centre on 8 October, and I so hope you can make it. If not, perhaps you have some protégés you could bring along? Let me know, matey.

Yours,

Newt

'Newt? Would that be Newton Burns, by any chance?' asked Danny.

'He's an old pal.'

'What…the presenter, writer, comedian…*the* Newton Burns?' asked Neil. 'He's practically the face of the BBC these days.'

'Yes, yes. And guess what? You've got the gig, chaps,' said Ken.

Eleven

Out of habit, Henry squeezed a lavender flower between his thumb and forefinger and took in his favourite scent. He then threaded the short stem of a small red rose through the buttonhole of his navy blue jacket and walked to the open-topped TVR, which was gleaming in the bright early evening sunshine. He folded his jacket carefully, placing it buttonhole-up on the passenger seat, then glanced around the garden, still in full bloom and looking magnificent, before climbing into the driving seat and firing up the engine's familiar throaty hum.

For the first time in a long while, he had decided to attend the monthly meeting of his Rotary Club in Windsor. Though an infrequent attendee these days, he liked to keep up with plans for the major events in the calendar – the summer ball in aid of a local hospice, the November fireworks extravaganza in conjunction with the Scouts, Christmas carols around the wards of St Luke's, and various twinning activities with associations in France and Germany. Not that any of that was of interest to him on this occasion. This evening he had a very specific plan for which a visit to the Rotary Club provided an ideal pretext for being away from the house.

As he drove slowly down narrow country lanes made narrower by burgeoning hedgerows, he thought through everything one more time.

His early arrival home from his island holiday had taken Jenny by surprise, knocking the wind out of her sails for a brief moment, but she had rallied beautifully. The sight of her sunbathing in a skimpy bikini, semi-naked in fact, with Jeffrey sitting nonchalantly in a garden chair reading a newspaper not two yards away, seemed somehow familiar. How many times had the two couples sunbathed together in Puerto Banus, the girls going topless without a care, while he and Jeffrey played pétanque or shuttlecock?

Jeffrey had apparently arranged to drop by to collect the hi-tech putter he had lent to Henry a couple of weeks previously. His golf score had been suffering, and he needed the putter for a medal tournament the following week. He called round on what happened to be the hottest day of the summer, so no surprise that Jenny was taking full advantage on the terrace at the time.

It was all very plausible, and the easy, casual manner in which they explained the situation was admirable. Or perhaps the story was entirely true, in which case it wasn't admirable at all. But somehow Henry doubted it. Something had flickered in Jenny's eyes that unsettled him. Jeffrey, wearing sunglasses, had remained inscrutable, but Jenny had looked, just for a fleeting moment, like a teenager whose parents had returned to find a forbidden house party in full swing.

At the time he had let it go. What else could he do? The three of them had even sat around with drinks for a while, their shadows lengthening across the terrace, the air rich with honeysuckle and night-scented stock. At last, Jeffrey had looked at his watch and declared that Suzi would be wondering where he'd got to. Henry had to remind him about the putter as he made for the door, which hadn't counted in Jeffrey's favour, but he had decided to let that go too. He was just in too good a mood to jump to paranoid conclusions at the time.

But what followed wasn't good. Jenny was edgy, showed little interest in Henry's holiday adventures – hardly asking any questions at all – and when he asked if she was all right, she snapped at him. The sun had brought on a headache, the takeaway tandoori he had planned was the last thing she could face, and all she wanted to do was lie down in a darkened room. So lovely to be home, Henry had thought.

In the weeks following, the pair had settled back into an uneasy co-existence. When they spoke they disagreed about everything, however mundane or seemingly innocuous. Henry reminded Jenny that the point of his solo holiday had been to allow the dust to settle following his redundancy. He was entirely serious about not wanting to stay on the corporate merry-go-round, and he felt that they could work out a perfectly good future for themselves that didn't involve the frenzy of the 'square mile' and the drudge of the daily commute. There had to be a *middle ground,* he explained.

But it fell on deaf ears. Henry grew increasingly frustrated, and not a little sad, at the barriers Jenny was putting up, and as he could find no reason for his wife's incalcitrant and unreasonable behaviour, he eventually concluded, with some conviction, that there was something going on between her and Jeffrey after all.

He had given Jenny several days' notice of the Rotary evening, which was an important part of the plan. He also informed her that he wouldn't be back before eleven-thirty.

At the Rotary Club, Henry was greeted like a prodigal son, and gently berated for his recent absence. A former chairman of the Windsor club, he had been one of the leading lights for several years, helping to establish a new charitable agenda and forge important links with a new generation of local businesses. One of his old quartets, The Plus Fours, had even serenaded the guests at a ladies' evening a few years back.

The business part of the evening was the usual perfunctory affair, working through matters related to the planning of various club initiatives, with thanks given liberally throughout to all those involved. The treasurer delivered his quarterly report, and someone gave a speech on health and safety, which unsurprisingly did not prove to be the high point of the evening. Under 'Any Other Business', some wag suggested that Henry Warrington should be required to pay a fine for 'failure to notify leave of absence', and the agenda was wound up with a toast to the future health and prosperity of the club. Then someone announced a ten-minute break, after which dinner would be served.

During the business meeting, Henry had scanned the room for familiar faces, nodding and exchanging little waves with several old timers. And over in the far corner of the room, partly obscured from view by what looked like a DJ's mixing desk, sat George Taylor.

Henry had a lot of time for George. He first met him twenty or so years ago when Henry was a rookie trader; being twelve years his senior and at the top of his game, George was one of the guys you could learn a lot from. Savvy, straight as a die, and with a clinical eye for a deal, George was the go-to guy for many a young kid starting off at his firm. Inevitably, Henry lost touch with George when his own career took off and he accepted a position with another firm, but they became reacquainted about seven years ago through the Windsor Rotary Club. Since then they had spent time together on various committees, played the odd round of golf, and shared many a dinner table, as well as the occasional very expensive bottle of red.

Finding out that George was Neil's father was one of those crazy coincidences in life. Singing with a twenty-something wasn't that unusual, as guys of all ages join harmony clubs, but finding out by accident that you've known his dad for donkey's years comes as a bit of a surprise.

During the break, Henry made a beeline for George, giving him the heartiest of handshakes, and insisting that they sit together at dinner.

'I still can't believe that you're Neil's old man. Come on, let's catch up,' said Henry.

Over dinner, Henry and George talked over old times. The morning when Henry almost blew a copper deal worth millions and George stepped in calmly, saving the deal and Henry's job without a second's thought. And the afternoon they cleaned up on orange juice concentrates and retired to Balls Brothers to polish off several bottles of 1961 Margaux.

'Of course, it's a long time since I saw any real action,' said George. 'They parked me in a back room years ago, though they flick the dust off me twice a week, which is good of them. But you're still at the crease, eh Henry? Still knocking them over the boundary rope, I bet!'

'No, George, no. Rain stopped play a few months ago, since when I've decided to pack up my bat and pads for good. As BB King would have it, the thrill is gone. I get much more of a kick out of simple things these days, George.'

'Like bloody barbershop singing, eh? That was a rum do, Henry. Coming home one evening to find you and Neil and two other herberts playing games in the back room.'

'It may seem like games to you, George, but we take it very seriously, I'll have you know!'

'Tell me about it. It's all that Neil does as far as I can tell. How can that be, Henry? He's twenty-three, just a year out of university, able bodied and as bright as a button. Yet he spends all his time pouring over sheet music and singing songs about Nellie Dean and the old mill stream! It beats me, Henry...'

'Music and singing are his passion, you know that. He's a cracking baritone, and a very talented arranger. And it's not all Nellie Dean, George! We sing lots of modern stuff – we're working on something by Take That at the moment.'

'Take what?'

'It doesn't matter. I forget I'm preaching to a confirmed non-believer, George – well, judging by the way you ran for the hills when we suggested singing you a song!'

Henry laughed, clinking his wine glass against George's.

George seemed suddenly serious.

'The thing is, it's all a bit of a lark, isn't it? I've no problem with you, you've worked hard, made your bit, and you're having some fun now, but Neil...he hasn't found his first job yet! And no sign of a girlfriend. His head's in the bloody clouds.'

George slumped very slightly forward, both hands flat against the tablecloth in front of him, as he took a deep breath.

'His brother was *so* different.'

Henry placed a hand on George's arm, and softened his voice.

'Neil is a super young man, George. Bright, talented, ambitious in his own way, and very considerate of others. He's really trying to find his way, you know. You should be proud of him.'

The old friends agreed it had been good to catch up, and promised to do so again before long. They gripped each other's forearms in farewell, an advance on the brisk handshake of earlier, but falling some way short of the full body hug that had become fashionable these days, and which George was having none of.

Henry performed a swift tour of the other dining tables, weaving between them to shake hands with more old friends, and he gave a final wave to the room as he made for the door, loosening his tie as he did so, and then taking the stairs nimbly two at a time down to the ground floor.

He checked the time as he made his way quickly to the car. Nine-forty. He would be back in Ascot by ten.

As he drove through the back lanes towards home, Henry thought about George. He was looking old these days; sorrow, and his ways of dealing with it, had clearly taken their toll. And he thought about Neil, his quartet pal, full of youthful exuberance and energy, and yet touched by the same sorrow. Father and son living under the same roof, and yet so far apart. They don't know it, but they hold the solution to each other's grief.

At two minutes to ten, Henry turned into the narrow road opposite the gated driveway to his house, did a three-point turn at the end of the cul-de-sac, and then parked near the top of the road with a clear view of the driveway entrance. He switched off the headlights, turned on the radio, tuned into Classic FM, and lowered the volume.

At twenty-three minutes past ten, Jeffrey Moss emerged from Henry Warrington's driveway on foot, turned left, and walked the fifty yards to where his titanium silver BMW 7 Series was parked, just around the corner.

At ten forty-five, the radio presenter introduced *Spem in Alium* by Thomas Tallis, and Henry turned the volume up a touch. Then followed *The Lark Ascending* by Ralph Vaughan Williams, and the full twenty-six minutes of *Appalachian Spring* by Aaron Copland, which brought the time to just after eleven-thirty. Henry started the car, drove it across the road, and parked in the second garage. He then let himself into the house.

Jenny had gone to bed, where she had probably been most of the evening, Henry realised with a sharp pang of sadness. He poured a large malt whisky, climbed the stairs, and made his way to the largest of the three guest bedrooms.

As he lay in the guest bed (far more comfortable than his own, as he had noted on many occasions), Henry imagined how things would unfold. He would keep it simple, with no high-handedness, no cute stuff. But he knew that whatever words he used would be inadequate, barely able to sum up the situation – how things had come to this. How could you put an end to the most significant relationship of your adult life in a simple exchange of words?

Whichever way he presented things, he knew it would

turn nasty. He could already see the look on Jenny's face – the immediate shock, followed by the quick-fire acid response; the venom, the rancorous outpourings of a woman who had lost whatever tenderness of spirit she once possessed, let alone whatever love she once felt for him.

In the end, Henry decided that confrontation would be futile. He went downstairs to the study, where he sat at his desk for about half an hour, pen poised over paper. Eventually, he wrote:

Jenny,

I can't believe it's come to this. I have tried to understand why we have grown so far apart, but you won't even talk. Now I know what you've been up to, and I feel deeply saddened and betrayed. Strangely, I don't feel angry, though I'm not sure why. I've always done my best for you and for us, but for some reason that hasn't been good enough for you. At least I see things as they are now, and my eyes have at last been opened to what a cold, calculating, vain, ungrateful, scheming, and utterly selfish individual you are.

I can't face you right now, but I'm prepared to talk so long as you can be reasonable. I'll be back at the weekend to collect some things.

Henry

Twelve

Vince stretched out his legs stiffly, sank back into his chair, and took a long, slow draught from his pint glass.

'That was a great session, wasn't it? Ken's a genius. Mad as a hatter, of course, but without question a genius. Why is it that there's such a thin line between the two, do you think?'

'He's probably neither. Maybe he's just a very smart and experienced musician with a slightly unconventional way of doing things?' said Danny.

'*Slightly* unconventional? This is a man who knows the key signature of every domestic appliance in his house. Electric razor? F. Electric toothbrush? F-sharp. The lowest speed setting on the food processor? D. I wouldn't mind betting his wife's got a box of vibrators under the bed, all tuned to a different pitch on the chromatic scale. You can just see it, can't you...*give me a G please Ken, and make sure it hits the spot!*'

They laughed until their sides hurt.

'As if my intercostals haven't taken a battering already today,' said Vince, as the laughter subsided.

Angie looked on from behind the bar, arms folded across her chest and shaking her head, but she couldn't help laughing along with them. She hadn't a clue what they were laughing about, but it was irresistibly contagious. She loved Vince for exactly this.

'I've got that feeling, a bit like after sex...a kind of natural high caused by those chemicals – what are they called? – dolphins, or something similar. I always get a natural high after a good, hard...quartet rehearsal. Know what I mean?'

'Endorphins is the word you're looking for. And yes, I do know what you mean.'

'But natural highs don't stay around for long...same again, gorgeous!' Vince shouted over to Angie. 'Are you okay to stay for a while, Dan?'

'Not seeing Ben until tomorrow.'

'Great stuff,' said Vince.

Thinking about how to broach the next subject, Vince balanced a beer mat on the edge of the table, flipped it with the tips of his fingers and caught it in mid-air. The direct approach was best, he decided.

'So...how are things working out with Hannah? Are you two finding time to talk to each other? Just tell me to shut up if you'd rather not—'

'It's okay. I...we...it's like we're...stuck. We're talking, but it's mostly about Ben. I see him to bed most nights, then sometimes Hannah and I talk for a bit, but it's not easy. We sit in the same room, and it's polite, but it's agony. I want to say it's all fine now, let's carry on like before, but the doubt is ripping me to bits.'

'Doubt?'

Danny looked deep into his glass.

'Ben was born about nine months after she...'

'Ah, I see. But you're Ben's dad, so why...?'

'I don't know for sure, do I?'

'Of course you do.'

'What the fuck do you know, Vince...?'

Vince looked deep into his own glass.

'Did I ever tell you about *my* dad?'

'No, why?'

'He married my mum when I was two. The bloke who got Mum pregnant did a runner when he found out. Then Mum was lucky enough to meet Bill, who became my dad. The sweetest man, with the biggest heart, you'll ever meet. My one and only dad.'

'But if your real—'

'Let me stop you there, Dan. Bill's my *real* dad. If the other bastard ever showed up, I'd blank him. He means nothing to me. Never did, never could do. It's that simple.'

'But—'

'I don't see any buts, Dan. You're Ben's dad, and that's that. Do you think that the result of a DNA test would change the way you feel about him? Change your determination to be there for him? I don't think so. And would it change the way Ben feels about you? Certainly not. Think about it... and drink up. It's your round.'

'It could be worse. At least I don't play golf,' said Danny, throwing Vince a deliberate curve ball in an attempt to change the subject.

'And what the hell's that supposed to mean?'

'Bertrand Russell. "The place of the father in the modern suburban family is a very small one, particularly if he plays golf".'

'Nice one! He also said "there is much pleasure to be gained from useless knowledge", which brings us full circle to when we last sat at this very table, talking music trivia. A lot's happened in a short space of time, hasn't it?'

'Just a bit. My marriage has hit the rocks, I'm sharing a flat with a lager-swilling amateur comedian and ex-PopMaster champion, and I've started singing in a barbershop quartet. You couldn't write the script.'

Vince turned a beer mat between his fingers and adopted a look of mock humility.

'You forgot to mention anything about me being a brilliant tenor...'

'Well, yes, that as well.'

Vince threw the beer mat on to the table and adopted a look of mock self-pity.

'Or anything about my crippling degenerative disease of the central nervous system...'

'Um, yes, that as well.'

'Other than that, you summed me up pretty well.'

Vince put an arm around Danny's shoulder and squeezed him for a second before letting go.

'Talking of which, you've not been too good on your feet lately, and you seem knackered more of the time,' said Danny.

'Damn it Holmes, you're good!

'Yeah, yeah, but what's the outlook?'

'Mostly dry with the chance of occasional heavy showers.'

'Seriously?'

'If I could tell you that, I'd have my mortgage on the two-thirty at Newbury as well. It's not an exact science. The general direction is south at the moment. I had a couple of years' remission, but it's progressive now. The disease has entered its Emerson Lake and Palmer phase.'

'Neil seems pretty supportive. Always there to lend you a hand when you're flagging.'

'Yeah, he's a good guy. You know his brother died of MS? So he kind of looks out for me. And he fancies me, of course.'

'Vince, behave, will you?'

'No, seriously, Neil's a star. Nothing that a job and a boyfriend wouldn't put right. And a heart-to-heart with old George. Are you getting those drinks in or what?'

Danny went to the bar, and Vince picked up his friend's mobile phone from the table. He quickly opened the address book, scrolled down to H, and found *Hannah Mobile*. He committed the number to memory, returned the display to the main menu, and replaced the phone in its original position, screen-side down, on the table.

Neil slinked into the dining room and sat down opposite his father at the breakfast table. George didn't look up from his *FT*, but made an unpleasantly loud swallowing noise as he knocked back a cup of piping hot tea and returned it empty to its saucer with a clatter of china.

'Morning, Father,' Neil said croakily, his voice letting him down, as it often did when uttering the first words of the day.

'More tea, please, my dear,' George shouted towards the kitchen, from where the smell of frying bacon and eggs was beginning to drift through the air.

Margaret appeared at the doorway, a wisp of her normally perfect coiffeur falling over one eye. She blew upwards at the offending curl.

'Yes, yes, just a minute! Aah, good morning, darling... not often we see you so early on a Saturday morning...what would you like?'

'Morning, Ma. I'll just help myself to cereal and toast,' said Neil.

'And to what do we owe this unexpected pleasure?' said George, lifting the lid of the teapot to double-check that more tea was indeed needed.

His father's feeble sarcasm, made far worse by the sight of him resembling an expectant pig whose trough is about to be filled, made Neil feel instantly antagonistic towards him. Right, bait the hook and cast the line.

'As I was saying, good morning, Father. I trust you're feeling bright-eyed and bushy-tailed, and I wish you well this fine Saturday morn as you anticipate the delights of the nineteenth hole that will surely follow the lacklustre perambulations of the first eighteen.'

'Smart arse. So, what interrupted your beauty sleep? I've not seen you up this early since Christmas Day ten years ago. Twenty-one speed racer, I seem to remember.'

Hooked in one.

'Good bike, that,' said Neil. 'Well, I'm seeing someone this morning about an assignment.'

'An *assignment?* What, are you bloody James Bond now? Who are you seeing...M?'

Bastard.

'I'm seeing a choral director who wants to commission a number of new arrangements. Could be a good break if I get the *assignment*.'

'Well, here's hoping that doing the dots for some local choir will catapult you to fame and fortune. What are they paying you...A hundred quid, two maybe?'

Complete bastard.

'Dear Father, when will you keep your bitter little barbs to yourself, you sad, sad man?'

George threw the *FT* on to the table, becoming suddenly animated, and looking up at Neil for the first time.

'How about when you come down from the clouds and realise that the chances of you earning a living from music are as good as my chances of flying to the moon.'

Neil felt a stab to his heart, but he wasn't about to give in.

'You enjoy pissing on people's dreams, don't you?'

'No, no I don't. Did I ever do anything to stifle Robert's dreams? He had dreams that the rest of us would find impossible to realise – an ordinary middle-class boy setting his sights on becoming a world-renowned surgeon – what were the chances? But he made it...yes, because he was brilliant, one in a million they said...but in no small part due to the support your mother and I gave him!'

Margaret appeared, looked at her husband and son in a forlorn, knowing way, and placed a plate of bacon and eggs in front of George without saying a word.

'Tea, dear?' George said gently, risking his wife's wrath.

'It's on its way. You two just carry on destroying whatever's left of your relationship, and I'll keep skivvying away quietly in the background. Wholemeal toast, Neil?'

Neil nodded and smiled at his mother, silently mouthing the word 'sorry' once he was sure that George wasn't looking.

Margaret returned to the kitchen, and George continued his rant.

'And let me tell you something else. I bumped into

Henry Warrington the other evening, at the Rotary Club. We had a good old chat. It may surprise you to know that when he first started work at my firm years ago I taught him the ropes, looked out for him, and watched as his career took off. He went on to be a big deal in the City. But he got things the right way round – he made a sound career choice, made his money, and now he's earned the luxury of sailing his boat, singing in a barbershop quartet, and whatever else he gets up to. All I want is for you to do things the right way round – get a decent job, a realistic job, and start earning your keep. Become self-sufficient. You can do your music on the side, no problem, but the idea that you're the next Andrew Lloyd-Webber just waiting to be discovered is... well, it's not going to happen, is it?'

Neil was angry now.

'No, I didn't know that about Henry, but we were talking about Robert. I don't doubt that you got behind Robert's dreams. Your wonderful first-born, who could do no wrong, and who was blessed with rare gifts. Of course you supported him, but how much support did he need? His brilliance was what got him there, and you were more than happy to ride the comet's tail, weren't you?'

'You arrogant little shit. I could knock your bloody block off!'

George got out of his chair, just as Margaret stepped in front of him, a fresh pot of tea in one hand and a white porcelain toast rack in the other. She placed the things on the table, and pointed to George's chair. He sat down. She then walked back to the kitchen, returning with a boiled egg in a white porcelain egg cup.

Margaret pulled out a chair from the table, sat down, poured herself a cup of tea, added a spot of milk, and stirred the cup gently with a small silver spoon.

'Now then. Neil, good luck with your assignment today. It sounds exciting! And please don't ever speak to your father like that again. It makes me sad and angry to hear that you think so little of him. But speak to him like that again, and I'll turn you from a baritone into a high tenor, just…like…that!'

Margaret smashed the top of her boiled egg with the back of a spoon.

'And George, enjoy your golf this morning, won't you. And unless you start to realise that Neil isn't Robert, and that he deserves your support every bit as much as Robert did, then I will have no choice but to leave you. Gentlemen, I have had enough, and you have both been warned.'

Thirteen

'Bloody hell, there it is. It really does exist, then,' said Vince, staring at Television Centre with a look of mild awe.

'You're having a laugh, aren't you?' said Danny. 'What do you mean, *it really does exist?*'

'Well, look at it. Iconic, isn't it? All those memories, growing up watching telly. *Blue Peter...Doctor Who...Sports Personality of the Year.* All in that building there. To me, it's on a par with Tracey Island from *Thunderbirds* and Marineville from *Stingray.*'

'What a load of nonsense you talk sometimes,' said Danny, glancing at his mobile phone for the time. 'Where's Ken? Wood Lane tube at six, we said. Do you think he's got lost or something?'

'Ken's always late,' said Neil, almost cheerily.

'Very reassuring. Well, let's give him five more minutes, then we'll walk over there and ask for Newton Whatnot ourselves at reception,' said Henry.

'Burns. His name is Newton Burns,' said Neil.

'Sorry, Newton *Burns.* It's just that I hadn't heard of him until Ken presented us with the invitation. I'm not much of a showbiz follower. I keep forgetting his name.'

'Deary me, Henry. You can't switch on the TV without seeing him. Sitcoms, panel shows, arts programmes, you name it. Ah, here comes Ken!' said Neil.

Ken was shuffling casually through the tube station concourse, looking down at a folded newspaper held at chest height. People were weaving around him to avoid collision, but Ken was oblivious to them all. As if deploying some sort of inner radar or homing device, he got to within three feet of the foursome before raising his head and smiling widely.

'Good evening, chaps. All present and correct, I see. Now then, are we ready to entertain the luvvies, fruit loops and sycophants over the road? Good, then let's go!'

Ken led the group over to Television Centre, where they negotiated their way past security before presenting themselves at reception. From there they were escorted to a small room on the third floor, allocated for changing and warm-up, and from where they would be collected at seven-twenty. The champagne reception for Mr Burns was to start at seven-thirty.

As they walked the corridors of Television Centre, familiar faces smiled at them from the walls. Vince made a point of naming them out loud.

'Eric Sykes, Hattie Jacques, Arthur Lowe, John Le Mesurier, Harry H Corbett, Wilfred Pickles, Billy Cotton, Morecambe and Wise, The Two Ronnies, Larry Grayson, Bruce Forsythe, Terry Wogan, June Whitfield, Terry Scott, Val Doonican, Les Dawson, Leonard Sachs, Danny La Rue—'

Then Vince stopped dead in his tracks.

'Whoa, whoa, wait a minute, stop! Who's this lot, then?'

Vince peered closely at an old black and white photo of four singers dressed in boaters, striped waistcoats and white flannels.

'No, surely not...well, bugger me...is that *you*, Ken?'

Ken barely glanced at the photograph, and muttered.

'Yes, could be. A long time ago. Probably *The Good Old Days.* C'mon, keep moving.'

'Okay, now I'm officially very nervous,' said Henry.

'I'm officially shitting myself,' said Vince. 'We land our first gig singing at a showbiz reception at the BBC, and look at this lot...an A to Z of small screen legends – and Ken's in there amongst them! How did all this happen? We're not meant to be here, are we? Wake me up, someone!'

'Calm down, calm down,' said Ken calmly, as they arrived at their changing room. 'I wouldn't have put you up for this if I didn't think you'd do a great job. Newt's an old friend, and he loves barbershop. I would have got my old quartet together again, but for the fact that two of them are dead and the other one's in an iron lung in Weston-super-Mare. Bring along your protégés is what Newt said, and here you are…you'll do just fine, chaps!'

The room was windowless and smelt of carpet underlay. It was empty except for a Formica-topped table, a portable fan, a few plastic chairs, a tin litter bin, and a clutter of cardboard boxes in one corner. As they entered, and the overhead strip lights flickered into life, Neil pushed past the others, picked up the litter bin, and wretched into it. The room now smelt of carpet underlay and vomit.

'I want to go home,' said Danny.

Panic was everywhere.

Ken placed the litter bin under a large cardboard box, then plugged in the portable fan and switched it on.

'Gentlemen, have a seat, please. We have about forty-five minutes. I'd like to say a few words. I'll keep it brief, then you can get changed and warm up, and by seven-twenty you'll be ready for action. Neil, sip some water, and everyone breathe slowly and deeply. First of all, let's just remind ourselves what you're here to do this evening – provide background music for a gathering of friends and colleagues, a party to celebrate someone's career. You won't be singing to an attentive audience. You're here to provide musical wallpaper. They don't want to listen to you; they want to chatter, drink champagne, eat prawn parcels, and exchange air kisses with people they have to pretend to like. However – and here's the thing – you will be appreciated if you sing well. And you *will* sing well. You'll see people looking your way, smiling politely, and even applauding gently now and then. This is the ideal gig for you guys – nobody's bought tickets to see you, you can relax and enjoy singing well together, and just have fun.'

'But Ken, this isn't a meeting of the local Masons or the Rotary...these people are...' said Danny, clutching his hands to his head.

'What, what are they...? Celebrities? Do me a favour. They're just a bunch of luvvies – some of them very nice luvvies, splendid people, like dear old Newt. Others are preening, narcissistic, arrogant arseholes. But that's life. You'd get the same mix at the Masons or the Rotary, though the arsehole quotient is undoubtedly a lot higher around here. Put that out of your heads. You are accomplished singers individually, and potentially something very special as a group. Start believing, boys. And, by the way, if you make a hash of this, I'll look like a right idiot, so think on!'

Ken smiled, picked up his newspaper, took a pen from an inside jacket pocket, and sat down to peruse the crossword puzzle.

'Right, get changed, chaps,' said Ken.

They changed in silence, into matching grey lounge suits with black open-necked shirts.

'At least we'll look the dog's bollocks, even if we don't sound like the dog's bollocks,' said Vince as they lined up to do some vocal warm-ups.

Ken directed the quartet as they ran through vowel-matching exercises, did a few scales in unison, and then sang *Heart of My Heart* and *Sweet Roses of Morn* in harmony.

'You're sounding sweet, chaps. Now, remember, it's an eight-song set, followed by a fifteen-minute break, then a repeat. Take your time between songs, accept whatever applause you get with a smile and a nod, and stay calm. Above all, enjoy yourselves. Now stand in a circle and put your arms around each other's shoulders.'

'Ah, Ken, what's all this?' Vince complained.

'Just do it. Now breathe together slowly. Okay, here's the pitch for your first song. Be aware of Danny, feel when he's about to sing and go with him. Let your voices lock, four into one. Hear the overtones, listen for a fifth voice. Okay. Now you're ready.'

Just then a pale, pretty young woman with cropped black hair and bright red lipstick appeared at the door.

'Hi, I'm Poppy. Would you like to come this way? Newt is really looking forward to hearing you. I'm really sorry about the room, but it was a bit last minute – it smells like someone's been sick in here!'

No one said a word, and Poppy led them to the lift.

'We're in the Reith Room on the eighth floor. I think I'll put you on the far wall, alongside the champagne table. That way everyone will get to hear you, but you won't be in the way.'

The lift stopped at the fifth floor. A slender thirty-something man with an orange face, accompanied by a grande dame in her seventies, got in. He was wearing a silver lamé jacket, skin-tight black jeans, and ballet pumps. She wore a bright blue pashmina and matching turban, and was festooned in ethnic jewellery. They all got out at the eighth floor.

Poppy led them along more corridors, whose walls were lined with the faces of more BBC luminaries, though not many of them instantly recognisable. Vince attempted to identify as many as he could as they walked towards the open doors of a large function room that was beginning to attract a trickle of people.

'Grade, haven't a clue, Yentob, no idea, nope, Birt, Dyke…'

Then Vince was distracted.

'Look out, there's that Danish weather bird…bugger me, is that an Attenborough over there?' he said.

Henry, Neil and Danny said nothing, their nerves more

self-contained, but they also couldn't help noticing the stream of well-known faces meandering slowly in the same direction. By contrast, Ken, bringing up the rear of their small group, was more interested in the solution to seventeen down than the gathering glitterati.

Poppy smiled her way through a small group hovering by the function room door, and shepherded her charges to the big open floor space within. Judging by the size of the room, a couple of hundred people might be expected, Danny calculated, as his empty stomach turned with a loud, hollow gurgle.

'I think this is just the spot, don't you, gentlemen?' said Ken, at last looking up from his crossword, and quickly taking in the proportions and layout of the available space.

Just then, a stentorian voice boomed from a corner of the room.

'Kenny, dear old Kenny, how the bloody hell are you, you old sod!'

And suddenly there was the larger-than-life figure of Newton Burns bear-hugging Ken right in front of them.

'I'm tickled pink you could make it! And these are your boys, are they? Well, a fine-looking quartet they are, I must say.'

Newton Burns shook each of them by the hand, asking their names, then stood back a couple of paces.

'Thank you for indulging my little penchant for barbershop singing. I can't wait to hear you. Now tell me, which one of you is the baritone?'

'That's me,' said Neil faintly.

'Well, my luck's in! I may need to borrow you, young man. You can help me brush up the bari part to *Heart of My Heart* and I'll join you for a rendition when I've had far too much champagne a little later on. I used to sing bari alongside Kenny many a year ago. Happy memories! Now, I'll leave you to it. Kenny, do come and mingle when you're ready.'

'You've pulled,' Vince whispered to Neil.

'Piss off, Vincent,' said a red-faced Neil.

'Right, chaps, line up facing this way. Back a bit. Over to the left a bit. Stop. Fine. Neil, you have the pitch pipe and the running order, yes? Okay, when you're ready...'

Neil blew a B-flat for the first song, and they started singing. Danny looked puzzled, Vince started straining to reach his notes, and Henry couldn't find his. They looked helplessly towards Ken, who signalled for them to stop. Poppy looked at them nervously from a distance.

'I believe you blew a B-flat, Neil,' said Ken softly. 'Try G-flat. That's the pitch note. No harm done. Off you go.'

Ken's coolness calmed the moment, and once the G-flat had sounded they were quickly into their stride, delivering a mellow easy-beat number for starters. The relief they felt after the first song was palpable, and they were pleasantly surprised to hear Poppy applauding and smiling what looked like a genuine smile. The next two numbers went by without a hitch, and they began to feel more relaxed. The room was filling up, and as people milled around the champagne table, an increasing number of them looked over at the quartet and gave understated signs of their approval: nods, smiles, a gentle ripple of applause.

After the fourth song Ken drifted into the middle of the room, where he seemed to be perfectly at ease in the assembled company. Just then, the orange-faced, silver-jacketed man from the lift walked past the quartet, delivering a barbed comment as he did so.

'I was expecting Westlife, not Pondlife,' he said with a sneer.

Vince turned to Neil.

'Don't blow the pitch, Neil,' he said, then stepped forward to follow the man across the room. '*Oi, you little twa—*'

Immediately Vince felt a restraining hand on his shoulder as Ken appeared as if from nowhere to steer him back towards the quartet.

'Shame on you, Vince,' said Ken in a firm but low voice. 'How dare you embarrass me and how dare you let your friends down. You're here to sing harmony. There's a clue in that word, my friend. Now calm down, take a minute, and carry on.'

Luckily, Vince's outburst went unnoticed, and the foursome managed to carry on to complete their first set, receiving generous applause from a small group who had gathered to listen more closely.

'We'll be back in fifteen minutes,' announced Henry, and they walked back out to the corridor in search of a quiet space away from the party. They gathered in a nearby stairwell.

'Well done, chaps, you did very well indeed,' said Ken.

'Apart from mouth almighty almost getting us thrown out, that is,' said Danny.

'You heard what that idiot said, didn't you? But you're right. I'm really sorry, fellas. I let you down,' said Vince, looking at the floor.

Ken smiled.

'No recriminations, chaps. The gentleman in the silver jacket was drunk, and he happens to be exactly the kind of arrogant arsehole I warned you about earlier. But, enough said. It won't happen again, will it Vince?'

'No. No, it won't. But, hey, did you see that Danish weather bird giving me the eye during *Witchcraft*? I'm in there, if I play my cards right,' said Vince.

If the first set went well, the second set was something of a revelation to them all. It was as if Vince's near incident had taken them as close to disaster as anything could, and suddenly the foursome felt liberated by the collective thought that nothing worse could happen from now on.

And they were right. They sang with ease, confidence and assurance, their voices blended better than ever, and they had a ball.

A couple of songs into the set, Newton Burns wandered over to listen, and a sizeable group gathered with him. Newton's evident enjoyment seemed to rub off on the others, and soon each song was being applauded loudly, and with hoots and whistles to boot.

Then Newton stepped forward and announced with carefully crafted humility that he was a frustrated barber-shop singer, and craved the indulgence of the room as he joined the quartet in a rendition of *Heart of My Heart*.

'It's highly unlikely that any of you will have heard this old barbershop number before, but if you have, my apologies in advance for what you are about to hear. And an extra special apology to my fellow baritone, the lovely Neil, whose job it is to remind me of all the right notes. Well, here goes...'

The crowd went wild as Newton Burns squeezed in next to Neil, and gave a more than passable performance singing baritone, albeit with his ear pressed ever so closely to Neil's face throughout the performance.

At the end of the set, Newton led the applause and thanked them heartily, before they were whisked away through the crowd by Poppy, and chaperoned back to their changing room.

They were all buzzing with excitement, and Poppy said she thought they had been wonderful as she led them back to the third-floor room.

'I'll wait outside while you change, then I'll escort you back to reception,' she said.

A dreadful smell greeted them as they opened the door, and Neil meekly admitted his contribution to the acrid aroma that filled their nostrils.

'Don't worry, I'll alert the cleaners,' said Poppy, stepping back into the corridor and closing the door on them.

They changed quickly, chattering excitedly about the evening.

Neil reached into the side pocket of his jacket for his pitch pipe and felt something that hadn't been there earlier. He took out a small white calling card upon which were the words NEWTON BURNS, with a telephone number beneath, in plain black type.

Fourteen

Henry and Jenny paced slowly and uneasily around the expansive parquet floor of the living room, neither wishing to sit down, neither able to be still. Henry stopped momentarily to look out through the large Georgian bay window. Jenny rearranged a vase of flowers on the mantelpiece, then fixed her hair nervously in the ornate gilt-framed mirror above it.

'You're not denying it, then?' asked Henry at last.

'No, I'm not denying it.'

'That's good. I mean, that makes things easier. And it's just as well. Jeffrey didn't put up much of a fight when I called in on him earlier today either.'

'Fight? You two…fighting? For God's—'

'No, that's not what I meant. I meant he didn't put up much resistance when I accused him of having an affair with my wife. And fighting would suggest that I'm *fighting over you*, and I'm not. So, what do you have to say for yourself?'

'I'm surprised you seem so happy to accept the situation.'

'*Happy*? Don't be so stupid, Jenny. Of course I'm not happy. I've never been more sad in my life. But that's not what I asked. I asked you to explain yourself.'

'What do you mean, you're not fighting over me?'

'Are you going to answer the question?'

'Why am I not worth fighting over? What do you mean, Henry?' said Jenny, her voice trembling.

'Answer me this one, simple question. Why are you having an affair with Jeffrey Moss?'

Jenny turned towards the mirror again, her back to Henry.

'It's not that simple, Henry, is it?'

Henry approached, stood over his wife's shoulder, and addressed her reflection.

'Okay, let me put this to you. We've had our share of problems down the years. That's to be expected. But the point of marriage, or so I was led to believe, is that you tackle problems together. You talk, you listen, you share, and you work things out. That's the deal. When did we stop doing that? What went wrong? Why turn to someone else after all these years?'

'I don't know, Henry. Maybe that's just it. *All these years.*'

Henry took Jenny by the elbow, and spun her round to face him.

'So, you're saying you're bored, is that it? Well, I'd be bored too if I had as much time on my hands as you. Taking it easy after your health scare is one thing – we agreed that was best – but four years on and you're taking the piss, Jenny. It's all *me, me, me.* Cosmetic enhancements, non-stop spa treatments, more shoes than Imelda Marcos, new cars, girlie weekends away, *Sex and the* bloody *City*…hollow, superficial nonsense, the lot of it.'

Jenny took a step backwards, and looked at Henry defiantly.

'We've been here before, Henry. Are you quite finished?'

Henry skimmed a hand across the top of his head in frustration.

'No, no I haven't. What the hell have I done wrong, I ask you? What's my crime? Working damn hard for too many years so that we can live a good life? So that you can live a double life, having it away with Moss behind my back! How could you be so scheming…so fucking heartless?'

Jenny squared right up to Henry, toe to toe.

'You sanctimonious bastard! You're far from perfect, Henry. You've become overbearing, and far too serious. You used to be fun to be around. And what happened to our sex life?'

'You took yours elsewhere, it seems.'

Henry backed away and, after a brief silence, continued.

'How the hell can you accuse me of being no fun to be around? Haven't you been listening to me? I'm the one who wants to get away, have a change of pace…have more fun together…well, that was my naïve idea, anyway. So why did you panic at the prospect? What scared you so much?'

'It seemed so unlike you. All that talk of escaping the rat race. I didn't want to see you waste your talent on whatever hare-brained scheme you were hatching…and I was scared.'

'You were scared all right. But let me tell you the real reason you were scared. You were scared that your carefully constructed way of life would be threatened. Husband out all day, bringing home the bacon, while you live a life of complete luxury, with uncomplicated access to a daytime lover in the form of that eager and compliant little prick, Jeffrey Moss. You had your cake and you were eating it with gusto. Well, no more. You've been found out, and it's time to face the music.'

'Meaning what, exactly?'

'I'm filing for divorce on the grounds of adultery, citing Moss as co-respondent.'

'Vin! Vin! Vin!' shouted Ben, as Hannah answered the door, her son by her side.

'Well, someone certainly seems to know you. Hi, I'm Hannah. Please, come on in, Vin.'

'Thanks. It's Vince actually. Ben was over abbreviating.'

Ben slapped Vince around the leg, then hid behind his mother.

'Good to see you too, fella!' Vince laughed.

'Ben! That's no way to behave. Now say hello properly, then go and play in your room, darling.'

Hannah led Vince into the living room, as Ben scurried up the stairs shouting 'Hi Vin, bye Vin!'

'It hadn't occurred to me that Ben must have met you, when Danny has him at the weekend. Tea or coffee?' asked Hannah, walking through to the kitchen.

'Yeah, he's a great little fella. Tea would be lovely, thanks. So, I guess it must seem strange me asking to come and see you. I think maybe I need to explain a bit more, huh?'

Hannah started assembling the tea things.

'I wish you would. All you said on the phone was that you had something important to tell me regarding Danny, so immediately I started worrying. What's it all about?'

Vince swept his smooth dark hair back with one hand. He felt suddenly nervous.

'Sorry, I didn't mean to alarm you. It's nothing serious, really. In fact, right now I'm asking myself what I'm doing here. Lovely place you've got, by the way.'

'Thanks. So, you have something you want to tell me about Danny, but it's nothing serious? Okay, so forgive me, but couldn't you have told me whatever this inconsequential thing is over the phone?'

Vince shuffled his feet, hands in pockets, struggling for an explanation.

'I wouldn't say it's inconsequential. No, I think it's very consequential – if that makes sense – *not serious* is what I said. And it's not so much telling you something, it's more a case of explaining something and asking you something. Something that, now I come to think of it, is almost certainly none of my business. Which is why I'm now wondering what the hell I'm doing here…as it were.'

Hannah looked at Vince with a mixture of incomprehension and pity. He was trying his best to explain, and being quite charming in the process, but making no sense at all.

'Here you go,' said Hannah, handing Vince a mug of tea. She picked up a biscuit tin and two side plates and led Vince back to the living room, where they sat, saying nothing, for a moment.

'How long have you known Danny?' asked Hannah.

'That's a good question. Just a few months, I suppose. Not long, now I think of it. But we've become very good friends.'

'We've been together over nine years.'

'Yes, he said. So, not much you don't know about him, I suppose?'

'Well, you might surprise me with whatever it is you have to say.'

'Shall I get to the point?'

'That's not a bad idea.'

Vince stood up. He had no idea what words to use, how to start.

'Is that you?' he asked, walking over to a bookcase, on top of which was a framed photograph of a young woman on a horse. 'Danny's told me all about your horse riding. Would I have seen you on the telly?'

'Possibly, if you've ever watched *Horse of the Year Show.*'

'I might have caught the last couple of minutes, waiting for *Match of the Day* or something.'

'Chances are not, then. You were about to get to the point...'

Vince gestured towards the framed photo again.

'Danny's so proud of you. His face lights up when he talks about you...and I can see why. I mean, well...so, getting to the point...'

Hannah grinned.

'You're a funny one. Look, I haven't got all day. Spit it out, Vince.'

Just start somewhere...anywhere, Vince said to himself.

'Right. So, I've only known Danny for a few months, but we're pretty close. And he's welcome to stay at my place while he's...you're...sorting things out. Listen, I don't want to take sides, but all I know is that he's ripped up inside with everything that's happened, and he wants to make things

131

right, but he's got a lot of wounded pride. Just...be patient with him, give him time. He'll get there. That's all I wanted to say.'

Hannah got up and gave Vince a hug.

'I should tell you to keep your nose out of my marriage, but that was the sweetest thing I've heard in a long time. And very brave of you.'

'Phew, thank God that's out of the way. I was bricking it there for a while,' said Vince, sitting down again.

'You're a very good friend. Danny's lucky.'

'Well, that's as may be. But he really is hurting, and his head's all over the place. If it wasn't for singing, I think he'd have gone mental by now.'

'Singing? Did you say *singing*?'

Vince squeezed his eyes tight shut and bit his bottom lip.

'Oh bugger, I wasn't meant to say that. It sort of slipped out.'

'Come on, Vince, tell me...'

Vince paused to collect his thoughts.

'If I explain, will you promise not to let Danny know I've told you? And, of course, I'd rather you didn't mention that I came to see you at all.'

'I won't, I promise. But you're not leaving until you spill the beans about Danny's singing! More tea?' said Hannah.

Fifteen

Neil sat at his desk, staring at the screen of his laptop. To be more exact, he sat staring at the small white calling card that he'd wedged between the keyboard and the screen. He couldn't count the number of times he'd read the inscription, and he now knew the telephone number by heart. His early assumption that the card had found its way into his jacket pocket by accident had given way to the obvious, yet nonetheless astonishing, conclusion that the darling of the British broadcast media, Newton Burns, had placed it there deliberately.

Vince had goaded Neil on the evening of the BBC gig, saying that Newton Burns had fancied him. That just made him cringe, though there was no doubt that Mr Burns had paid him a lot of attention and more than a few compliments at the time. Neil had laughed it off as showbiz behaviour, but then again it was well known that the nation's favourite raconteur was gay. In fact, unlike many celebs, Burns's sexuality was never a subject of much prurience or media scrutiny; it was as much a part of his accepted public persona as his shoulder-length white hair, his tendency to slip into French, or even Latin, in the middle of conversation, and the trademark yellow braces without which he was rarely seen.

So, Neil could only conclude that Newton Burns was interested in him. That ought to be flattering. Except that Neil had always gone out of his way to play it straight in public. Okay, he camped it up with Vince, because he knew Vince found it amusing, but for the most part he tried not to wear his sexuality on his sleeve. He had discussed this with Vince once, saying that he didn't ever want to be pigeon-holed. Vince had simply laughed at him and, seizing the comedy moment, told him that pigeon-holing was the latest gay craze, and that he thought Neil was missing out on some great fun.

Sod it, Neil thought at last. Dial the number. He reached for his mobile phone, then put it down again. Calling one of the most famous people in the country out of the blue might not be such a smart idea. Text. That's it. Send a text. He picked up the phone again and, after several minutes, managed to type:

> Hello Mr Burns. It was lovely to sing for you recently, and I hope you had a great evening. I found your card and was wondering if maybe you'd mislaid it. If so, sorry to bother you. I won't contact you again. Just saying Hi (and Ken sends his best regards) – Neil Taylor

Neil's thumb hovered over the send key. He took a large sip from the glass of white wine on the desk in front of him, and pressed the key.

With that out of the way, Neil went back to work on a new song arrangement. He fired up the music composition software, and reached for a pad of paper pre-printed with music staves. Then, swivelling his chair to his left, he switched on an electronic keyboard and made a few adjustments to the sound settings. His preferred way of working was to play with ideas as they came to him on the keyboard, record on to the computer via a MIDI interface, and then generate the basic score using the composition software. However, he sometimes preferred to write the dots down longhand on to paper, scribbling notes above and below the staves, and in the margins, as thoughts occurred to him. Somehow, he managed to bring it all together in the end.

Just as his hands were poised above the keyboard, his phone's text alert wailed a four-part harmony rendition of *Tonight* from *West Side Story*, causing him to jump. With his heart in his mouth, he looked at the message, which read:

> You will soon be able to upgrade your phone. Come back to PhoneHouse UK and we will match the best price your network can offer.

He keyed in the word STOP and hit send. Then, with the phone still in his hand, *Tonight* wailed at him again. The text read:

> How's my favourite young baritone? You took your time (lol). Would like to meet up. Have some interesting suggestions for you. How does Saturday evening look? Newt.

'I *bet* he's got some interesting suggestions for you!' said Vince, barely able to conceal his amusement.

'Yes, yes. That's it, isn't it? Just a crude, sexual come-on, nothing more,' said Neil, frustration showing in his voice.

'That's about the size of it, I'd say,' said Vince.

'Thanks for that. You do realise that he must be my father's age? Don't you think there's a chance that he might want to discuss things of a more artistic or creative nature? I thought perhaps he might have some advice on pursuing a musical career...he was very taken with our singing, and he knows I'm looking for openings for my composing and arranging. I just thought...'

'Looking for openings...yes, without a doubt. Look, why worry about it? He's invited you to dinner, you'll have fun. How many people can say they've got a date with one of the country's biggest celebs? Not just that...he obviously likes you in *that* way, so why not just accept it? Look, go with the flow and see what happens. You never know, you could end up being a very close friend…you might even get to penetrate his inner circle…'

That was it. Vince now had a fit of the giggles.

Neil glanced over towards Angie behind the bar, who was smiling a big smile. She shrugged her shoulders as if to say *what do you expect from Vince?* and Neil instantly dropped the po face and started laughing along with his friend.

Neil arrived at the chic but unassuming Mayfair restaurant on the dot of eight, and asked to be shown to Mr Burns's table, as had been agreed.

The waiter led Neil through the dimly-lit dining space, which not only exuded elegance, but also afforded a good deal of privacy, with lots of secluded corners and alcoves. The place seemed to be full of *types*. There were a few very well-dressed Middle Eastern gentlemen dining with implausibly glamorous and impeccably made-up young women. Then there were a number of high-tan, high-roller types, more casually dressed, but with wealth written all over them. A few media types, what looked like a footballer and his WAG, and (yes, he was certain) an ex-Chancellor of the Exchequer. Neil had always been good at surveying a room, and people-watching was one of his favourite pastimes.

They arrived at a private booth, where Newton Burns's large frame was hunched over the table. Both elbows were planted on the red linen tablecloth, one hand holding a mobile phone to his left ear, the other idly playing with a long strand of white hair just above his right ear. The waiter gestured, and Neil slid along the leather banquette, to take his place opposite Newton. He felt as though he was intruding momentarily, but Newton looked up, smiled, and finished the call with 'Sorry, must go. Dinner guest just arrived.'

'Neil, there you are! Glad you could make it. Now then,

does champagne take your fancy? It does mine! The usual please, Marco.'

Neil had been considering an orange juice, but there didn't seem to be a choice. He started talking nervously.

'Mr Burns. Hi. Wow. I can't believe this. How are you? Did you have a good time at your party? You seemed to be having fun. And I couldn't fault you on *Heart of My Heart.* You're a great bari. Still got it…not that you ever lost it, I dare say! And Ken seemed happy with the way it all went. Mind you, we nearly didn't get past the first few songs, as Vince – he's our tenor – nearly had an altercation with one of the guests…not that anyone noticed. Well, then…'

Newton Burns loosened his tie. 'Please, call me Newt.'

'Oh, right. Newt. Seems too familiar somehow, but sure.'

'Well, I hope we can become more familiar with one another. That's the idea of having dinner, isn't it?'

'Well, yes, I guess it is. In fact, I was wondering why… why the card…why me? Very flattered, no question. But, you know—'

'Relax, Neil. It's not the most unusual thing in the world to take a shine to someone and invite them to dinner, is it? Now, what do you fancy to eat? Two Michelin stars – just missed out on a third this year – but damn good fodder nonetheless. The tasting menu is very good if you haven't tried it. Bit of everything. Shall we?'

Neil allowed himself a joke.

'Is it all slug porridge and quails' eggs in hydrogen?'

'Scoundrel! No, you're confusing this place with a certain culinary laboratory in the wilds of Berkshire, I believe.'

'Yes, I know, it's just down the road from where I live. Never eaten there, but it's a stone's throw from my place.'

'Is it, indeed? Interesting.'

Neil took a sip of water and cleared his throat.

'Talking of interesting…you said in your text that you had some *interesting suggestions* for me. I hope you don't mind me asking, but what did you have in mind exactly?'

'Ah, straight to the point. I like it! Well, I have a couple of things in mind, Neil. One of them is to do with a script I received recently.'

'A script?'

'A screenplay that I very much like the look of, and one that requires a fair bit of musical input. It's about a group of harmony singers – that's what drew me in. And that was one of the reasons I got in touch with darling Kenny – to sound him out on what looks like a very interesting project. Ken mentioned that you're a dab hand at arranging harmony scores, and that's exactly what I need for this project. So I thought...why not? I'm all for encouraging young talent.'

Neil could barely believe his ears.

'Are you...are you making me some sort of offer?'

'I guess you could say that. If you're as good as Ken suggests, I'm happy to give it a go if you are,' said Newt, allowing Neil a few moments to take it all on board before continuing.

'However, I did say that I had a couple of things in mind. The project is one of them, but it would be wrong of me not to reveal my second motive. I'd like to get to know you a lot better, Neil. *A lot better.*'

Sixteen

'Henry's filing for divorce.'

Jenny spluttered as she lit her first cigarette in four years. She sat uneasily at the large kitchen table, turning the stem of a wine glass between the fingers of her right hand, and blowing huge plumes of un-inhaled smoke high into the air at five-second intervals. She had summoned Jeffrey as soon as Henry had broken the news, and he now sat quietly across the table from Jenny looking mildly disturbed at what he was seeing.

'Yes, I rather thought he would. Look, put that out, would you? You haven't smoked for years.'

'Don't tell me what to do, Jeffrey.'

'It's your life,' said Jeffrey, rather too casually for Jenny's liking.

'Yes it is. And yours too, Jeffrey. Yours too.'

'Sorry?'

Jenny blew a cloud of smoke in Jeffrey's direction.

'This is not just about me, Jeffrey. It's about *us*.'

'Is it?'

'What in God's name is wrong with you? Of course it is! And we need to decide what we're going to do about it.'

There was a moment's silence. Jeffrey opened his mouth as though to speak, then hesitated. He waved a dismissive hand at a wisp of smoke as it drifted past his nose.

'I, er…well, the thing is—'

'Yes, yes, speak to me, Jeffrey. Speak to me.'

'Well, I'm not sure it *is* about us.'

Jeffrey's gaze had been distracted by the smoke trails

filling the kitchen, but now he looked directly at Jenny as he spoke.

Jenny reduced her voice to a slow, patronising drawl.

'Am I hearing you correctly? Have you lost your faculties? You have been having an affair with me. We have been found out. You are the co-respondent in a divorce petition. *You – Me – Us.* Do you see?'

'I understand all of that, Jenny. What I don't understand is your over-emphasis of the word *us*. As though there is an *us* any longer. We've been found out, remember. You said it yourself.'

Jenny's right hand twitched, releasing the stem of her glass, which fell sideways without breaking, spilling white wine in a delicate rivulet across the surface of the table. Jeffrey took a paper tissue from his jacket pocket and started to mop up the spillage, moving the wine glass out of Jenny's reach as he did so.

Jenny's head lowered slightly over the table, and she spoke with a more measured voice.

'I had assumed that…with Henry and I, and you and Suzi, no longer together…I had naturally assumed that…'

'That's just it, you see. Suzi and I aren't splitting up. That's not happening.'

Jenny let out a sardonic laugh as she raised her head.

'*I take it you have told Suzi about all of this?*'

'Yes.'

'And she waved it away without a care, did she? *Never mind, darling, let's forget all about it, shall we? Now, what would you like for dinner this evening, hunny-bunny?*'

'Do you have to be sarcastic? No, it wasn't like that. If you must know, our relationship…well, it isn't like you think. We've always had an…open marriage. We both, from time to time…and, well…we're both okay with it. Always have been. So, as I was saying, Suzi and I aren't splitting up. Sorry, but that's the way it is.'

'I can't believe this! How many years have we known each other…I mean, as couples? Five years? And why haven't either of you mentioned your *open marriage* before now? What a load of hogwash, you conniving little—'

'Look, it's true. We never mentioned it because it's, well, a private thing…and we never intended to…not with friends.'

'But you bloody did, didn't you! You two-faced, lying shit! You couldn't resist coming after me when I was vulnerable, leading me on, and letting me believe—'

'Believe what exactly?'

'That there might be a future between us…what else?!'

'Ha! You're having a laugh, aren't you? Don't sit there and pretend for a second that you ever intended to leave Henry. I would never have started anything if I thought you did. No, no. You can play that game if you like, but it won't wash with me, Jenny. You were more than happy to keep all your plates spinning at once. You knew what you were doing, and you thought you could get away with it for as long as you wanted. Christ, you've got some nerve throwing that at me!'

'You've manipulated me from the start, you slimy bastard!'

'Not a bit of it, darling. You wanted it every bit as much as me. More so. Don't you play the *poor little me* card. I'm not having it!'

'So, that's it then, is it? All finished between us.'

'Yes.'

'You total bastard.'

Jeffrey stood up to leave.

'Look, I'm sorry. I…'

'*Just get the fuck out of my house!*' Jenny screamed.

'Thanks for coming over, Henry. Thanks.'

Jenny coughed as she lit her second cigarette in four

years. She sat in the same chair at the large kitchen table, with Henry sitting where Jeffrey had been just the day before. That meeting hadn't gone to plan, and she was left reeling from the fallout. Who else could she turn to but Henry? Perhaps they could find a way out of this mess after all?

'That's quite all right,' said Henry. 'I said I'd be happy to talk so long as you can be reasonable. I can't believe you're smoking. Put it out, Jenny. You don't need to do that.'

Jenny smiled feebly and extinguished the barely touched cigarette on a nearby saucer. No thoughts of blowing defiant smoke clouds in Henry's face. She needed to be conciliatory, not confrontational as she'd been with Jeffrey.

'You're right. Sorry, I'm in a bit of a state just now.'

'Well, yes. I see. How have you been otherwise?'

'Hanging in there. Would you like a drink?'

'Coffee would be nice if you're having one.'

Coffee wasn't what Jenny had in mind.

'Coffee, yes, of course. Coffee coming up.' Jenny tried to redirect her thoughts from the drinks cabinet to the espresso maker, but the thought of all the fuss defeated her. 'Instant okay?'

'Fine.'

'And how have you been? How's the flat? Not too pokey, I hope.' Jenny tried to show concern for Henry's predicament, but all she could think of was her own.

'It'll do for now. So, did you want to talk about the divorce? The settlement? It makes sense to work things out now if we can. Avoid any complications later,' said Henry, discomforted by the insincerity in Jenny's voice.

'Yes, yes. I just wanted to take stock, see where we are and what the options are. I mean…is divorce inevitable? Have we thought it through sufficiently? Is there maybe a chance that we could put all of this behind us and start again? Clean slate, so to speak. You see, darling, I've been thinking about everything and I realise that I've made a terrible mistake.

If you could forgive me, I thought that maybe we—'

Henry raised an index finger to his lips.

'Shhh. No more, Jenny.'

'But I…we—'

'Jenny. It's over. Let's talk about the settlement, shall we?'

Jenny felt a wave of panic sweep over her.

'But there doesn't need to be a settlement if we can… if I promised to get my act together, change my ways. I'll be a better wife, I'll never cheat on you again, Henry. I promise…'

'I could never trust you again,' said Henry, getting to his feet. 'Let's talk another time when you're ready to face up to things. I'm sorry. I have to go.'

Seventeen

'That was Neil,' said Vince, tucking his phone back into his jeans pocket. 'I'm afraid he won't be able to make it. He sends his profuse apologies and said it's the first and last quartet rehearsal he's ever going to miss. He's been called up to town at short notice for a meeting with some composer or other. Possibility of some serious work by the sound of it. So, just us three musketeers, then.'

Vince sat down in his favourite armchair, opposite Henry and Danny, who were tucking into coffee and ginger biscuits.

'Did he say anything more?' asked Henry.

'Nope. He's very excited, though. Almost certainly some spin-off from his rendezvous with Newton Burns. Good luck to him!'

'What…he met up with Newton Burns after our gig?' asked Danny.

'Yup. Invitation to dinner in Mayfair, the full enchilada,' said Vince.

'What, they went to a Mexican? Bit cheap, isn't it?' said Danny.

'No, you bloody chump. *Full enchilada*…as in, *the full nine yards…the full monty*…no expense spared. French place, two Michelin stars. Then they went off to some private members club in Soho, apparently. No more details just yet, but it all sounds promising.'

'Wow, that's fantastic. What a turn of events! This could be the making of the young fella!' said Henry. 'Here's to Neil!' and they all raised their coffee cups in salute.

'No Jaffa Cakes, Vince?' said Danny.

'Not at the rate you consume them, no. Make do with ginger biscuits, you greedy sod. Anyway, I guess we'd better crack on regardless. There's a lot we can do as a threesome. For example, we can focus on lead-bass duets. The lead and bass are the heart of any quartet. The engine room. If you two can become as tight as a gnat's chuff, then we're well over halfway there. Then all we need is for Neil to apply his baritone Polyfilla and yours truly to sprinkle a bit of tenor magic dust on top.'

'Oh, as easy as that! I see where we've been going wrong now. What was Ken thinking all this time?' said Danny.

'You may jest, but Ken would say the same. Let's give it a go, anyway. We'll warm up a bit, then run some duets with *Heart of My Heart*, and see where that takes us. On your feet, lads.'

Henry and Danny got up from the sofa and stood in the middle of the room, while Vince strained to get out of his chair, then fell backwards into it.

'Whoa there,' said Danny, reaching out a helping hand. 'Are you all right, pal?'

Henry looked on with concern. 'Just a stumble, Vince?'

'Something like that,' said Vince, though the look on his face suggested otherwise. 'Look, let's crack on, shall we?'

Vince started working with Danny and Henry, and after about forty minutes of running lead-bass duet sequences, Henry thought that they were making progress, and said so.

'Sounding good, partner!' he said to Danny.

Vince felt he needed to say something, and his facial features contorted as he searched for something that didn't come easily to him. Diplomacy.

'Yes, it's getting there, lads. But Henry, you're coming in flat a lot of the time, and it's buggering things up.'

Henry looked shocked.

'Flat? Me? Flat?'

'Pancakes and mill ponds spring to mind,' said Vince, now in full diplomatic swing.

Henry struggled for words.

'But, no one's ever…not even Ken…flat, you say?'

'Flatter than a Yorkshireman's cap. It's on the pick-ups. And you're scooping up to the note, which is why you're coming in just under it. Get rid of the scoop, aim for the top of the note, and you won't be flat,' said Vince.

'Scoop, you say? Scoop?'

'Ice creams and tabloid headlines spring to mind,' said Vince, who was beginning to enjoy this diplomacy stuff.

Danny, who had been staring at the carpet for the last couple of minutes, interjected.

'Okay, so let's try that same passage again, Henry, and we'll both aim for the top of the note. It's not just you. If we both think sharp, we'll nail the note straight away.'

Vince blew pitch, and the other two started singing again. Vince's right hand shot up, signalling *halt.*

'Sorry to say it, but you're scooping again, Henry. A bloody big raspberry ripple this time. With a flake in it.'

Henry's face betrayed a mixture of frustration, humiliation, and rising anger. Danny stepped in again to avoid an impending diplomatic incident.

'Remember what Ken told us about onions?' said Danny.

'I remember the one about the Thai masseuse and the banana – that was one of Ken's best – but I can't recall anything about onions,' said Vince.

Henry gave Vince a look. Danny ignored Vince and continued.

'Well, it goes like this. Think of a note as having many layers, like an onion. If you come in a few layers down, you'll be slightly flat. Aim for the outer layers…the very outer layer…that's where you need to be.'

'Not one of Ken's best,' said Vince.

'Put a cork in it for once, will you, and blow the B-flat,'

said Danny. 'Now, Henry, pick up from the start and hit the first note full-on, straight to the outer onion skin. Make the pitch pipe sound flat, if anything...Vince, blow the pitch again after Henry sings the note, then sing it again Henry, then blow pitch again, and so on...keep alternating until I tell you to stop...pitch, sing, pitch, sing...okay, go!'

Henry nailed the note ten times in a row.

'Great job!' said Vince, at the end of the sequence. 'I knew you could do it, though I was beginning to think you might be tone deaf there for a while...'

'Thank you, Mr Kissinger,' said Henry, gracefully.

'No worries,' said Vince. 'I don't know about you two, but I'm suddenly a bit knackered. Shall we have a break? I'm just going to my room...tablets, and what not... help yourself in the kitchen. I'll be back in a bit.'

Henry collapsed back on to the sofa.

'Blimey, that was harder work than I thought it would be. The first time I've been accused of singing flat. I feel embarrassed, to tell you the truth.'

'Ah, but that's the thing. We're all guilty of coming off the boil from time to time,' said Danny. 'Nothing that a bit of drilling can't fix. Though I'm not sure Vince is the best coach in these situations.'

'Subtlety's not exactly Vince's middle name, is it?' said Henry.

'Er...no. I've become very familiar with Vince's ways since I've been living here, I can tell you.'

'That must be difficult. How's everything coming along?' asked Henry, glad of a change of subject.

'Phew...where do I begin?'

'Well, I hope you and your wife can work things out... Hannah, isn't it? I do hope you can get back to normal. I'm in a similar situation myself just now, so I can understand what you must be going through. Jenny and I have...well, it's over for us, I'm afraid.'

'Shit, Henry, I had no idea. How long have you been bottling this one up? I mean, do the other guys know?'

'Vince, most certainly not. At least, I haven't said a word to him. Neil might have worked out some of what's going on, I'm not sure.'

Danny shook his head.

'Well, we know you lost your job and went away to sort things out, so we...well, I...assumed everything was fine now. At home, anyway. Obviously not. I'm sorry, Henry.'

'I'm not. Well, I'm sorry it's come to this, but knowing what I know now, it's difficult to be anything other than resigned. We're finished, and I know it's for the best, no matter how difficult things are right now. But your situation's different, I guess...'

'I think so. I hope so. We're trying to patch things up, but there are obstacles to overcome. Stuff from the past. We're getting there slowly,' said Danny.

'Well, I'd put my foot on the gas if I were in your position. How much longer do you want to live here with Mr Subtle?' said Henry, giving in to a fleeting urge to have a dig at his tormentor.

'Ah, Vince has been great, really supportive. Heart of gold. Talking of whom, he's been in there a while. I bet he's nodded off. Let's wake him from his slumbers.'

Danny walked over to Vince's bedroom door and knocked gently.

'Vince...sorry to bother you, but Henry and I were wondering if you'd care to re-join us in the living room for a bit more yodelling.'

'Come in, Dan. Please...come in.'

Danny opened the bedroom door to find Vince lying on his back in the middle of the room, staring up at the ceiling.

'What the bloody hell are you doing down there?'

'Just now, I'm wondering how long it's been since anyone

took a feather duster to the ceiling. But while you're there, can you help me up? I've been trying for the last ten minutes, but it seems that my legs have stopped working.'

Eighteen

'Sorry I'm a bit late, babe. The by-pass was dreadful, and parking wasn't much better,' said Angie, breathing heavily.

'No worries, no worries,' said Vince. 'My, you're a sight for sore eyes!' He folded his *NME* and threw it on to the bedside table, then hoisted himself up with a lot of heavy breathing of his own, along with the odd muttered profanity.

'Oh, babe, look at you…here, let me help you up…' said Angie, fussing momentarily and to no great effect, before bursting into tears.

'Bloody hell, Ange, what's come over you? Hey, come on. Here, have one of these.'

Vince threw an open box of Kleenex towards the foot of the bed. Angie blew her nose and waited while her upper body stopped convulsing.

'It's just the shock of seeing you laying in a hospital bed, all crumpled up with your *NME*.'

'They didn't have *Q* or *Mojo* in the hospital shop.'

'You know what I mean. What happened, you poor bugger? What have the doctors said? What's the story?'

'Well it's not "morning glory", I'll say that much. What can I tell you? One minute we were rehearsing round at my place. Then suddenly I came over all lethargic, and then next thing I'm on my back staring at the cobwebs and wondering why I can't feel my legs. Not one of my better Saturday mornings. Mind you, we sorted out Henry's problem, so it wasn't all doom and gloom.'

'Henry's problem?'

'Flatting and scooping. Bloody dreadful it was, but I think he's cracked it now.'

'Oh, Vince, you beautiful, crazy bastard! What are you like? Laying there with no legs and all you can talk about is someone else's singing problems.'

'Woah, steady on, girl. We're not quite in Douglas Bader territory yet. *No legs* is slightly overstating the case, I think. Dysfunctional, I'll give you, but they were definitely still attached last time I looked.'

Vince raised the bed sheets and took a look.

'Mind you, it's not all dysfunctional down there. Wey hey! Draw the curtains, darling. I have a little favour to ask...'

Angie raised the back of her hand in a gesture of disapproval.

'Vince! Behave yourself! Now tell me sensibly what the situation is. What have the doctors said?'

'It's not a big deal.'

'That's what they said? Your legs have stopped working and it's no big deal?'

'Well, kind of. Look, honey, I know the score. With MS, this sort of thing can happen. It won't be permanent. Not yet, anyway. I can already feel some sensation returning, I promise you. This is just one of those set-backs I have to live with. Give it a few days and I dare say I'll be able to get around okay; maybe with a stick, maybe without. I just don't know exactly how this episode will play out, but I'm sure as hell not going to lie here getting depressed about it. Come here, give me a kiss!'

Angie leant forward to kiss Vince on the lips.

'Not quite where I had in mind, but it'll do for starters,' said Vince as they embraced.

Then, reducing his voice to a whisper, Vince said, 'I love you.' It was the first time Angie had ever heard him say those words, and she burst into tears again.

*

Later the same day, Vince received visits from the rest of the quartet, with Neil leading the highly premature mourning, or so it seemed to Vince at the time. He resisted the temptation to take the mickey out of Neil too much, given his history with Robert, and for the second time that day Vince wondered whether his infirmity was making him soft.

Danny very thoughtfully brought him a box of Jaffa Cakes. Henry was more traditional with an offering of grapes, which he assured Vince were not sour. In fact, Henry went as far as thanking Vince for pointing out and correcting his flatting and scooping, and said he was now a much better bass for all of that.

Neil asked if Vince felt well enough to sing a song, and he asked the duty nurse if she or the other patients on the ward would mind if the quartet sang a gentle number 'to lift the spirits'. Vince was all for it, but advised against Henry's choice of *After You've Gone*, on the grounds that the old fella in the corner bed wasn't expected to see the week out.

The duty nurse was initially reluctant, but came round to the idea that lifting the patients' spirits was a lovely thought. She also happened to love barbershop singing, and she pulled up a chair for a ring-side seat. They sang the gentlest number they knew, *Lullabye (Goodnight My Angel)* by Billy Joel, which was greeted by warm smiles of appreciation from the patients, and a few tears from the duty nurse. Vince's ability to make women cry seemed to know no limits that day.

Just as the guys were preparing to leave, Ken arrived with a bunch of bananas. He made light of Vince's predicament, telling a couple of anecdotes that had the guys stifling laughter for fear of breaking the mood they'd created with *Lullabye*, and for fear of being chucked out by the new nurse who'd just come on duty, and whose demeanour seemed a good deal less benevolent than the previous one.

After the laughter subsided, Ken brought the conversation

round to a more serious point.

'Well, chaps, I probably don't need to remind you that there's just less than a month to prelims, and the stark question before us is...will we be able to make it?'

They looked at each other in silence for a moment, then they all looked at Vince.

'What are you all looking at me for? I'm not letting the side down, if that's what you're thinking. My legs might be temporarily incapacitated, but my voice has never been in finer fettle. Carry me there, wheel me there, I don't much care, but *there* I will be. In any case, I'm planning to do a Lazarus in the next couple of days. I've no intention of lying here for much longer, and I can already feel some sensation returning in my right leg.'

'So, with a bit of luck, we'll be all right, even if our tenor remains deficient in the leg department to the tune of one,' said Ken.

They all knew where this was going, and they listened and laughed along as Ken regaled them with his rendition of Peter Cook and Dudley Moore's *Tarzan* sketch.

Nineteen

Though they'd all made light of Vince's predicament at his hospital bedside, the reality was that they were all deeply concerned for his state of health. While they could only admire Vince's mental strength and fighting spirit, they all knew that his condition was deteriorating at a worrying rate. None of them would have placed a bet on Vince's chances of a quick recovery based on what they'd seen in Ward 12 of St Luke's that Sunday afternoon. But, true to his promise, Vince had rallied magnificently in the days following, and within a week was able to get around reasonably well with the aid of a walking stick. His right leg had recovered well, but his left was still letting him down a bit.

Of course, they were all eager to get as much rehearsal time in as possible before prelims, but they agreed that it was only fair to allow Vince to set the pace. He tired easily, and needed regular respites. He had taken sick leave from work, though he soon started working from home, and he'd even surprised his colleagues at Bowman-Lamy by turning up at the office unexpectedly one lunchtime.

'Rumours of my demise have been greatly exaggerated,' he told everyone, for which he received spontaneous applause. Ever the showman.

One thing was very clear. Vince was determined to play his full part in the final push towards prelims, and if anything, the pace he set put the rest of them to shame. For three weeks they rehearsed for two hours every Monday and Wednesday evening, and for three hours on either Saturday or Sunday morning. Their two contest songs were in good shape, they had ironed out one or two technical problems with the balance of voices, and they felt there was more artistry in their performances every time they sang. Ken was encouraging as ever, but didn't flinch at identifying even the tiniest of mistakes, and helping them correct their shortcomings.

And now the day had arrived. Forty quartets from all around Britain converging on the Birmingham Conservatoire for a day's contest that would see just sixteen qualify for next year's British championships. Would they make it through?

Would they even make it to Birmingham was the more pressing question right now. Vince and Neil had travelled by train the day before, and were safely ensconced in a comfortable city centre hotel. Meanwhile, Danny, Henry and Ken were waiting for an AA recovery vehicle in a service station off the M40 just north of Bicester.

Ken was apologetic. His Volvo estate had served him well from new, but that was twelve years ago, and he was rueing having missed the last annual service.

'We could have come in the Bentley,' Henry said, but that seemed to make matters worse, and now Henry felt the need to apologise.

'Sorry, that must have sounded ungrateful, or arrogant, or both...I didn't mean it that way.'

Luckily they had planned to make a whole day of it, and so had set off at 8.30am. They broke down (or, rather, failed to re-start) at 9.20am, but they weren't due on stage in Birmingham until 3.42pm. Nobody was panicking just yet.

At 11am, Danny said 'I'm starting to panic.'

The AA man arrived at 11.15am, an hour later than the original ETA they'd been given. It turned out to be one of the busier Sundays for accidents, with pile-ups on the M4 east-bound near Slough, and on the anti-clockwise carriageway of the M25 near the Sunbury/Wraysbury exit. The Home Start service was also reporting unusually high call-out rates for a Sunday morning. Flat batteries were up fifty per cent for the time of year.

Ken told the AA man that he wasn't convinced the detailed road report was helping them much, and they all felt relieved when he eventually got down to business and started running mechanical checks. While the AA man busied himself under the bonnet, Ken suggested that Henry and Danny do some duetting to make use of the time. Ken blew pitch, the duo started singing, and they all heard the AA man bang his head against the underside of the bonnet.

'Do you know any Meatloaf?' asked the engineer, rubbing the top of his head. They politely declined the request.

Eventually, the AA man announced that he could get them going again, and that they were lucky because the part he needed was the last one in stock in his van.

'Excellent. And please proceed with all due speed, as we're as keen to get going as a *bat out of hell,*' said Ken.

They were on the move again just after noon, and they made it to Birmingham city centre at around 1.20pm without further incident. After several circuits of several inner ring roads, they eventually found the turning for the car park, and by 2pm they were entering the hallowed halls of the Birmingham Conservatoire.

Neil and Vince were waiting for them when they arrived, and though Danny had kept them informed of their progress by regular phone calls, they both looked mightily relieved to see their friends. They went straight to the reception desk to check in and receive the latest timings for the afternoon session.

'You've made it just in time,' the lady at the desk told them. 'Three quartets dropped out earlier on, and your stage time has been brought forward to 3.05. You'll be collected by a courier from the dressing room at 2.35, and escorted to warm-up room B. From there you'll be taken to the backstage holding area at 2.55. Good luck, gentlemen.'

So, any plans they'd had for an extended warm-up and some relaxation time prior to taking to the stage were now out of the window. They had barely half an hour to get ready, and so they made for the dressing room as fast as they could, weaving their way through the milling groups of singers and their supporters, Ken nodding and smiling at lots of familiar faces as they went along. Ken knew just about everyone in barbershop circles.

They changed quickly into their stage clothes in the large but crowded dressing room, jostling amongst other contestants, and tripping over shoes, suit carriers and hold-alls scattered everywhere across the floor. They made sure Vince had a seat, and tried to clear a decent space for him to change comfortably. When they were all ready, Ken lined the four of them up to check that their appearance was up to scratch, before reaching into a carrier bag for a bunch of six bananas.

'Energy, chaps. Energy. One each, and two for me.'

They ate their bananas and sipped water in silence, then Ken called them to order again.

'Right, chaps. Nearly time. When you leave this room, I can't come with you, so this is it. You've worked hard for this, and I know you're ready. When you get to the warm-up room, just run through the first few bars of both songs a couple of times. Then I want you to stand in a circle and put your arms around each other's shoulders. You know the routine. Breathe together slowly. Let the nerves drain away, and let the energy flow. Lock voices. Listen for a fifth voice. And enjoy yourselves.'

Just then, they heard someone shout, 'From The Edge?' and a courier was beckoning them to follow him out of the dressing room. They each shook Ken's hand, then marched in line behind their guide, along corridors and through several sets of double doors, sipping nervously from bottles of mineral water, until they reached their warm-up room.

'Gentlemen, you have just about seventeen minutes and one of my colleagues will be along to take you to the backstage area. Best of luck,' said the courier as he closed the door behind him. Suddenly they were on their own.

'My mouth is completely dry, no matter how much water I drink,' said Neil.

'I can hardly breathe,' said Danny.

'My legs are…'

They all looked in fear at Vince.

'…absolutely fine,' said Vince. And the tension instantly dissipated.

Then they ran the preparation routine exactly as Ken had asked them to.

At 3.03pm they were waiting in silence in the wings, stage left, having said their last words and taken their last sips of water.

'Stand by,' whispered the stage manager.

They listened as the Master of Ceremonies made his announcement.

'Stewards, close the doors, please. Ladies and gentlemen, contestants number twenty-eight, from Maidenhead A Cappella…please welcome…From The Edge!'

Neil led them on to the stage to take their positions as warm applause greeted them from the auditorium.

The next six minutes were a blur.

'How did we do?' asked Danny as they left the stage.

I can't remember a thing,' said Vince.

'Me neither,' said Henry.

Neil said that he thought they'd lost pitch halfway through the ballad but recovered well, and that they'd allowed the tempo of the up-tune to run away a bit towards the end of the song.

They all felt a bit dejected hearing Neil's analysis.

They changed, then went into the auditorium to watch the last few quartets perform, and to listen to the announcement of the results. They found Ken, who greeted them with what looked like a half-hearted thumbs-up.

'Well done, chaps…it's going to be close.'

When the MC took to the stage to announce the results, their hearts were in their mouths. The tension was almost unbearable. They listened as the names of twelve qualifying quartets were read out. Then the thirteenth and fourteenth.

Then the fifteenth…

'From The Edge!' announced the MC.

They sat there stunned at what they had just heard.

'That's it, chaps, you're through,' said Ken. 'You're on your way to Harrogate!'

Part Two

The Road to Harrogate

Twenty

As she sat at the window table of her favourite café, Margaret felt a sudden pang of loneliness which took her quite by surprise. And, never one for too much introspection, and certainly nothing even remotely approaching self-pity, she wondered where on earth this new feeling had come from.

Blowing the froth on her cappuccino to one side for ease of entry and the avoidance of an unwanted dairy moustache, she sipped her coffee with a growing sense of gloom. It wasn't that she was bored. Today alone she had done half an hour of stretching exercises, made breakfast for George, packed him off to work with a thick slice of home-made gala pie for his morning snack, sent lengthy emails to two old friends – one in Buenos Aries, the other in Skelmersdale – listened to *Woman's Hour*, and made considerable progress on her forthcoming presentation to the WI, which currently went by the working title of *A Dancer Domesticated.*

Margaret was one of the busiest ladies in the village, what with her senior citizens' ballet class, the WI, the cricket club, the reading group, and two afternoons a week at the charity shop. Add to that wifely and motherly duties, albeit somewhat scaled-back compared to, say, ten years ago, and what you had was one very active, busy lady of a certain age. One very active, busy, frustrated and lonely lady of a certain age. *Stop it, Margaret,* she said to herself. *That's beginning to sound just a little bit self-pitying.*

She took another sip of coffee, bit into an amaretti biscuit, and allowed the thought to cross her mind that there was probably nothing wrong with thinking about herself and her lot in life, just for a while. Most people thought about themselves all the time, it seemed to her. By contrast, the last time Margaret had dwelt on her own existence for more than five minutes was probably twenty-five years ago. So, what brought all this on, she wondered?

In her *über*-analytical way, it took her just a minute or so to render the problem, if it was a problem, down to three essential ingredients: the march of time, a yearning for one great life achievement, and the disintegration of the relationship between her husband and her one surviving son. She played that back, and wondered why she hadn't included "loss" as one of the key ingredients. Robert's loss was probably the single most momentous happening in her life; it coloured her, it ran through her, it was part of her. But because it was a familiar constant in her life, she decided it didn't belong in the equation.

She also questioned whether "the march of time" was relevant. Time does march on, ever faster as you get older, and that was true for everyone who ever lived. So, she dropped that one too. Which left two essential ingredients.

She thought about the first one: a yearning for one great life achievement. Really?

When she looked back, she knew that she had achieved a lot in her life already. Aged seventeen, she joined the corps of the Paris Opera Ballet, the only English girl in the company at that time. In Paris, she lived what, to most people, would seem an exotic life. Mixing in rare social circles – not just dancers and choreographers and classical musicians, but painters, poets, philosophers, jazz musicians. The Paris set. She didn't court it, it was just where she found herself. And she adored every minute. Her career as a dancer took off. By nineteen she had progressed from *quadrille* to *sujet*, and by twenty-one she made *première danseuse*. She danced Juliet, Odette-Odile, Beauty, Manon. She worked with Nureyev. People travelled from afar to see her, and especially to see her world-renowned arabesque.

And she found love, too. First with Dmitri, a startlingly talented young Russian dancer, and then Hubert, a wealthy Parisian socialite. She never had worked out exactly what Hubert did, or how he came by his money.

By her mid-twenties, and finding herself unattached, Margaret had started to miss England, and so she moved to London where she spent a season as guest artist with the Royal Ballet, before settling at English National Ballet, where she spent a further five years – the rest of her dancing career. Somewhere along the line she met George, then a young, brash City type, who had charmed her with his quick wit and his abundant generosity. They married, she retired from dance, they moved to Berkshire, and then along came Robert. Neil came along much later, and it was when he was a toddler that Margaret retrained as an English teacher, and spent several happy years, latterly as head of department, at a private boys' school in Windsor. All of that spanned half a century, which, when she thought of it like that, came as quite a shock.

So, what else am I am yearning to achieve, Margaret wondered? I've packed a decent amount of living into my time, she thought. I'd quite like to write a book, I suppose. Memoires, possibly. But then *quite like to* is hardly a yearning, is it? In any case, though it only just occurred to her this way, she had already started assembling her memoires for her WI presentation next month. So, what was this yearning for one big life achievement?

She parked it impatiently, and went on to the second essential ingredient: the disintegration of the relationship between her husband and her one surviving son.

She was too tired now to re-hash, in her mind, the whole sorry story of how Neil and George had come to fall out so badly. She knew every step along that particular road, and at the centre of everything was, of course, Robert. It seemed

165

utterly wrong that Robert, who they all loved so dearly in their own different ways, should be the cause of the schism between Neil and George. Of course he wasn't the cause at all. He was a reference point, a benchmark, a shining example of how wonderful one human being could be. And that was the crux of the matter. Comparisons are invidious, but we all make them. And George was guilty of it, certainly. How could Neil help simply being himself?

And it had come to this. Margaret felt like a referee in a boxing match most of the time, and she feared that one of them was about to deliver the knock-out blow. Except that she couldn't let it happen. She had given them each an ultimatum. One more low blow, one more punch after the bell, and they'd be disqualified. But she knew that her ultimatums were ultimately hollow. Would she really leave George or turn her back on Neil? Of course not. But at least she'd made the strength of her feelings abundantly clear, and for the moment, both men were in their corners, breathing heavily and spitting blood.

Margaret went back to the first essential ingredient: the one great life achievement.

Then she skipped back again to the second.

And then came her *eureka* moment. They were one and the same.

The reason she had failed to articulate the subject of the first essential ingredient was because it is, in fact, the same as the second. So, by a process of logical reduction, she had identified the single thing that was making her feel lonely and frustrated, and it was far from rocket science.

If she did nothing else of any note in whatever remained of her life, she absolutely had to repair the relationship between father and son. It's what Robert would have wanted.

Neil's feet had hardly touched the ground since the dinner with Newton Burns. During an exquisite meal that lasted three hours and as many bottles of vintage champagne, he had found himself mesmerised by the wit and charm of someone he had long admired – as did most of the nation – but had no reasonable expectation of ever encountering in real life. Through his numerous TV and theatre appearances, the people's polymath had become a ubiquitous figure in modern British culture. And there he was, all white hair and yellow braces, clinking glasses with Neil, offering him what sounded like the biggest career break he could ever have dreamt of, and making it abundantly clear that Neil was the object of his amorous intentions.

There seemed little doubt that the career break and the amorous intentions were linked, but was Neil being naïve in questioning whether one could be achieved without giving in to the other?

Much as he admired and respected Newt (it still sounded wrong to call him that), he was well into his sixties, and though he looked good for his age, this made Neil feel very uncomfortable. Vince had casually suggested that he should *just go with the flow and see what happens*, but how could he? Aside from feeling uneasy about the advances of a man more than old enough to be his father, there was a much more straightforward problem with all of this, Neil concluded. He needed to know that he was a talented enough musician to be able to make a success of the project without any conditions or attachments.

To be fair to Newt, he wasn't putting any pressure on Neil, except in the work sense. He had lined up a series of meetings in London with the composer, musical director, script editor, and copyright lawyer, and Neil threw himself into the project with a passion. This was, without question, the most thrilling thing that had ever happened to him.

After a couple of scoping meetings, the project started to become clear. Neil would be hired as musical arranger, working on four-part harmony arrangements of nine original songs written for the screenplay. He was also invited to work as part of a research team, whose job it was to ensure that every aspect of the script's musical content was accurate to the last detail. Neil was assigned the task of researching the history of modern a cappella singing, something he felt he already knew a good deal about. He couldn't believe his luck. This job really was made for him.

For two weeks, Neil immersed himself in the research. He started with the most obvious of starting points: that *a cappella*, being Italian for "like the chapel", describes one of the oldest forms of Western music, with its origins in the praise of God. He traced the development of the form, from Gregorian chant, through shape-note singing, and the emergence of a book of vocal spirituals called *The Sacred Harp*. Along the way, call-and-response singing from Africa influenced these vocal traditions to become American gospel. Then, secular singing emerged alongside the ecclesiastical tradition, and the evolution of popular American vocal music began.

This was where Neil's interest really started to peak. His choice of dissertation subject in his final year at Manchester had been informed by his involvement with the university a cappella society, and was entitled *The Influence of American Barbershop on Modern Pop Idioms*. A little pretentious now he looked back on it, but his belief in the influence of barbershop singing, a form that had become marginalised and often ridiculed in recent years he felt, remained undimmed.

This was a labour of love for Neil, as he researched, documented, and summarised all of the significant historical milestones. In 1936, Norman Rockwell's *Barbershop Quartet* cartoon appeared on the cover of *The Saturday Evening Post*. In 1938, at a hotel in Kansas City, two travelling businessmen from Tulsa laid the foundations for what became the Society for the Preservation and Encouragement of Barber

Shop Quartet Singing in America, a name so painful that it cried out for a catchy acronym. Unfortunately, the best the society could come up with was SPEBSQA, which remained in place until some bright spark decided to change the name of the organisation to the Barbershop Harmony Society, and hence the acronym to BHS, in 2004.

From there, Neil documented barbershop's continuing influence on the development of modern vocal music. The Dapper Dans at Disneyland; the release of *Mr Sandman* by the first big female barbershop quartet, The Chordettes; The Buffalo Bills taking barbershop mainstream in the motion picture *The Music Man*; the influence of The Four Freshmen on the Beach Boys. And then, a line traced through to The Nylons in the 1970s, Manhattan Transfer in the 1980s, and later to Bobby McFerrin, Boyz II Men, and beyond.

At the end of the exercise, Neil delivered a concise twenty-page report, complete with references, and then turned his attention to the real business of working on the song arrangements. But not before pausing to reflect upon how Newton Burns and the project were affecting everything else in his life.

He was relieved to be able to avoid his father, so little time was he spending at home, but he missed the quartet, whom he hadn't seen since they had qualified for the British championships a month ago. And what of his mother? What was Margaret thinking? He felt considerable guilt at not telling her about the new developments in his life. He felt, rightly or wrongly, that if he confided in his mother, he would somehow be building a bridge to his father. And he wasn't ready for that.

Twenty-One

Angie looked down at her breasts as she stood in the shower, and wondered if they were beginning to drift south. They had always been her prize assets, certainly ensuring her popularity with men, and they had played a very significant part in her working life, too. She preferred not to refer to her work as a career, though it seemed everybody else did these days. In her time as a topless model, Angie's assets opened doors – metaphorically, of course, though she suspected they could do so literally as well, so firm were her famous 34 DDs.

And so it came as a shock to see that her treasures were beginning to give in to the law of gravity. Perhaps they'd been on the slide for a while. Now in her mid-thirties, Angie had given up the glamour game a few years back. She knew she could have carried on for a while longer, but she'd grown tired of being seen as little more than a pair of boobs, and she felt the need to do something more rewarding. The financial rewards she'd enjoyed as a model had been considerable, and she'd managed to save enough money to know that she could keep the wolf from the door for a good while should the need arise. But what she most needed was the kind of reward that came from giving, nurturing, caring for others.

What she wanted most of all was a child, but she had known since the time of her second serious relationship, some ten years ago now, that she couldn't have one of her own. In one of life's great ironies, it saddened her to know that her most admired features would never be pressed into service for the purpose for which nature had intended.

Angie had become an *au pair* for a while, working for three different families, and tending to the needs of three sets of preposterously over-privileged children – the offspring of a commercial property developer, then a telecommunications entrepreneur, and finally a newspaper proprietor. In each case, Angie had impressed both the wife and husband in the interview, had devoted several months to skivvying for their ungrateful brood, and had been released by the wife on spurious grounds. In each case, the real reason for her dismissal was the wife's displeasure at the amount of attention the husband was paying to the hired help.

She then trained as a nursery assistant, her main part-time job to this day, and one she really enjoyed. The things small children said and did cracked her up, and she spent most of her time at work laughing. Her charges often reminded her of Vince.

Then there were the three afternoons at the old folks' home, which she had somehow fallen into by accident. She enjoyed that too, and it was remarkable to see how, in many ways, the old folks behaved in much the same way as the kids. They too often reminded her of Vince.

The nursery children and the old men in the nursing home shared a fascination with Angie's breasts. Both seemed to take every opportunity to use her bosom for a pillow. He knew a song about that, Vince had once said.

The old fellas at the home were particularly amusing, following Angie, or rather her chest, around the room with their eyes, and then purring with excitement whenever the need for Angie's assistance brought her bosom within close proximity. Just the other day, as she was helping an old fella to the loo, she felt his bristly face rubbing against her tunic for the best part of five minutes, and when she looked at him his eyes were closed, he had the biggest smile on his face, and he was showing definite stirrings in the downstairs department. She didn't mind, and she always saw the funny side. And what was it with old fellas' balls? If women's breasts had a tendency to drift south with age, that was nothing compared to what happened to blokes when they were getting on. Huge, pendulous objects swinging around in sacks of endlessly stretching skin. She had once tried to demonstrate the appearance to Vince by suspending two kiwi fruits in the leg of a pair of tights, with hilarious results.

The balance of Angie's working week was made up by a few shifts at The Ship, which she'd come to think of as part of her social life as much as a source of income. At least she knew she would get to see Vince, he being one of the pub's most ardent regulars.

She had first met Vince during her brief spell at The Candy Store, east Berkshire's answer to Stringfellows. She was taken by his carefree attitude, his ability to make everyone around him laugh, and his Mediterranean good looks. But what really did it for her was his singing. Out of the blue he had serenaded her with a heart-achingly beautiful rendition of Harry Nilsson's *Without You*, made all the more impressive by his ability to maintain eye contact throughout, never once allowing his eyes to drop to the level of her bare breasts. That was it. Game over.

Since then she and Vince had become an item, albeit a rather unconventional item. Having made the initial running, and with instant success, having hooked her right away, Vince had proceeded to demonstrate a coolness and a reluctance to move things on in the traditional way. Yes, they became lovers and, over time, very good friends, but at no time did Vince give the impression that he wanted a committed relationship that involved anything so conventional as living together.

She had learned of Vince's MS early on, and had seen him go through a couple of tricky periods when his mobility had been impaired. She knew that he'd once had to use a wheelchair, though that was before her time, and she prayed he'd never have to again. He seemed to bounce back after every episode. However, this latest episode was worse than any she'd seen before. She knew that he'd been knocked hard, and that it had taken a monumental effort of will to make it to the quartet competition in Birmingham.

She loved Vince's tenacity, his never-say-die spirit, and his loyalty to his friends. She loved so much about him, and was never afraid to tell him. And yet, until that day at his bedside in St Luke's he had never even come close to reciprocating. She saw fear in Vince's eyes that day, but she also heard something that she never thought she'd hear him say. Those three words meant more to Angie than anything in the world.

After the high drama of prelims, Vince had almost collapsed with exhaustion, though he had done his utmost to conceal the fact from Ken and the lads. In qualifying, he had described their efforts as heroic, though the others were unanimous in telling him that there had been only one hero, and that was Vince himself.

There were now six months before the British championships in Harrogate, and while the others still attended most Wednesday chorus nights with Maidenhead A Cappella, for Vince this was the ideal time to pay closer attention to his doctors' advice, and opt for a period of complete rest. He didn't want to, and as chairman of the club he felt he was neglecting not only his singing but his official duties too. But chorus director James Pinter and the rest of the executive committee would hear none of it. They wanted him back only when he was fit and ready.

In addition to texts and emails congratulating him and the quartet on their joint achievement, he also received a personalised get-well card, hand-crafted by Lizzie and signed by all the guys in the chorus. The cartoon figure on the front of the card was of a man clearly unable to stand up, which amused Vince considerably: he couldn't work out whether this was a reference to his MS or his fondness for a few beers, until he noticed that there was an empty pint pot on a bar behind the cartoon Vince. He loved the club, and couldn't wait to get back there. And he loved his quartet buddies, but that would all have to wait for a while.

For the time being, Vince knew that bravado had to take a back seat, so he took full sick leave from work (his GP and his specialist had insisted) and began a new regime aimed at speeding his recovery. He took care to eat well, drink less, take moderate, appropriate exercise, adhere closely to his medication regimen, and get lots of early nights.

Angie was on hand more than usual to guide and encourage him, and though he gave her considerable stick for treating him like one of her infants, she had quite rightly given as good back. She told him that in his current condition he was more like one of the old fellas at the nursing home and that, if he had any doubts about that, he should check out his scrotum in a mirror. They laughed until it hurt, and they ended up in each other's arms before making slow, gentle love on the sofa. Needless to say, Danny wasn't there at the time.

Danny was spending less time at Vince's flat now, and though he hadn't officially moved out, it was obvious that he was edging closer to a resumption of home and family life. Vince knew from Danny that he and Hannah were on better terms, but that they still had a way to go. However, Hannah had encouraged and welcomed Danny's return home for Christmas, and Ben had shown such excitement at the prospect that Danny knew it was right to give it a try.

Not wanting to put a hex on Danny's chances of finally patching things up with Hannah, Vince had repeated his mantra '*mi casa, su casa*' saying that he was welcome back any time. But Vince really hoped that his own visit to see Hannah that day might have done the trick and that his good friend would remain back where he belonged.

The one thing that Vince was dreading was boredom. He looked forward to rest, and to blissfully deep sleeps, and to feeling the strength return in his legs. He didn't look forward to the long daylight hours and the horrific prospect of becoming a daytime TV addict. No *Jeremy Kyle, Loose Women* and *Midsomer Murders* for him. He'd seen the effects on other people who'd allowed themselves to go down that road. They invariably had the life sucked out of them.

He would be selective in his TV viewing; either that, or cut the plug off the mains lead. Better still, he would subscribe to Sky Arts and watch only music documentaries. He'd seen them listed in the TV pages and had often considered how wonderful it would be to have a TV diet consisting solely of programmes about the birth of the blues, the Motown sound, Johnny Cash at San Quentin, and the food consumed by Elvis Presley the day he died on the toilet.

He also decided to catch up on reading. Not just music biographies and histories, but classic fiction that he'd missed out on, including the likes of Charles Dickens and Jane Austen.

Vince fancied that even then he would find he had spare time on his hands. There was lots of interesting music software that he'd been meaning to find out about, but that would mean spending far too much time on the computer, and that usually meant the internet, and that usually meant indecent distractions and the onset of carpel tunnel syndrome.

And then it dawned on him. He would take up painting. He'd always enjoyed painting at school, though inexplicably he had given up Art in favour of Latin at 'O' Level. Either he had fancied himself as a classics scholar back then or, more likely, his Art teacher had begged him not to waste any more of the school's precious art supplies. It was perhaps true that his enthusiasm had outstripped his ability at the time, but he had always had fun sploshing paint around like Jackson Pollock. And the desire to take up art as a hobby had always stayed with him.

This time around, he imagined he'd go more in the direction of Botticelli. And his first painting, should she be persuaded to agree, would be a life study of Angie. She had hinted that she felt she was starting to lose her figure, which he had assured her was ridiculous. And what better way to prove it than to capture her naked beauty on canvas? She deserved it, and the time was now. He only hoped that he was up to the job.

Twenty-Two

Hannah climbed over a stile and made her way to a far corner of the parched field, where a large chestnut mare and its rider were trotting around in circles. As she got nearer, the rider looked increasingly familiar until, to her amazement, she realised that it was Danny. What's more, he was singing a love song with a melody so beautiful that it made her want to cry. She shouted his name and started running towards him, waving her arms above her head. But when he recognised her, Danny flicked the mare's flanks with his heels and, rapidly gathering pace, raced straight past her in the direction she had come from. She turned to watch the mare jump a hawthorn hedge at a gallop and disappear into the fields beyond.

Hannah woke up from the same disturbing dream for the third night running, got out of bed, and went downstairs to the kitchen to make hot chocolate and shake the images from her head. It didn't need an analyst to explain the dream, the imagery was obvious, but maybe if she went over everything again, she could prevent it from recurring. She felt bad enough at the moment without nightmares making things worse.

Her thoughts went back to her early riding days. If there was one thing that riding had taught Hannah it was that you had to get straight back on the horse after a fall. She had done so many times as a young girl learning to ride, and then throughout her career. Until that fateful day when getting straight back on the horse was no longer an option. In a way, her fling with Ian three years ago had been a serious fall from which she thought she'd recovered. Big stumble, remount, trot on, nobody noticed. But she'd been wrong. It was as if she'd been secretly caught falling off the horse on CCTV camera, and the tape had turned up three years later.

Why the hell had Ian kept the stupid birthday card with its intimate message all this time? Simple neglect, perhaps. Or could it be that he kept it as a keepsake of a time that meant more to him than she had ever supposed? At the time there had been no signs that he had wanted anything more than what they had. She didn't doubt that he'd have preferred to spin things along, continuing to heap praise and adoration upon her for as long as it served his carnal purpose, but the thought that he might have continued to carry a torch hadn't occurred to her for a second.

She had quickly put an end to things before they could get out of hand. Thankfully he hadn't harangued her about it (beyond an appeal to see her *just one more time*, she seemed to remember) and so she assumed that he'd returned to normal, having had the common sense to do away with any evidence of their tryst. The bloody idiot.

Hannah remembered the moment she realised that what she had done was wrong. How the hell could she do this to Danny? No, it had to stop, and it did. And yet, three years on, she was in the dock facing charges for the same offence. Not just the simple charge of having an extra-marital fling – to that she held her hands up – but the much more serious charge that, as a result of the fling, she had subsequently given birth to a baby that wasn't her husband's.

To Hannah, honestly, it didn't matter one way or the other. Ben was as much Danny's as hers, whatever the biological realities happened to be. When she had told him so, Danny accused her of 'hiding behind the smug certainties of motherhood', and while that comment incensed her at the time, she couldn't help but reflect on what he'd meant.

While mothers may claim to carry the greater burden of bringing children into the world (nine months of growing discomfort, followed by the agony of giving birth), the fact is that no mother who ever lived could have a moment's doubt about the maternity of the little bundle of flesh and mucus that eventually emerges from between her legs. The same could not be said for the father and paternity.

So, while she was incapable of empathising with Danny, she sympathised, and she understood why he was in so much pain. She wasn't going to give up on him, she loved him too much. But the ball was in his court. She was as close to certain as she could be that Danny was Ben's biological father, but while any doubt remained in Danny's mind, he had important choices to make. He could trust and believe. Or he could decide that, whatever the reality, it didn't matter. Or he could insist on getting a DNA test done, with whatever consequences that might bring. She had no idea which choice he would make.

But one thing was for sure. They would get through this. Hannah was determined that they would, no matter how much difficulty and heartache there was along the way. And her determination had been galvanised the day that Vince had paid her a visit. It took some bottle to do what he did, and she was so happy that Danny had found such a true friend.

What Hannah hadn't bargained for was the revelation that Danny had joined a singing group. Danny, singing, at last! She found it hard to imagine how this had happened, particularly at a time like now. For years she had been on at Danny to find an outlet for his obvious talent. He lived for music, and whenever he was off guard he would sing like a bird. None of your karaoke or pub singing, but lyrical and passionate. Early in their courtship he had made her a mixtape of him singing three songs a cappella: Roy Orbison's *You Got It*, Elvis Costello's *Good Year for the Roses*, and Elton John's *Blue Eyes*. She cried when she first played the tape, and she knew she wanted to be with him always.

However, Danny had always dismissed Hannah's urging that he should take singing more seriously by taking lessons, joining a group, or whatever. To her frustration, he had always retreated into his shell, more wary than ever that she might catch him next time, and over the years she got to hear his singing voice less and less often. And now, having arrived at the biggest crossroads in their relationship, and in real danger of breaking up (though not so long as she had a breath left in her body), she discovers that Danny has had a Damascene conversion and decided to launch a singing career *without her knowing*! And what's more, she was sworn not to let Danny know that she knows!

But Hannah knew that one day soon she would be able to share in Danny's new adventure. She looked out of the kitchen window at the gathering light and knew that the nightmare wouldn't return.

Danny felt the time was right to spend more time back at home, with Vince in need of peace and quiet, and with Christmas around the corner. How could he not be there with Ben at Christmas time? It was a no-brainer. And he had to admit that he and Hannah had been getting on much better of late.

When they had discussed it, Danny had been touched by the warmth and enthusiasm that Hannah had shown. She stopped short of excitement, as he had expected; she was keeping a level head about everything, for which he was quietly grateful. They hugged, and it reminded him of their very first hug.

When he returned home, Ben was like a thing possessed, running up and down the stairs, waving his Everton scarf above his head, and shouting out loud everything he wanted for Christmas. Danny grabbed hold of him, and gave him the biggest hug ever. He closed his eyes for a moment as Ben writhed and giggled in his arms, and when he opened them he caught a glimpse of Hannah's profile as she walked into the kitchen; how he missed that smile, that turned-up nose.

'So, sausage, tell me again what you'd like Father Christmas to bring you,' said Danny as he sat Ben down on the sofa.

'Transformers.'

'And?'

'Football.'

'Anything else?'

'Daddy, where have you been, Daddy?'

Danny felt the need to swallow hard.

'Nowhere, silly billy. I can't be here all the time. I have to go to work and stay somewhere else sometimes.'

'Why?'

'Because daddies and mummies are busy people. Sometimes they have to go away to get things for home.'

'Mummy didn't go away.'

'Well, I didn't go away for long, and I'm here now.'

Danny plucked at Ben's Everton scarf, which he was now clutching to his chest.

'How about we ask Father Christmas to bring you a new blue for Christmas? This one's all old and tattered.'

'Noooooo! My blue! *My blue!*'

'Okay, okay, I know. Then how about an Everton shirt with Ben and number nine written on the back?'

'Yeaaaah! Yeaaaah! Daddy! Daddy! Daddy!'

Danny felt his eyes filling up, and he turned away for a second. *Think of something else. Think of something else.* And it occurred to him to wonder whether his boyhood football team had ever given him as much pleasure as it was giving to his son right now. He allowed a memory of a freezing cold evening at Goodison Park, standing at the Gladwys Street end with his own dad, to flash across his mind. Everton

0, Manchester City 2. He stiffened at the thought, and any trace of tears quickly vanished.

'Okay, sausage. I'll let Father Christmas know. An Everton shirt with Ben, number nine, on the back. Now, let me go talk to Mummy for a bit.'

'Football. Number nine. No new blue,' said Ben as he scurried towards the stairs and up to his room.

Danny went to talk to Hannah.

'He's so excited about Christmas, it's brilliant,' said Danny.

'He's happy to have Daddy home,' said Hannah. 'It means the world to him.'

'I guess it's up to us not to screw things up for him then. I couldn't stand that. I remember what it's like as a kid when your parents fall out at Christmas. One year after Christmas lunch, Mum and Dad had a blazing row and Dad hit the whisky. He eventually collapsed on the couch like a dead man while we sat watching *The Morecambe and Wise Christmas Special* pretending not to notice.'

'I might be able to trump that,' said Hannah. 'One Christmas Eve when I was about ten, Mother left the house inexplicably and didn't come back until the day after Boxing Day. Father was beside himself, didn't know what to do. Christmas dinner that year was egg, chips and beans followed by rice pudding out of a tin.'

With a laugh they agreed that they were both long overdue psychotherapy for their respective childhood Christmas nightmares, and they vowed (sealed with a peck on the lips) that there was no way they would jeopardise Ben's Christmas. But that was easier said than done, so they decided to set some simple rules.

'I promise I won't go over old ground, we'll only start arguing,' said Danny.

'And I think it would be best if we slept in separate rooms, don't you?' said Hannah.

They put Ben to bed, then continued talking, catching up on this and that, over a bottle of wine. Nothing heavy, no mention of *it*, just familiar, friendly conversation.

And as Danny was opening a second bottle, he started singing.

'That sounds lovely,' said Hannah. 'Is it a lullaby?'

'Sorry, I wasn't even aware I was singing,' said Danny. 'Yes, it's a lullaby. Billy Joel.'

'You should sing it for Ben.'

'Good idea,' said Danny.

'I'd like to hear it, too,' said Hannah.

Danny topped up both their glasses and sang the song just for Hannah.

Twenty-Three

Lying flat on the ground on one of the southern slopes, Cat was examining what she believed to be a species of mushroom not normally found on the island. She had spent the last two days studying mushrooms and little else, as she was expecting a visitor from the British Mycological Society.

Just then a breeze picked up, and she heard the sound of a helicopter engine in the distance. How far had the spores travelled on the wind, she wondered?

Turning over on to her back, Cat stared up at the autumn sky as sunlight appeared between the shifting clouds and warmed her face. Fifteen years, she thought. How time flies.

Cat first visited the island as a biology student on a field trip from Cardiff University. Her specialist subject was ornithology, and she spent a month catching and ringing birds in Heligoland traps around the island, and mapping the movement of numerous species as part of her thesis on avian migration patterns.

At the time she had felt a little daunted at the prospect of a month marooned on a remote rock, but all her reservations had disappeared the moment she set foot on the island. There was no jetty in those days; the boat dropped anchor as close to shore as the tide would allow, and then passengers were ferried on to the beach in a flat-bottomed pontoon in a sort of peacetime equivalent of the D-Day landings.

She liked the island and its quiet, magnificent beauty, immediately. It was the first time she had been anywhere where there were no cars, and the absence of traffic noise, and of city din in general, had an immediate tranquilising effect. In this place, nature was everything.

She learned more about ornithology, and many aspects of zoology and botany, in a single month than she had learned in her previous two years at Cardiff. She also made some good friends, locals and visitors alike, and most importantly of all, she came away from the island knowing that she would return many times in the future. She had found her spiritual home.

After university Cat embarked on a series of laboratory jobs, working for a yoghurt manufacturer, then a pharmaceutical company, and then in a medical research facility. This wasn't what she'd had in mind as an undergraduate, and she longed for a job outdoors, where she belonged.

She continued to be a keen twitcher in her spare time, and eventually, through her association with one of the leading ornithological societies, she landed a job as an assistant keeper at a bird sanctuary in south Wales. Following that, she had a two-year stint as a ranger on a private estate in north Devon.

Then, one day, she saw a job advert she never thought she'd see: assistant warden on the island. Was her CV good enough? In the end, it hardly mattered. Upon application, Cat was invited to an interview with the warden and the island estate manager, and in the space of an hour she had convinced them that she was made for the position. She already had an extensive knowledge of the island's native and non-native species, both on land and in the coastal waters, and she could talk for England on ecological matters as they pertained to the island, including the role of farming and other forms of human intervention. Added to this, she knew the history, geography, geology and archaeology of the island like she'd studied nothing else all her life. She got the assistant warden's job, and within two years she became the warden.

More and more she referred to the *magic* of the island,

which, while hardly scientific, increasingly seemed the only word to adequately describe the way she felt.

Over time she learned, despite her scientific training and natural scepticism, that she could touch the granite and connect with the past. She could sense where socially or historically significant events had taken place simply by being in that place. And she could locate archaeological artefacts by feeling the energy they emitted. She had discovered Neolithic worked flints, several items of Bronze Age pottery, and most notably a previously unknown early Christian burial site. Increasingly, she worked alongside archaeologists, who had come to trust Cat's instincts, powers, or whatever it was that she had.

Sometimes she could also sense when things were about to happen. And today, she knew that Henry was returning to the island.

Henry's first visit to the island had begun with a rough, two-hour sea crossing that had set a tone of high adventure from the off. Now, with the boat out of commission for the low season, transportation from the mainland was an easy seven-minute helicopter ride.

One of six people squeezed into the small aircraft, Henry peered out at the impressive mass of the island as it hove suddenly into view, looking very different from his last memory of the place. The sparkling emerald greens, bright yellows, and shimmering blues that made up the island's summer palette had made way for more subdued greens, and a predominance of greys: sea, sky, granite rock.

The helicopter made an elegant descent and the softest of landings in the field north-west of the church, and the passengers were ushered safely from the machine and across to the track that ran due-west from the village.

Henry stood for a moment, looking back at the helicopter with its rotor still turning furiously, as it prepared to shuttle back to the mainland to collect a few more island visitors. As the helicopter rose sharply and spun through a hundred-and-eighty degrees, the sun appeared suddenly from behind distant grey clouds, lighting up the field that stretched back towards the village, and Henry felt as though he had returned to a place he already loved. He knew the smell of the air, the sweep of the landscape before him, and the feel of the ground beneath his feet.

He looked towards the church, with its clock tower out of view, and hoped that it was still three o'clock.

This time, Henry's accommodation was an unassuming flat-roofed, part-rendered granite building that had been used as a stable, a piggery, and a hay store at different times in its past. It stood in front of a battlemented wall, on a hilltop overlooking a sheltered valley, with panoramic views out to sea. He unpacked, made a mug of tea, and sat on the stone steps at the front of the house. He looked back across the sea in the direction of the mainland, which was completely obscured by heavy banks of rain falling way off in the distance.

Raining over there, dry over here. That summed things up pretty well, he thought. His last encounter with Jenny had affected him quite badly, though he had toughed it out with her. When he heard her plea for reconciliation his heart ached. But he knew he had to move on, and that meant returning to the island.

Henry slipped back into a familiar morning routine, getting up to watch the sun rise over the sea, making tea, and returning to bed to read for a while. Then he would fall into a semi-slumber for a short time, allowing ideas to bubble around in his head as he made plans for the day ahead. Sometimes, if he fell into a deeper sleep, he even completed unfinished dreams.

As he lay in bed that first morning he reflected upon his

first visit to the island, and found himself thinking about Cat. Though he had thought about her only once or twice since his summer visit, she had made an impression on him; she seemed to embody the freedom he felt in this place. He had kept her gift, the little grey stone, about his person ever since, and it had become a sort of talisman. It was his connection back to the island, and it had somehow ensured that he would return.

That morning, Henry revisited some of his favourite island landmarks, including the castle, the old lighthouse, and the battery point. He resisted the temptation to sing as he went, and for now his pitch pipe remained firmly in his pocket. He strode around the island, just breathing the air, listening to the sounds of nature, and allowing his troubles to evaporate. Everything seemed much more familiar than was reasonable to expect, and it felt as though he had been visiting the place for years.

After a couple of hours exploring the west coast, he headed back towards the tiny village to collect some supplies from the shop. But first he decided to visit the church, which looked dark and bleak in the distance, its hard lines silhouetted against a glowering grey sky. How different it looked compared to the last time he saw it. He was learning that everything on the island looked different depending on the weather, and today was Henry's first taste of the nasty stuff. After a bright enough start to the morning, rain clouds were now sweeping in from the west, preparing to let loose on the island. The first torrents started to fall just as he reached the church gate, and he quickly went inside for shelter.

The interior walls were of brick, rendered here and there, and with green and black patches of damp prominent in several places. The floor of the aisle was made up of a mix of terracotta, white and black tiles. The pews were made of rough, dark wood and looked particularly uncomfortable. At the back of the church was a baptismal font made of sandstone, standing upon a granite base, and topped with a carved wooden lid. On the walls surrounding the font, several display cases contained samples of rocks and minerals from the island, and hand-made posters told the story of the island's geology in words and pictures.

Henry walked up the aisle (he was sure he would never do that again!) and sat in a front-row pew. The rain was battering hard against the slate roof, and he looked up at the wooden-clad ceiling for signs of leakage. High on the wall behind the altar was an impressive stained-glass window with a large central panel depicting the crucifixion. To his right was an ornate wooden lectern in the shape of an eagle, and to the left was a sandstone pulpit into which had been carved the words "Thy Word is a Lantern unto My Feet".

Henry sat cold and motionless for maybe fifteen minutes before reaching into a pocket for his pitch pipe. He wasn't religious, but he knew one or two blessing songs and a gospel medley from the chorus repertoire, and he couldn't resist singing one. He absolutely loved church acoustics. He blew an A and started singing softly.

Oh Lord my God, when I in awesome wonder
Consider all the worlds thy hands have made
I see the stars, I hear the rolling thunder
Thy power throughout the universe displayed

Though he sang very gently, Henry was astonished at how the sound bounced off the walls, resonating and filling the space around him. He felt an involuntary shiver run down his spine. And then he heard a voice from the back of the church.

'Beautiful, Henry. Very beautiful.'

He looked around to see Cat standing by the font, smiling at him.

'Good God...I mean, heaven's above...I mean...hello again!' said Henry.

The rain had faded, and a weak sun was showing signs of emerging from behind the clouds as they left the church. Henry stopped and looked up at the clock tower. Three o'clock. He checked his wristwatch. Eleven thirty-seven.

'Excellent,' he said, and Cat looked on in amusement.

'How come you were in the church?' asked Henry. 'Not the usual place for a nature warden at half eleven in the morning, I wouldn't have thought!'

'I was passing on the quad, and I noticed a couple of sheep wandering into the porch. You must have left the gate open. So I stopped to shoo them out, and then I heard an angel's voice from somewhere. I wondered whether this might be the moment of my celestial calling, so I popped inside to repent my sins just in case. Imagine my surprise when the angel turned out to be the big fella with the lovely deep voice!'

'Ha!' was all Henry could think of to say.

'Listen, I can't stop now. I've got some honcho over from the British Mycological Society. He's desperate to see our wood blewit rings.'

'Seems like a fungi.'

'I gave you that one on a plate.'

'Best served that way, I think.'

'What?'

'Mushrooms. Best served on a plate? Sorry, I couldn't resist.'

'I see you've been sharpening your sense of humour since you were last here. Listen, I must go. I'll be in the pub around six-ish if you fancy popping in later.'

'Will do. Have a good day.'

'You too, music man.'

Henry re-ran their brief conversation in his head, and detected more than a hint of Vince in there. He wasn't usually so ready with the puns.

Later in the pub, they resumed the conversation once

the familiar gaggle of regulars had thinned out. To Henry's surprise, most of them remembered him, and his pitch pipe still seemed to be the subject of some amusement. He felt like he was fitting back into a social group he didn't even know he had.

'So, how's things?' asked Cat, at last.

Henry thought for a moment before saying anything.

'Well, from a subjective point of view, I'd say that things have gone from bad to worse.'

'Oh dear.'

'And from an objective point of view, I'd still say that things have gone from bad to worse.'

'Ah. Care to elaborate?'

'Are you sure? The first time we met, I seem to remember that specifics didn't really feature much in our conversation. It was all a bit mystical, if you know what I mean.'

'Mystical?'

'Well, if not quite mystical, then vague. I mean, you seemed to know that something was troubling me, and you gave some very kind advice, but I never did say what it was all about.'

'I didn't need to know. I could see that there was something troubling you. The eyes, mostly. So, would it help to tell me more?'

'How long have you got?'

'That bad, eh?'

Henry had no idea why he was about to reveal details of his personal life to someone who was practically a stranger, but it seemed completely natural.

'Well, okay, here goes. In a nutshell…last time I came here I'd just lost my job after years with the same company, and I'd taken a bit of a knock. I needed some space to work out what I was going to do next. I was also a bit disturbed by things that were happening in my marriage. But that was nothing compared to what I discovered when I got back

191

home. It turns out that my wife has been having an affair with someone I thought was a friend, and I now realise what an idiot I've been. I suppose things have been messed up for a long time, but I just couldn't see it. Anyway, now it's over for good. And I've no idea what I'll be doing next. Apart from having another pint of this bitter. You for another?'

'Er, yes, thanks. Blimey. So, all my high-flown advice last time must seem a bit lame now, I dare say.'

'No, no. It was helpful. *If your heart says fly, then fly*...isn't that what you said? Well, I guess that's what I've done. I've stopped off here for a little while, like most of the migrant birds on the island. The difference is they know where they're flying to next. Me, I haven't a clue.'

Henry got up to go to the bar.

'How long are you here for?' asked Cat, as Henry returned with the drinks.

'Just a week this time.'

'Do you fancy finding out a lot more about the island while you're here?'

'Sounds great. What do you have in mind?'

'You could be my unofficial assistant for the week, if you like. Come with me and I'll show you the island at close quarters – show you how special this place really is. Unless you'd prefer to do your own thing, of course.'

'No, no. I'd be mad to refuse.'

Henry was excited at the prospect of discovering more about the island, and he felt privileged that the nature warden of all people had given him the opportunity. But more than anything, he looked forward to spending time with Cat, who was beginning to intrigue him almost as much as the island itself.

In the days that followed, Henry found himself at various times in the roles of labourer, scientific observer, and student. He helped load Cat's Land Rover with all sorts of surveying equipment, scuba gear, and any number of objects he was hard pressed to identify. Then he stood back and watched as she went about in search of this or that species, identifying, measuring, photographing, and scribbling in notebooks.

One morning they took a motorised dinghy around the island, stopping every so often to pull something out of the sea, or put something back in. The same day, they went snorkelling in wetsuits off the jetty, Henry flapping around hopelessly and blowing large amounts of seawater through his snorkel, while Cat slipped elegantly beneath the surface to examine something interesting below, returning for air what seemed like an age later. Everything she did was impressive in an understated, professional kind of way, and Henry felt like an imbecile apprentice beside her.

However, every hour he spent roaming the island with Cat was a pleasure, bringing to light some revelation or other. She gave Henry a running commentary as she went about her work, so that he understood everything he was seeing. She told him the common and Latin names of every animal, plant or fungus they stopped to observe, describing the various ecosystems they inhabited. And she described the geology and topography of the island as they walked, connecting everything together in the form of a grand story that told of the island's rich and diverse natural history.

Cat also expounded on the social history of the island, taking Henry to sites of historical significance, including shipwrecks, smugglers' hideouts, and hidden graves.

'The island is a treasure chest,' she said. 'Stand anywhere, and I'll tell you something amazing that's happened within a twenty metre radius.'

And so she did, proving her point time after time in what quickly became Henry's favourite game. Finding some apparently featureless stretch of land, he would stop still and say, 'Okay, here,' and listen as Cat reeled off some fascinating fact.

'You're six feet away from a yellow flowering plant that only grows on the island, nowhere else in the world... ten metres behind you, there's a crankshaft from a plane that crashed here during the Second World War...you're standing on a Saxon burial mound, you bloody oaf...'

It was the time he was standing on the burial mound that Cat suddenly looked at him differently, walked towards him, and kissed him very gently on the lips.

Four days flew by, and Henry was having the time of his life. But the kiss seemed to change things, and he needed some time alone to think.

The next day, he walked all the way to the north end of the island, along the dramatic west coast. About halfway, he stopped to rest on a high cliff top, looked down at crashing waves four hundred feet below, and felt the sharp lash of a westerly wind against the side of his face. Turning inland, he looked across the rough terrain of dry heath and gorse that filled the late autumn landscape, stretching as far as he could see to the north and across to the east. A solitary peregrine surveyed its territory high above.

Henry thought of home, saw Jenny's lying eyes and Jeffrey's smug face, and felt his heart sink.

Then he thought of Vince and Neil, Danny and Ken, and heard laughter and the sound of ringing chords, and his mood lifted again.

Then he looked at the magnificent beauty all around him, and he thought of Cat, and that kiss. Something stirred inside him. Something he hadn't felt for a very long time.

Twenty-Four

Wedging the last fatty chunk of pork chop into his mouth, George chose that moment to ask his wife a question that had been puzzling them both.

'What the dickens do you suppose that son of ours is up to these days? He's never here, and when he is you can hardly get a word out of him.'

'Don't speak with your mouth full, George,' said Margaret.

'Sorry, dear,' said George, causing pork fat to dribble down his chin and on to his tie.

'Honestly! Another one for the dry cleaners. So, why the concern about Neil all of a sudden? I'd have thought it best for you two to stay as far apart from each other as possible right now.'

George wiped his chin with a napkin, and dabbed half-heartedly at his tie.

'What makes you say that? Just showing natural parental curiosity. What's he up to, do you think?'

'Take it off and give it here, George. I'm not sure, but he's clearly got a lot on with his music at the moment. You can't move in his room for files, notebooks, sheet music, theory books, you name it. I've asked him, but he's being quite vague. Some project or assignment or other.'

George undid his tie, pulling it out from beneath his shirt collar, and dangling it over the dining table for Margaret.

'Everything's a bloody project or an assignment these days. Whatever happened to job, or career, or profession? Do we even know if he's earning money? It's about time we started charging the boy rent.'

'George, how many times have we been through this? Whether you believe it or not, Neil has been trying hard to find something suitable, and until he does, I think the least we can do is to cut him some slack by not charging him to stay in the family home. Let's not go there again, shall we?' Margaret was quietly pleased that George was showing some sort of concern for their youngest, even if it was of the begrudging kind. But she was wary of taking George's words to mean too much. She had witnessed years of decline in the state of father-son relations, and things had got to the point where she didn't even know if reconciliation was possible, let alone the reconstruction of any sort of bond between them.

While George eagerly helped himself to a gigantic portion of summer pudding with double cream, Margaret worked through the facts as they pertained to the case (she was starting to feel like a detective with a case to solve).

Neil isn't Robert, fact. Neil is, in his own way, as much of a prodigy as Robert, fact. George is a stubborn, pig-headed booby, fact. Okay, what next?

The answer to that question came as a shameful surprise. She decided to search Neil's room for evidence of what he's up to, and use anything she can find to persuade George to start viewing their son in a more sympathetic light. With any luck she might find a letter from a successful job application, or maybe a contract of employment, which she could put under George's nose over dinner.

This didn't make Margaret feel good about herself. She had never pried into Neil's affairs. They were close enough for Neil to want to confide in her, but she always felt that there should be boundaries one didn't need to cross. Of course, she went into Neil's room often, to change the bed linen, vacuum the areas of carpet not concealed by musical equipment, books and CDs, and flick around with a duster. But she never opened drawers, or went looking for things. And here she was, planning a forensic examination of her son's room.

But first she decided to try a little cross-examination on George, as he relaxed into a post-prandial torpor.

'Isn't it remarkable that Neil should find himself singing in the same group as your old chum Henry?'

'Mmm, say what?'

George's eyes had glazed over as he sat back in his chair, one hand resting upon the stuffed protuberance of his belly, the other gently teasing a glass of red wine.

'I was saying, isn't it remarkable that Neil should end up singing in a quartet with your old friend?'

'Oh, Henry. Yes, quite a turn-up for the book. I hardly knew where to look when I walked in on them that day.'

'Don't you think you were a bit impolite, rushing off the way you did? They even offered to sing for you...'

'Impolite? Ah, well, never meant it that way. I was delighted to see Henry. Just a bit embarrassed I suppose. Not sure why, but I wasn't about to be serenaded in my own conservatory by an old friend, my youngest son, and two other charlies.'

'Why the cynicism all the time, George? Why can't you just accept things the way they are? Chill out.'

Margaret reckoned that was probably the first time she'd ever used the expression *chill out*. Certainly to George, who was now looking at her with a mixture of surprise and suspicion. Margaret expected a sharp retort, but then her husband's demeanour changed, and he looked momentarily sorrowful.

'We nearly came to blows, Margaret. Neil and I. We nearly came to blows.'

'I know, George. I was there. I came between you, remember? Oh, why so much animosity, darling? Why—'

George's mellow moment had passed, and he interrupted sharply.

'Not again, Margaret. You know where I stand. When the boy shapes up, gets a proper job, gets himself a young lady, and—'

'He's GAY, George! When will you accept that Neil is gay?'

George threw his napkin on the table and got up slowly. 'Excuse me, I must…' said George, but left the sentence hanging.

Margaret knew she'd hit the brick wall of George's denial once again, and felt suddenly tired of it all. However, her attempt at cross-examination had given her another idea.

George and Neil share at least one thing in common, and that's Henry. However unlikely it may be, father and son are connected by a common friendship, so perhaps Henry could be helpful in sorting things out between them? She decided to contact him, though she wasn't quite sure what the pretext would be.

The following day, Margaret got up at seven o'clock as usual, and made breakfast for George before seeing him off to work. They barely spoke at the breakfast table, though the air was more resigned than frosty, following the previous day's exchanges.

She then did half an hour of stretching exercises and, after showering and dressing, made a large mug of green tea, which she took to the computer. She wrote emails to two old friends – one in Melbourne, the other in Pontefract – then found herself looking back at the presentation she'd given to the WI. It had been received very well, and now Margaret allowed herself the indulgence of clicking through the slides and imagining how the story of her early life as a dancer must have come across. The personal feedback had certainly been glowing. Emily Pickford, who had invited her to speak at the WI lunch, seemed thrilled. But then she was a bit of a balletomane, travelling up to London to the Opera House or the Coliseum whenever she could, and taking pride of place in the front row at Margaret's senior citizens' class. Not a bad job, Margaret concluded, as she reached the final slide.

By early afternoon, Margaret was starting to feel fidgety. She had a reading group meeting early in the evening, so there were a few hours to fill. And while she never had any trouble finding useful things to do, she knew the reason for her restlessness was that she was putting off the distasteful task she had set herself the previous day. So she decided to get the vacuum cleaner out and do a quick tour of the house, leaving Neil's room until last.

She pushed the extension hose with its large brush head around the carpet in her son's room, avoiding knocking over a pile of books, two music stands, and an electric piano with especially wobbly legs. She bent down to pick up a small white card on the floor, throwing it on to Neil's desk, where it landed face-up.

She glanced at the card and saw a familiar name. NEWTON BURNS. There was only one Newton Burns as far as she was aware. The one everybody knew from TV. The one she knew better than most. The one who had been the lover of her gay best friend when she moved to London from Paris just over forty years ago. What was Neil doing with his calling card?

Margaret switched off the vacuum cleaner and sat on the edge of her son's bed to compose herself.

Even by recent standards, Neil was having an especially busy day. As he did quite often these days, he had stayed overnight in a modest hotel in Bayswater (thankfully, an allowable expense) ahead of an early morning meeting at The Dorchester with the composer and script editor. They talked through the first couple of songs in the screenplay, discussing their context within the overall storyline, the mood the composer wanted to convey, and how the harmony arrangements should reflect all of that.

Though he had confidence in his own ability as an arranger, and was comfortable working to a brief, Neil found this sort of collaboration challenging, learning that even the smallest nuance of meaning or intent within the story could impact the way he approached the harmony chart. If the composer had written in a minor key to convey melancholy, for example, this immediately set Neil a challenge with the harmonies and how to structure the chords in such a way that his work would not only reflect, but amplify, the composer's intentions.

After the meeting, Neil visited Newton Burns's small office in Soho to pick up a copy of his contract, all signed and sealed at last. Newt was away on location somewhere, and wouldn't be around for at least the next three weeks. Neil had felt bold enough to ask Newt's PA about his schedule, and discovered that he was filming a documentary abroad for BBC2, would then be hosting two awards ceremonies (one for ITV, the other for Sky Arts), and then recording the latest in a long-running series of TV adverts for a pre-mixed cocktail drink. Newt being so busy came as a relief to Neil, as it meant that he could concentrate on his work rather than worrying about his next liaison with the great man.

Neil left the Soho office with a spring in his step. He felt exhilarated and relieved to have a contract with Newton Burns's film production company at last. Though he'd spent hours on the project already, the legal team had taken ages finalising the terms and conditions, something which he had been assured was not unusual. He had been hired for six months on a full-time basis, with a retainer that secured his part-time involvement with the project until the end of the production phase. There was also the possibility of spin-off work, but with little by way of detail. If all went well, he could be employed for the best part of a year. And if all went very well, and the film was a commercial success…he could barely allow himself to think that far ahead.

For now, Neil looked forward to the rest of the day, and a bit of catch-up. He was very aware that he'd been a stranger to friends and family for a while, and now that he had the contract, he wanted to make up for it. His first port of call was to see Ken for lunch. He owed him a lot, as it was Ken who had recommended him to Newt in the first place. He hadn't needed to do that. He was a true friend and mentor, and Neil wanted to thank him properly.

Ken had sounded flustered on the phone when Neil had asked him to lunch, as though embarrassed by the invitation, and so Neil had pretended that he wanted to discuss possible songs for the quartet's appearance at the British championships the following May. That did the trick.

When Neil arrived at the Chinese restaurant, Ken was already seated at the table, studying *The Times* crossword page, and eating something deep-fried.

'Neil, dear chap, take a pew. How are we? Been busy? Tell me about it! Spent last night coaching the ladies in Southampton again. The bass has lost about half a stone, which I'm not sure is helping matters. Detracts from the comedy value of being called The Weightwatchers, if you ask me. Lady basses need to be on the big side, I've always thought, and I fear she's not as powerful as she used to be. The foul-mouthed tenor hasn't changed much, mind you. She told this joke about a magician's assistant and a set of billiard balls that was a bit near the knuckle. Banana fritter?'

'Banana fritter?'

'Go on, help yourself. They're delicious.'

'Thanks. So...lovely to see you! Thanks for coming...'

'Glad to, glad to. As you said on the phone, the championships are still a few months away, but the sooner we choose the songs, the better off we'll be. Now then, I have here...'

Ken reached under the table for a briefcase, which he placed on his lap, and then took out a bulging yellow cardboard folder.

'...a few suggestions.'

Neil wasn't in the mood for wading through song suggestions, but didn't know how to divert the Ken juggernaut.

'Oh, before we start, Mr Burns sends his best regards to you and Bella,' said Neil, thinking that this might present a useful diversion.

'Ah, dear old Newt. You've seen him recently, I take it?'

'Well, yes. You know you spoke to Mr Burns – Newt – about me being a keen arranger? Well, he invited me to work on a project, a new screenplay, arranging a bunch of songs in four-part, and it's really exciting, and I just wanted to say thank you so much, Ken. Thank you!'

'That's excellent...they've got salt and pepper squid.'

Neil knew that Ken had heard every word, but that he wasn't good at taking thanks.

'Shall we go for the feast and share, or go it alone?' asked Neil, with what he felt was a better chance of an appropriate response.

'Screenplay, you say? Lord, not one of those raincoat numbers of his? Back in the old days, dear Newt was quite heavily involved in the underground film industry. Lots of underdressed young men all over the place. Art films they called them, but they were filth really. At a time when the board of film censors were all over everything. Fruity Newty we used to call him.'

'Ah, I see. Interesting. No, it's not one of those films. I don't suppose many films of that type would call for nine original songs arranged in four-part harmony.'

'No, I see your point. Feast, I think. Bit of everything, so long as they throw in the salt and pepper squid as a starter, and banana fritters at the end.'

'More banana fritters?'

'Not now, we'll have them at the end with some lychees, shall we?'

Then Ken asked Neil a question he hadn't been expecting.

'Has Fruity Newty made a pass at you yet, young Neil?

Because Fruity Newty always feels it his duty to go after fresh booty…'

Neil was taken aback, though whether it was Ken's unexpected frankness, his adeptness at rhyme, or his incongruous use of the word 'booty' that shocked him most, he wasn't sure.

'I, well, er…I think he has taken a bit of a shine to me, but I rather hope that…well, that we don't let that get in the way of what is, after all…well, a professional relationship. Ken…did you know that Newt – Mr Burns – was, well… interested in me in that way?'

Neil took a mouthful of water and cleared his throat.

'Neil, my dear boy. Old Newt lives in a world very different from mine, but I've known him for many years, and he's essentially a good egg. He appreciates talent, he loves music, and he has an eye for young men. But then so did the ancient Greeks. Don't worry. Newt wouldn't take advantage. If you're on the payroll, then it means he trusts you to do a good job, and I'm happy to have put in a good word.'

'Thanks, I appreciate that, Ken.'

'*I Can't Give You Anything but Love,*' said Ken, staring into his lap.

'Sorry?'

'Just a thought for a contest song. A nice easy-beat number that I think will suit the quartet very well.'

Ken picked out some sheet music from the file on his lap and handed it to Neil.

'Ah,' said Neil.

And then Ken started singing the song, a little too loud for Neil's liking. The first line, beginning with the words '*Now that it's your birthday…*' Ken sang with particular gusto, attracting the attention of the head waiter, who appeared from nowhere to offer his congratulations and ask if he could take their order. Neil didn't have the heart to tell him that it wasn't his birthday.

Neil and Ken thoroughly enjoyed the feast for two with extra salt and pepper squid and banana fritters. The extra dessert was delivered to the table with special attention to detail, a lit birthday candle having been inserted into each banana fritter.

Neil's next stop was Foyles on Charing Cross Road, to collect two books he'd ordered a month ago. Then, as the shopping mood was upon him, he ambled around Oxford Street and Bond Street, nipping into arcades and department stores to get inspiration for Christmas, before taking the tube to Knightsbridge.

He bought just one item all afternoon: a 150g tin of Russian *Chatka* crab meat from the food hall at Harvey Nichols. Apart from good caviar, this was Margaret's favourite treat. Caught in the deep waters of the Bering Strait, the King Crab was the most sought after variety in the world apparently, and his mother had developed a taste for it many years ago. Something to do with a Russian boyfriend, Neil seemed to recall her saying.

With that, Neil headed back to Paddington and the train to Maidenhead. He looked forward to seeing his mother and finding out what had been going on in her life recently; she always had some new story to tell him about, or at least some spicy village gossip. However, he still felt reluctant to tell her about his new venture for fear that his father would get wind of it and do his usual hatchet job on him. Neil couldn't bear the thought of George dismissing his precious project and ridiculing his ambitions yet again, so there was a limit to what he could tell Margaret, much as he wanted to tell her everything in glorious detail.

Sometime very soon Neil would tell all, but for now he would just say that he was beginning to earn reasonable money from a couple of freelance assignments, and that he was in a position to start paying rent. Margaret would probably resist, but Neil would insist. He was paying his way from now on and, whatever his father might think, he was proud to be able to do so.

Neil called Margaret as his train was leaving Paddington, and she offered to pick him up at Maidenhead station forty minutes later. Neil persuaded his mother not to go straight home, but to drive to a country pub some way out of town, where they could relax and chat without the shadow of his father hovering over them. Facing George was something that couldn't be avoided much longer, but Neil needed just a bit more time to steel himself. They had both promised Margaret to be on their best behaviour the next time they were in the same room together, but it still wasn't going to be easy.

Neil sensed that Margaret was slightly ill at ease as they took their drinks to sit beside an open fire in the lounge bar.

'This is cosy, Ma. Cheers!' Neil reached to clink wine glasses with Margaret.

'It's so lovely to see you, darling. You're hardy ever home, and when you are, you keep such strange hours these days. I know you've been keeping out of your father's way, but still...I've missed our little chats.'

'Me too, me too. But all's cool. In fact, more than cool...'

Neil told his mother about the freelance work, which was both untruthful and not very interesting, and he could see that Margaret knew he was keeping something from her.

There was tension in the air now.

Margaret sipped her wine slowly, searching for words. She was desperate to ask about Newton Burns, but didn't want to jeopardise everything by revealing that she had been digging around in her son's affairs.

'Is there anything – or anyone – else you'd like to tell me about, darling?' was the best she could manage.

'No, no. It's all cool,' said Neil.

Twenty-Five

After just three weeks of his new lifestyle, Vince was sleeping well, finding more energy throughout the day, and his legs were feeling less feeble. Not that he was exerting himself much, except for a gentle spin on his newly-acquired exercise bike once a day, and a session of muscle strengthening exercises that involved an enormous blue elastic band. Red meat and dairy foods were out, while fish, chicken and beans were in. Lager was something he craved, but limited himself to one or two bottles a day.

Pushed to say what else he was enjoying about his new lifestyle, Vince felt that he could point to two bonus items. One, he had found the time to organise his possessions and generally get the flat into shape. Two, he had lost some of his beer belly, which Angie had said was beginning to make him look like a Twiglet.

He wasn't sure he'd understood the Twiglet analogy at first, until Angie had invited him to stand side-on in front of a full-length mirror. Patting his belly, she'd told him that he was perfectly proportioned except for the bump, which made him look like a specimen of the aforementioned salty snack. That had been enough for Vince to lay off the lager more than he'd have preferred, but he had to admit that the effects were showing.

He felt virtuous, and yet he felt bored. He knew this would happen. To his dismay, the promise to avoid daytime TV was faltering, and he found himself falling under the spell of delights such as *Celebrity Sheds*, *Truncheons and Tasers*, and *A Passion for Plywood*. At first he would watch five minutes or so before switching off with a stern self-reminder not to stray again. Then he started switching on to catch up with the news, only to find himself, remote control in hand, flicking back to *Celebrity Cross-Stitching*, *Lager Lout Britain*, and *The World's Weirdest Vegetables*.

He subscribed to Sky Arts, as he'd intended, and was delighted at first to discover a wealth of music documentaries to keep him happy. *Queen: A Kind of Magic*, *The Making of Dark Side of the Moon* and, yes, *The Day Elvis Died*, all captured his imagination. Until he discovered that gems such as these were on a frequent repeat loop, and that he had to wait weeks for fresh material.

He turned to reading, deciding to borrow from the library rather than invest too much up front in what was, after all, a journey into the unknown. He was a keen enough reader, but rarely strayed much beyond musical non-fiction. He started with Dickens' *Bleak House*, but the plot made his head spin, and he found himself slip-ping into a state of depression. He turned to Austen's *Pride and Prejudice* to see what all the fuss was about, but found himself irritated by the manners and morals of nineteenth-century landed gentry, and unable to shake the image of Colin Firth's smirking face from his head.

Deciding that classic English literature probably wasn't going to do it for him, Vince switched his attention to comedy, and discovered Spike Milligan's war series, which he found instantly hilarious. He hadn't laughed so much since he was last with the quartet. And that was a big part of the problem. He missed rehearsing and singing with the guys more than he could have imagined.

Perhaps the enforced lay-off after prelims was not such a good thing after all? It was entirely for his benefit that they all decided it was the right thing to do. However, having made good progress so far, Vince now felt that a resumption of quartet duties was just what the doctor ordered – or just what the doctor would have ordered if the doctor knew anything about harmony singing.

The trouble was, everyone was tied up. Neil was up to his ears with the Newton Burns project (he had several new and reassuringly distasteful jokes for Neil when he next saw him); Danny was busy patching things up at home (and quite right too); and Henry seemed to be away most of the time (what was going on there, he wondered?).

Of them all, Danny was probably best able to spare an hour or two, and so Vince called him to suggest a bit of lead-tenor duetting as soon as he could make it. They set a date for Danny to come over to Vince's flat the following week.

'You've still got a key. Just let yourself in,' Vince told Danny. 'I'm not going anywhere.'

In the meantime, Vince decided to get serious about painting. He had already bought a lot of art equipment on the internet, and he now had a full set of oil colours, brushes, knives, three different sizes of canvas, a palette, and an easel. He decided to work wet-on-wet, which he'd read was a very forgiving method of painting, as it allowed for fresh paint to be applied on top of still-wet paint, so avoiding the tedious process of waiting for layers to dry.

He began by sketching bowls of fruit and other inanimate objects in charcoal, before moving the compositions to oil on canvas, and he worked meticulously in both media. He resisted the temptation to give up when things didn't come easily, and he really enjoyed the discipline and concentration required in observing something in still life, calculating its colour and form, and transferring his interpretation on to a blank space. It was invigorating, and he felt excited at the prospect of taking things to the next stage. That, of course, would require Angie's consent.

When Vince first hatched his plan to paint Angie in the nude, it seemed a wonderful idea. It still did. He could think of nothing more uplifting, other than perhaps a rein-forced underwire 34 DD bra. He allowed himself a snigger at that one, as he had so few outlets for his puerile humour these days. However, the point was that Angie was yet to find out that she was to be his muse, the subject of his artistic endeavours, and he had to find a way of convincing her that this was an opportunity not to be missed.

He knew that if Angie had a weak spot it was her current conviction that she was losing her looks. This was not something that Vince concurred with, but he knew that it was only by playing the vanity card that he could convince Angie to disrobe and let everything hang loose in the precious name of art. Vince expected Angie to be difficult to persuade, but when it came to it, things went more smoothly than he'd imagined.

'You know I've bought all this painting gear?'

'Yes?'

'And I've been practising on bowls of fruit?'

'A-ha?'

'Well, how about you getting your kit off and letting me paint you in the altogether? You're in your prime, and it would be fantastic to get you down on canvas for posterity. What do you think, Ange?'

'Mmm, I'm not sure. How do I know you'll be any good?'

'Well, there are no guarantees. But look at that study of two plums and a banana over there. I'd say that was a pretty decent representation, wouldn't you?'

'I thought it was your meat and two veg.'

'Ha bloody ha. Look, I'm serious. I want to capture your loveliness for all time.'

'Well, only if you're quick about it. You usually are.'

'That's harsh. Anyway, a work like this can't be rushed. Three or four sessions at most. And I'll turn up the thermostat if you like.'

'How could I resist? So, when do you want to start?'

Vince decided he would do a bit of homework before

launching into his great work. Up to now he had practised on fruit and little else, and he'd promised Angie that he wouldn't spend hours experimenting while she sprawled naked on his DFS cowhide three-seater, even if the thermostat was cranked up.

Up to now he had resisted spending too much time on the computer, other than for downloading music tracks and the odd bit of internet shopping. Now, in the interests of art, he found himself exploring a number of websites dedicated to the beauty of the female form. This was an exercise he felt was best conducted while Angie was out of the flat, for fear that she might misconstrue his motives. However, he was driven by the need to observe the great variety of shapes, sizes and skin tones that the female of the species had to offer. And he was unstinting in his research, spending several hours over two days sketching in front of the computer screen in an attempt to perfect his technique. The curve of a woman's hip, the soft slope of her inner thigh, the gentle undulation of her stomach – these would be so much more difficult to paint than apples and pears.

On the second day of his research, an hour or so into his work, Angie arrived home to find Vince examining the naked forms of a blonde and a redhead, both slender and beautiful, engaged in what can only be described as an intimate act. To give Vince his due, he had made a rough sketch of the scene in pastels on a large art pad to the right of the computer, and Angie was curious to examine his efforts.

'Do you see how I've captured the arch of the blonde's lower back there...and I do think the foot resting on the shoulder is very well rendered. What do you think, Ange?'

Angie resisted the temptation to question Vince's motives, deciding instead to encourage him. While the images he'd chosen to study were somewhat dubious, Angie had to admit that he had several half-decent sketches to show for his exertions.

The day of Angie's first sitting arrived.

Vince set up the easel with a pre-stretched twenty-four by thirty-inch canvas locked into position. Alongside he placed a small table for all of the materials he would need: pencils, paints, thinners, brushes, palette knife. To create as much distance as he could between himself and his subject, he positioned the easel and table as close to the living room door as he could, and pushed the sofa back against the window wall opposite.

Angie appeared from the bedroom in a dressing gown.

'Ready when you are,' she said. 'It's nice and warm in here, anyway…'

'You can say that again. Do you mind if I turn it down a notch? I'm beginning to sweat here,' said Vince.

'Leave it, it's just fine. I'm the one taking their clothes off, not you.'

'Well, I'll have to join you. I can't paint like this,' said Vince, taking off his T-shirt and jeans.

'I don't suppose Rembrandt painted in his boxer shorts. How can I take you seriously looking like that?'

'It doesn't matter, just ignore me. So, if you'd like to get ready…'

'How do you want me?' said Angie, as she let her dressing gown fall to the floor.

'Er, yes, very nice. Well, just lie on your left side, put your elbow on the arm of the sofa, and lean your head on your left hand – make a fist – that's it. Fantastic…what a sight. Wowzer. Now then, let me just get my…blimey, it's still hot in here…'

'Come along, Vincey. Let's get to it.'

Vince thought Angie's voice sounded more sexy than it had ever sounded. And she called him *Vincey*. And, just look at her, she's absolutely bloody gorgeous…Vince was feeling flustered and more than a little excited.

'Vince, STOP IT! Look at you! You've got a…put it away, will you…'

Angie was pointing towards Vince's crotch.

He looked down to see his manhood poking proudly through the hole in his boxers.

Just then he heard a noise behind him, and he turned towards the door, which was opening.

'Only me...' announced Danny. 'I've brought some Jaffa Cakes...'

Twenty-Six

Danny was delighted to get a call from Vince suggesting they get together for a bit of singing practice, and he looked forward to seeing his good friend. As it turned out, he saw more of his good friend than he'd bargained for, and his girlfriend too. He wasn't sure he'd know where to look the next time he saw Angie pulling pints in The Ship, and he hoped that the sight of Vince's evident excitement wouldn't leave any permanent mental scars.

In truth, Danny found the whole thing hilarious, and so very Vince. They had all frozen still (and stiff, in Vince's case) for about a second, before bursting into a kerfuffle of screams, apologies, and scampering about. Danny retreated into the hallway, closing the door quickly behind him, shouting yet more apologies as he did so. The last thing he remembered saying was, 'Sorry...another time...hope to see more of you next time!' which seemed hardly possible in the circumstances.

Christmas back home with Hannah and Ben had been a success. From that first evening when, to his own surprise, let alone Hannah's, he had sung for her, things seemed to click into place. It was as if his singing had helped bring them closer together. However, he didn't tell Hannah about the quartet or the chorus. Easy though it would have been to reveal all, he felt he needed to keep that to himself just a while longer, as though it was his safeguard against things going wrong again.

Christmas Day was wonderful, watching Ben tear into his presents, and sharing the simple pleasures of good food and wine, games and stories. On Boxing Day, Danny took Ben to see his first big football match, Fulham versus Everton at Craven Cottage. Ben was more excited than he'd ever seen him (if that was possible), and he wore his new replica shirt with pride as they watched the Toffees stride to a 3-1 victory. Danny wasn't sure whether Ben had seen any of the goals, as he barely stopped talking for the entire ninety minutes, but it hardly mattered. Danny felt he was building a real bond with his son, and he wiped away a tear as he remembered watching Everton with his own dad all those years ago.

Yes, things were going well. Up until now.

Danny and Ben returned from the park, and they stood in the hallway taking off coats, hats and scarves. Ben sat on the bottom step of the hall stairs as Danny grabbed his son's wellington boots, huffing and puffing as he pretended they were stuck fast. Ben howled with laughter as his dad's face reddened with mock exertion, until finally Danny pulled off both boots, tumbled head-over-heals backwards, and then sprung to his feet like a circus acrobat. Ben laughed even louder.

'What's going on, you two?' Hannah shouted from somewhere inside the house, but not in a way that suggested she wanted to join in the fun. There was a dark tone to her voice. Was it irritation or something else?

'Hang your things up, Ben, there's a good lad. I'll just see what Mummy wants…'

Hannah was sitting at the kitchen table with a glass of whisky. Her hair, usually loose and flowing, was swept back tight against her head. She looked up as Danny approached, and barely managed a smile.

'It's a bit early for that, isn't it? What's up?'

Danny pointed to the glass. Hannah glanced at the only other object on the table, her mobile phone, like it was a recently discharged handgun.

'Nothing.'

Danny looked at the large wall clock, went to the kitchen door and shouted to Ben.

'You can have half an hour of CBBC, Ben.'

He returned to Hannah.

'So, what's happened? And please don't say *nothing*.'

'I should lie to you at this point, but I'm not going to,' said Hannah, knocking back the whisky, and glancing again at her phone.

'Okay, what's the bad news? Who called?'

'Ian.'

'Ian. I see.'

'No, you don't see.'

'So, would you please explain what's going on? I promise I'll keep calm.'

'He wants to see me.'

'What the *fuck*?! How come the bastard's still got your number? What the *fuck's* all this about, Hannah?'

'That's your version of keeping calm, is it?'

'No, that's my version of being angry and upset.'

'Look, I'm going to tell you exactly what happened. Now will you just listen?'

Hannah gestured for Danny to sit down.

'Let's hear it,' said Danny, taking a chair.

'He called half an hour ago, completely out of the blue. Emma has kicked him out. It sounds like he's about to lose his job. He sounded desperate. He says he's contemplating...he says he's on the brink, and that I'm the only person who can help...'

'When you say *out of the blue*...when was the last time you heard from him...or saw him?'

Hannah looked angry.

'If you're suggesting that I've had any contact with him since...since back then, then I'm *very* disappointed in you. I haven't seen or heard from him in all that time.'

'I had to ask.'

'Yes, and now he pops up just as things are getting better between us. How very convenient! How sodding wonderful is that?' said Hannah.

'The fucking loser,' said Danny.

'That's helpful.'

'It's not meant to be helpful. Are you suggesting we should help him? Why does he deserve help? The selfish, blackmailing bastard. Ignore him.'

'How can I ignore *that*?' said Hannah, pointing at her phone.

'What did you say to him? How did you respond?'

'I told him to get help from someone else. Professional help. I told him not to call again. And then he repeated that he's on the brink, and that if only he could see me… He…sounded so…*what could I say*? I said…I said I'd see him. Just once.'

'You want to see him?'

'No, of course not.

'Then why—'

'Because he might…he might be serious.'

'And why is that your problem?'

'We're talking about a human life, Danny.'

'So, you still have feelings for him?'

'No!'

'Then ignore him.'

'How can I? What if he—'

'Then I'll come with you.'

'Oh, don't be ridiculous, Danny. What would you do, start a fight?'

'You never know, I might knock some sense into him.'

'Don't be stupid. Look, I agreed to see him just once, and that's what I'm going to do. Get him to see sense, find some help, and leave me alone once and for all.'

'If you see him, I'll—'

'You'll do what? Leave me and Ben again? Don't you

dare give me that! Are you trying to blackmail me as well, Danny? *Are you?*'

'No, of course not.'

Danny started to get up from his chair.

'Sit down! Sit down! Stop being such an arsehole, Danny! I need your support here. I'm in an impossible situation, and I need you to believe me...I love you, I have no feelings for him...it was a mistake, I fucked up, but faced with this, what can I do?'

Danny sat down, and put his head in his hands. Then he looked up, and into Hannah's eyes. He saw that they were pleading with him to understand. And he saw that they were full of love.

Twenty-Seven

'I'll see you next time,' was all Cat had said as Henry left the island.

They walked together in silence up to the helipad in the field beyond the church, where the helicopter was waiting, rotor blades spinning furiously. Henry and his fellow passengers were summoned to approach the aircraft, he and Cat embraced, and he impulsively reached into a pocket for his pitch pipe, which he pressed into Cat's hand. Then he walked forward, head bowed, and without looking back, boarded the helicopter. Seconds later he was airborne, the island was falling away beneath him, and Cat disappeared out of sight. He had no idea when 'next time' would be, but he knew that there would be one. He'd expected to feel sad, but instead he felt calm and contented.

Henry's good mood continued even as he returned to his little flat in an unprepossessing part of town, just a couple of miles from the home he'd shared with Jenny for the last dozen or so years. His route took him directly past their home, and he even considered calling in to…well, quite, he thought, to do what exactly? He felt a sentimental pang as he thought of Jenny in better days, but any idea that he could just pop in for a friendly chat without things turning sour quickly vanished.

He drove on, back to his temporary bolt-hole, where he opened all the windows, changed the bed linen, made a pot of tea, and sat next to the front window overlooking a betting shop, an Indian takeaway, and a small corner pub, none of which he had really noticed before. With no plans for the evening, he decided that he would walk across the road, place a bet, order a takeaway, and have a pint or two while he waited for his meal. Life suddenly seemed simple and wonderful, and he smiled a contented smile.

The fact that he had a potentially messy divorce looming, was out of work, and had given away his beloved pitch pipe seemed insignificant details. He would get through the divorce, he could find work if he wanted to, had enough money if not, and his beloved pitch pipe was safe in the hands of someone he had known for next to no time but had managed to transform his outlook on life completely.

There were three messages waiting for him on the telephone answering machine. The first was from his divorce lawyer suggesting a date for a meeting, and the second was from Danny asking how he was doing and when he would next be at chorus rehearsals. The third message took him by surprise, as it was from Margaret Taylor, who had never previously called him. Her tone was worried and apologetic as she explained that she would like to meet up to see if Henry could help with a family matter. It didn't take much working out that this had to be about George or Neil, and probably both. Henry called Margaret right away.

That evening, Henry walked into his local bookmakers, perused the racing pages pinned up around the walls, and then looked up at one of the television screens showing greyhound racing from Walthamstow. Noticing a dog called *Treasure Island* running in the next race, he placed a £20 win bet at odds of 8-1, and five minutes later he left the shop £160 richer. In the Indian takeaway restaurant he ordered all of his favourite dishes, knowing that there would be enough food for breakfast and lunch the following day. In the pub, he was delighted to find St Austell bitter on draught, which had been his favourite beer in the island pub.

As he approached the window table, and before she was aware of his presence, Henry could see that Margaret Taylor was forlorn, like he'd never seen her before. Her elegant face was lined with worry, and Henry instantly felt sorry for her.

Rather than catch her off guard, he called out from some distance across the café floor.

'Margaret! How lovely to see you!'

Margaret looked up, her face now beaming like someone had flicked on a switch, and they embraced. She explained that this was the place she always came to when she needed to think or just get away from everyday troubles. On the table in front of them were Italian pastries with coffee and biscotti.

They spent the first few minutes exchanging pleasantries, but it didn't take long for Margaret to get to the point.

'I'm so grateful you agreed to meet me. I feel very awkward, Henry. This isn't easy for me, and it's a delicate matter, but I think you may be uniquely positioned to help with what has become a very distressing situation. I'm not sure where to begin...'

Henry decided to help Margaret get over the hurdle of her embarrassment.

'I know that things aren't great between George and Neil. I presume it's got something to do with that? If so, I'll do anything I can to help. George is one of my oldest friends, and Neil is one of my newest, but they're both dear to me. Take your time, and I'll see what I can do.'

Margaret composed herself.

'It started when my first-born, Robert, died. I won't say more than that, except that ever since that day, George and Neil...well, they haven't exactly seen eye to eye. And it's grown steadily worse, to the point where I honestly think they could happily kill one another.'

Henry had thought about George and Neil a lot, and had clear ideas on the matter, but would it be too presumptuous to express them? The cry-for-help look on Margaret's face gave him the answer.

'I saw George at a Rotary get-together recently, and

he said something of the kind. I know that Robert meant the world to him, but I also know that he loves Neil dearly and wants him to make a success of his life. But his head gets messed up when he remembers Robert and he takes things out on Neil. George's coping mechanism is to re-channel his grief into frustration. Frustration with Neil. Poor Neil.'

'That's very perceptive of you. How come you've been able to read the situation so clearly?' asked Margaret.

'I know George. I owe my professional career and a large part of my success to him. And I want the best for Neil. He's a quarter of one of the most important things I've ever been involved with. I've been able to see things from both sides.'

Margaret looked slightly abashed, and said nothing for a mom-ent as she hesitated over her next question.

'Do you know anything about Neil's association with Newton Burns?'

A surprising change of direction, Henry thought.

'Well, yes. The quartet sang at a party for him recently. Didn't Neil mention it?'

'Sadly, no.'

'Why do you ask?'

'It's just that I found Newton Burns's business card on Neil's bedroom floor when I was cleaning. So I figured they must have met. Except that Neil didn't say anything, and I guess I feel disappointed, because he's always confided in me – up to now. Oh, and it so happens that Newton was a friend of a close friend many years ago, and I know what he's like. His association with my son worries me.'

'But surely you know that Neil is working for him now?'

'What! Good lord, I hadn't the foggiest.'

Margaret spluttered, returning her coffee cup to its saucer with an unsteady hand.

Henry again felt sorry for Margaret.

'It's early days, I suppose. Maybe Neil doesn't want to

jinx things by getting too carried away and telling everyone,' he said in a feeble attempt to make Margaret feel better.

'Henry, I'm his mother. He could have...but never mind...so how on earth did Neil come to be employed by Newton Burns?'

'Do you remember Ken, our coach? Of course you do, he came to your house for one of our first rehearsals...'

'Yes, yes, what a character!'

'Quite. Well, Mr Burns is an old pal of Ken's – they go back donkey's years in the music business – and Ken recommended Neil as an arranger for a musical film project. A bit of a long shot to hire a rookie, I suppose, but Ken's word seems to mean a lot to Mr Burns. And it all seems to be clicking into place. Neil's working away on a bunch of songs and he's loving it. Four-part harmony stuff. Right up his street. Beyond that, I'm not sure of the detail.'

Margaret reached into her handbag for a paper tissue, dabbed at her eyes, and blew her nose loudly.

'Dear me, Henry. I had no idea. I really didn't.'

'I'm sorry.'

'Don't be sorry. I'm so happy for Neil...except that...'

'Yes?'

'Well, Newt always had a reputation for pursuing young men. I've seen him in action, and I dare say he hasn't changed much down the years.'

'Ah, I didn't know about that. But, if you'll forgive me saying this, I think you should trust that Neil knows what he's doing.'

'I do hope so.'

'He *is* twenty-three, Margaret.'

'I'm sure you're right.'

'And, of course, this gives you an opportunity with George.'

'Sorry, I don't quite—'

'Well, if he found out that Neil has been given a big break

by one of the country's most influential media personalities, I think he might see things a little differently,' said Henry.

Margaret stood up and threw her arms around Henry, kissing the top of his bald head.

'Thank you, Henry. You don't know how much that means to me,' said Margaret.

Twenty-Eight

Vince pushed open the double doors leading from the public bar to the function room, and was greeted by an enormous cheer.

'Let's do that properly!' shouted James Pinter. 'Three cheers for your returning chairman…Hip hip…'

The assembled chorus of Maidenhead A Cappella was delighted to see Vince again after his enforced absence, and there were several calls from the risers for him to say a few words.

Vince joined James in front of the chorus, cleared his throat, and held up his hands.

'I can't tell you how good it is to see all your ugly mugs again. I missed you all. And thanks so much for all your well wishes, cards, and emails. I'm feeling a lot better, and the thought of Wednesday night rehearsals, and to getting back with the quartet too, has kept me going. I still need to take it easy, and I'll be using this blinking stick for a while, but I can't think of any better medicine than being here with you lot. Now I'm going to sit back here and listen for a while. Carry on, Maestro!'

James resumed the rehearsal, and Vince took a seat along the far wall, facing the chorus. Lizzy got up to hug him, and whispered, 'Welcome back, young Vincent.' A few of the wives and girlfriends also greeted him and, as he sat down, Vince noticed the unmistakable form of Cliff "Tonsils" Thompson waving an enormous bronzed arm in his direction. From the risers, Danny, Henry and Neil variously smiled, waved, or gave a thumbs-up in his direction. Ken was there too, but he seemed miles away.

'Right, back to business, gentlemen,' said James. 'Let's get in at bar thirty-four again, just before the key change. Keep it bright, leads, and stay on top of that pitch. Baris, back off a bit. Tenors, you're on the root, so you can afford to come out a bit more. Basses, just keep doing what you're doing. Pitch...and...'

During the break, Vince was joined by the rest of the quartet. This was the first time in a good while that all four of them had been at chorus rehearsal on the same evening. Danny had continued to attend throughout, but Neil had often been too busy with work, and Henry had missed a few Wednesdays as well, most recently having visited his mystery island again. Vince felt out of touch with what they were all doing, though he had seen Danny once or twice, most recently to explain what had been going on the day he let himself into the flat and caught him and Angie in a ridiculously compromising, if comic, situation.

They all agreed it was great to be back together, and they sang a quick song "to blow the cobwebs off", at Vince's suggestion.

At the end of the evening, James sprang a surprise by congratulating the quartet again on their qualification for the British championships, and inviting them to sing.

'I heard you warming up during the break, lads, so there's no excuse...gentlemen, back together again...I give you...From The Edge!'

The quartet gave a passable performance, though they admitted to feeling a bit rusty. The chorus gave them generous applause, after which Ken approached them, looking somewhat stern.

'I think we need to schedule a few quartet rehearsals, chaps. You'll need to be a lot better than that to stand any chance of impressing the judges in Harrogate.'

'That's a bit harsh,' said Vince with a smile.

'Just being realistic, chaps. It's four months to the finals. You haven't sung together for weeks. Assuming you're all fit and able to put the time in, I suggest that you start ramping things up again PDQ. And I'm more than happy to resume my taskmaster duties, if you'd like me to.'

There was no question about it. They all thanked Ken for his support, and his honesty, and they agreed to start rehearsing again on a regular basis.

'Are you sure you'll be up to it?' Neil asked Vince, looking nervously at his walking stick.

'Are you sure *you'll* be up to it, now that you're so busy with Mr Burns?' Vince replied with a wink. He decided to keep his more lewd innuendos for another time soon.

Just then, they were joined by the huge figure of Cliff Thompson, this time dressed in a pink polo shirt and voluminous red tartan trousers, and flashing dazzling white teeth in a generous display of American bonhomie and expensive dentistry.

'Now, pay no mind to dear old Ken, here! I saw you fellas at prelims, and you sounded even better just now... I do believe...'

Ken put a hand on Cliff's vast shoulder.

'But Cliff, the chaps only just scraped through at prelims, and they'll need to be an awful lot better if they're to have any chance in May.'

'Oh now, there you go raining on the parade again, Ken. I do believe these fellas have been through quite a lot recently,' said Cliff, looking at Vince's walking stick by way of explanation.

'Yes, yes, quite so, but if Doctor House here is well enough, then it's time these boys got a move on,' said Ken, a little irritation showing in his voice.

'Doctor House! Nice one, Ken,' said Vince.

'Okay, fellas. It sounds like you're in great hands! Knock 'em dead! I'll be lookin' out for y'all,' said Cliff, giving them a round of high fives before shuffling off towards the bar.

'I still find it hard to believe he comes from Slough,' said Vince.

Finding a regular rehearsal place proved a little tricky. Neil wasn't entertaining any idea of using his parents' house for fear of George turning up at any time. Space at Vince's flat was more of a problem than ever, with the recent addition of an artist's studio, an exercise bike, and a rail of clothes belonging to Angie. Henry's place had even less room than Vince's, and he was under orders from the landlord not to disturb the neighbours.

Danny was still under the impression that Hannah knew nothing about his singing adventures, so his house was out of bounds too. Quite why Danny felt the need to maintain the pretence with Hannah he was no longer sure, particularly after singing for her at Christmas. Yet, he held back from telling Hannah about the quartet and the chorus. Though he didn't like to admit it to himself, he was keeping his singing a secret just as Hannah had kept her affair a secret. Little did he know that Hannah knew all about it, and that Vince was complicit in the whole matter.

Ken came to the rescue, offering to host the quartet rehearsals whenever they wanted.

Ken lived in a remote spot in the Buckinghamshire countryside, surrounded by farmland. He lived with his wife Bella in a rambling old farmhouse set in a couple of acres of woodland, with just a church and a pub within a half-mile radius.

Danny and Vince drove up the long driveway, which was peppered with potholes and overgrown on both sides by dense bramble and other wild shrubs.

'Somehow, I couldn't imagine Ken living in a town house. Look at the place! Straight out of a Stephen King film. I'm not hanging around after nightfall when the

227

zombies start coming out of the woods,' said Vince.

'Don't be so ridiculous. That's a fine old house. You're looking at a couple of million's worth there, I'd guess,' said Danny.

Danny parked the car beneath an enormous oak tree alongside two other cars – Neil and Henry had already arrived – and the great hulk of a boat covered in a moss green tarpaulin.

Ken greeted them at the doorway, shaking hands with them both.

'Welcome, welcome, come in, join the others...we're just discussing the finer points of female anatomy.'

'Sounds interesting, Ken. It's a subject close to my heart,' said Vince.

'I can vouch for that from recent experience,' Danny added.

Ken ushered them into the sizeable hallway, the walls of which were covered in picture frames containing a variety of old photographs, vibrant watercolours, and a hotch-potch of diplomas and certificates. He led them through a large kitchen that smelt of freshly baked bread; a cauldron of soup bubbled on top of an old Aga stove, at the foot of which two King Charles spaniels were sleeping peacefully. Pots, pans and utensils hung everywhere, just above head height, and the shelves were lined with glass, terracotta, and ceramic jars of all shapes and sizes.

'Now this is what I call a home, Ken,' said Danny.

'What? Yes, quite. The old place could do with a bit of a facelift, I dare say – not unlike the dearly beloved – but we're very happy here. Come on through,' said Ken.

He led them into a magnificent music room with polished wooden floors, high ceilings, and crystal chandeliers. A grand piano stood alongside a full-sized harp, a bank of synthesisers, and a complete drum kit. Arranged in stands along one of the walls were a double bass, a cello, a Fender

Stratocaster, and a Martin acoustic guitar. Elsewhere, several carrying cases looked like they might conceal a trombone, a clarinet, and a full set of diatonic harmonicas.

Vince's jaw dropped as he took it all in.

'Bloody hell, Ken. This is...wow, I didn't know... I mean...do you play this lot?'

'I've dabbled down the years. Now, here we are. I was just explaining to the other chaps about Penny's boobs,' said Ken.

Henry and Neil waved from a Chesterfield about ten yards away.

'Lovely big room, Ken. Is that Henry and Neil over there? I can just about make them out,' said Vince, tapping his walking stick against Danny's leg for no particular reason.

They joined the others and Ken resumed a monologue that had been interrupted by the arrival of Danny and Vince.

'Yes, as I was saying...boobs. What struck me yesterday was that, glad to say, Penny had piled on all the weight she'd previously lost, and a bit more, and her bosoms were looking particularly ample. It made all the difference.'

'Ken, sorry, but what are we talking about?' asked Vince.

'Weightwatchers, of course. My ladies' quartet down in Southampton. Never let it be said that boobs don't matter to a lady bass. They do, and I have the proof.'

After twenty minutes or so listening to Ken, Neil suggested that it might be an idea if they did a bit of singing.

'Excellent idea,' said Ken, as though singing had been the furthest thing from his mind.

Five minutes later, once Ken had been successfully diverted from a story about the time he coached a quartet naked for a wager during the long hot summer of '76, he was all focus.

After a few warm-up exercises and singing through a couple of standards, they got down to the hard work.

'Now, I've dug out some of my notes from last time, which might help,' said Ken, 'but don't be alarmed if some of what I say comes as a surprise. I was quite gentle on you leading up to prelims, and we didn't work on all the things I would have liked. However, now that you're heading for the big league, I won't spare you. Things have to be said.'

'Such as?' asked Henry.

'Okay, let's see…you sometimes have a tendency to scoop at the beginning of phrases, particularly on your bass pick-ups,' said Ken.

Vince and Danny both stifled a laugh, and Henry inspected his fingernails.

'Yes, so I'm told. And I have a tendency to go flat as well, apparently. But I've been working on it in my own time, believe me,' said Henry with good humour.

'Ah, excellent, so at least you're aware of the problem, which really is excellent,' said Ken. 'And Vince, what are we going to do about your head voice?'

'Sorry, Ken, I'm not sure…'

'Well you don't seem to have one as far as I can tell. You're much too keen to welly everything in full voice, when you really should be floating into a light falsetto at the top end, don't you think?'

'Oh, well, no…I wasn't aware…but, short of asking Angie to tighten my nuts for me, what can I do about it, Ken?'

'Well, now that I've made you aware, you can practise… and practise…and practise some more.'

Ken proceeded to give Neil and Danny similarly helpful notes, and they worked on techniques to help them improve the areas Ken had highlighted. They then worked on a song together, trying to remember and implement everything that Ken had suggested. After two and a half hours, Ken called a halt to proceedings.

'I think that's enough for today, chaps. What you've got

now is a much better platform on which to build. I hope you agree.'

They all agreed, though they all felt like they'd been put through the wringer.

'That's what they call tough love these days, I believe. Now, who'd like one of Bella's famous cocktails? I'll just go and find her...'

As Ken disappeared, the others looked around the room, taking in a lifetime in music. Aside from the many musical instruments occupying the floor space, the walls and several shelves were full of framed photographs, and Vince quickly found the one they'd seen on the walls of Television Centre. Ken was singing in a quartet, dressed in traditional barbershop outfit, and sporting a fine handlebar moustache. The inscription read '*The Good Old Days, October 1971*'.

'Ah, the good old days indeed,' said Ken as he re-entered the room. 'Chaps, I don't believe you've met Bella...Bella, this is Vince...Henry...Neil...and Danny.'

Bella shook hands with them all, and then stood back and closed one eye, measuring them up.

'I've heard a lot about you, and Kenny's got great hopes for you. I must say, you do look good together.'

Bella was no more than five feet tall, with an asymmetric white bob, painter's overalls, and an aura of serene authority. Though her face was lined, her bright blue eyes were still youthful, and she looked at least a decade younger than her years.

'Have you been painting?' asked Vince.

'He's a sharp one,' Bella quipped, nudging Ken with her elbow. 'Was it the paint splashed overalls or the fan brush in the top pocket that gave me away?'

Vince looked a little intimidated, but appreciated the challenge.

'It's just that I'm a bit of a painter myself.'

Danny snorted in a vain attempt to stifle another laugh.

'Wonderful! So, what do you like to paint?' asked Bella.

'This and that,' said Vince.

'Not to mention a bit of the other,' Danny couldn't help adding.

'Oh, come on now. You can do better than that! It sounds like there might be a saucy little story you're not telling me about. Now, I'm just going to wash up and then I'll make us all a nice cocktail. After which, you can enlighten me about your artistic endeavours, Vince. Margaritas okay with everyone?'

'Banana daiquiri for me, please,' said Ken.

'Of course, dear. I won't be long. Make yourselves at home.'

While Bella was away, Ken answered questions about his musical career, and especially about *The Good Old Days* photograph and how it came to be on the walls at the BBC. Ken delighted in telling them the story of how he had been a nightclub singer in the early '70s, and had somehow been invited to join a harmony group. They were spotted by a television talent scout who was working on the BBC nostalgia show *The Good Old Days*, which celebrated old time variety acts. Ken's quartet, called The Affable Chaps, were asked to perform as minstrels or in traditional barbershop outfits, and they appeared in several series of the show.

'Yes, that was a great little group. I sang lead, Mike Barton bass, Gary Moorhouse tenor, and dear old Newt baritone,' said Ken, slightly dewy-eyed.

'Newt? My God, really?' said Neil with surprise.

'Yup, there he is, second left. On his way to much greater things. But we've all got to start somewhere.'

'I see you're on first name terms now then, Neil?' said Vince, but Neil ignored him.

'And here comes my little Marie Lloyd,' said Ken, as Bella returned carrying a large silver tray with six cocktail glasses.

'You haven't called me that in years, Kenny! Have you been reminiscing again? Come and help yourselves,' said Bella.

They sat in the music room for another hour listening to Ken and Bella tell stories, including how they met at the City Varieties Hall in Leeds, where they were recording *The Good Old Days*. Bella had been appearing as a tribute act to Marie Lloyd, the legendary music hall performer who was renowned for her ability to add bawdiness to the most innocent of lyrics.

'It was the feigned innocence and the hidden smuttiness that attracted me to her,' said Ken. 'Not much has changed, I can tell you.'

The stories kept coming, and they were all thoroughly enchanted by the Ken and Bella double act. Thankfully, Vince was spared from having to tell them about his artistic endeavours, and for once he was happy to take a back seat in the presence of these master storytellers. They all laughed until their faces hurt.

At last it was time to leave, and they made plans for their next rehearsal.

'Looking a little bit further ahead, I have a suggestion to make, chaps,' said Ken. 'You need to get as many serious rehearsal sessions under your belts as possible from now on. May will be here before you know it. However, what you really need is more contest experience. You have only ever sung in competition together once, at prelims, and it will really help if you can get some additional contest time in between now and May. So...are you all free the third weekend in March?'

As far as they could remember, they all were.

'Excellent, because that's the weekend of the Holland Harmony Festival, and I have taken the liberty of entering you in the barbershop category. You'll get some great competition from around Europe, just what you need to step up your game. Double-check your diaries chaps, and get back to me. But, assuming you're all free that weekend, it's Amsterdam here we come!'

Twenty-Nine

'How's the lamb?' asked Hannah.

'Slow roasted to perfection. And this red goes brilliantly. Have you been watching *Saturday Kitchen*? This has all the hallmarks of James Martin.

'Jamie Oliver. I prefer my chefs *Naked.*'

Danny found the remark surprisingly arousing. Perhaps it was the capital N in Hannah's voice that did it.

'I find that remark a bit of a turn-on,' he said.

'Ben threw up at nursery today.'

'Not *quite* so arousing as your previous remark. Nothing serious, I take it?'

'Just one of those things, they said. He'd been running around a lot after lunch. Something and nothing. I asked Mum to keep an eye on him and I took some Calpol over. She'll call if he seems under the weather, but he's fine.'

'I must admit that I've been a bit worried about him just recently,' said Danny with a slight frown.

'What do you mean? What's been happening?'

'Well I hope it's just a passing fad, but...actually, the more I think about it the more disturbing it seems.'

'Christ, Danny, what is it?'

'Well, apparently his friend Peter told him that Manchester United are better than Everton, and now he keeps talking about Wayne Rooney.'

'Ha! If my memory serves me correctly, you could barely stop talking about him yourself not so long ago!'

'That was years ago when he played for us. He was at Everton from the age of nine, we taught him everything he knows, and he famously wore a T-shirt saying "Once A Blue, Always A Blue".'

'And?'

'Well, he went and signed for Man U and became a red. I'm not having Ben doing the same. Whatever happened to loyalty, I ask you?'

'Didn't I read somewhere that Wayne Rooney still supports Everton, that he still goes to see them when he can, and that he bought his little boys an Everton strip?'

'Well, yes, that's right. But what's your—'

'My point is that it's possible to stay loyal to your first love even if you stray.'

'Stray? He's been there eight years.'

'Oh, don't be so obtuse, Danny. Okay, my analogy wasn't brilliant, but I'm trying to tell you something…I'm, I'm… meeting him tomorrow afternoon.'

'Wayne Rooney?'

'You know who.'

'Sure, I know.'

'Have you seen my MCC tie, Margaret?' George shouted from the bedroom.

Margaret was sitting in the lotus position on the floor of one of the guest rooms that she used as an exercise and relaxation space. Her sanctum, as she often reminded George. She breathed deeply.

'Margaret, I need my MCC tie…have you see it?' George shouted even louder.

'Sanctum, sanctum,' Margaret repeated calmly as she exhaled, enjoying what sounded like the beginning of a chant. She got up and walked to their bedroom.

'Is that the blue one with the white stripes?' she asked, knowing very well that it wasn't, and knowing that it would drive George just a little bit more mad.

'What? No, no! MCC members' tie. Red and gold…

the old *egg and bacon*! Been that way since 1860…blue and white, indeed!'

'In that case, it's at the dry cleaners along with half your other ties. And it was beef gravy, not egg and bacon, as I recall.'

'What! But I wanted to wear it for the Pakistan match,' said George, sounding like an exasperated child.

'George, I'm no cricket fan, but I thought it was a summer game. What are England doing playing at Lord's in February?'

'No, no, they're on tour, it's on television. I just wanted to wear my egg and bacon to watch it, that's all.'

'I despair of you sometimes, George. I really do. So, are you home for supper this evening?'

'Well, yes. But *supper*? I'm not sure I like the sound of that. It suggests that we're having just the one course. No starters? No pud?'

'I thought we'd have something a bit lighter for a change. Who has a three-course dinner every evening in this day and age, I ask you?'

'We do! And damn proud of the tradition.'

'It's not the same with Neil hardly ever here to eat with us, and well…that much food every evening isn't good for you. You could do with losing some weight, George, to be honest.'

Having lit the blue touch-paper, Margaret stood well back.

'So, I've Neil to thank for not getting a proper dinner this evening, have I? Well, isn't that marvellous? And what about the bloody bread-winner, Margaret? What about me?'

'Neil pays his way, George. Didn't I mention it?'

'Pays his way? Since when?'

'He started paying rent recently. He told me he's earning reasonable money from a couple of freelance jobs. Arranging.'

'Flower arranging, is that it?

237

'That's beneath even you, George.'

Margaret felt her heart rate quicken. George was spoiling for a fight, and she was ready to give him one.

'Oh come off it, Margaret. How far will he get doing odd jobs, for pity's sake?'

'He told me he's got a couple of freelance jobs—'

'Yes, you just said so—'

'But I found out what he's really doing. He's working for Yellow Braces, the film production company. He's been hired as an arranger for a new film musical that goes into production next year. He was hired directly by the head of the company. That's Newton Burns, in case you didn't know. The film is very close to Newton's heart apparently, and it seems that he's aiming big with this one. Offers have gone out to the A List. The Hollywood drums are beating, so I'm told.'

'*The* Newton Burns?' said George, slightly flustered.

'I doubt there could be more than one.'

'I see. But why…why didn't Neil say as much…why all this nonsense about freelance jobs?'

'Put yourself in Neil's shoes. Why would he want to tell *you?* Why would he risk you humiliating him once again? And why would he give you the satisfaction of knowing that he's fallen on his feet? You've done nothing but put him down for years, George.'

'But, I…always wanted the best for him. Always wanted him to be a success…just like Robert…'

'And he will be, George. But not like Robert…like Neil.'

'Has it gone too far, do you think? Have I pushed him away for good?' said George, with the first semblance of humility, and Margaret could see from his face that the penny had dropped at last.

'No. Neil's not a vindictive boy. All he's ever wanted is his father's approval. It's not too late to do that, George,' said Margaret.

*

Newton Burns's PA told Neil that he could go through now.
He knocked firmly on the office door and walked in, doing
his best to look assertive.

Newt was on his feet walking towards him with a grin
like a Cheshire cat. His enormous frame engulfed Neil's in
a showbiz-style embrace, and he beckoned for Neil to take
a seat.

'Sorry about the wait, but I was on a call with the New
York office. I bet you were out there feeling like a contestant
on *The Apprentice*! So, how's my favourite baritone, then?'

'Great, just great, thanks. I'm really enjoying the work,
and I think we're making good progress,' said Neil. He
hoped he sounded confident, but he was trembling inside.

'Yes, I thought it was about time I found out how it was
all going, what with me being away a lot recently.'

'Oh, how was the documentary...and the awards...and
the TV commercial?'

'Good grief, you are well-informed. Very good, all very
good. I particularly love doing the telly ad. We're getting
a bit of a cult following. Who'd have thought it? They're
saying we're the new Leonard Rossiter and Joan Collins...
what a hoot!'

Neil didn't get the reference, but smiled nonetheless.

'Well, I'm very pleased to hear that you're enjoying the
project. Very pleased indeed. But it won't surprise you to
know that I've been taking reports from within. And Neil,
I'm sorry to say...*you're fired!*'

Neil's heart leapt as Newt pointed at him, Sir Alan
Sugar-style.

'I'm sorry, I couldn't resist,' said Newt, reaching for some
printed notes on his desk. 'In fact, I'm told that you're doing
a fine job...let me see...they love your work on Song Two...
*beautiful interpretation, shows a delicacy of touch and a fine ear
for detail*...Song One...*great intro, meticulous reworking of bars*

*twenty-eight to forty-nine…great idea to give the tenor the melody in the middle eight…*and there's lots more like that. I won't embarrass you further. Well, the team seems happy, which means I'm happy. Are you happy?'

Neil felt the tension in his stomach disappear and a huge sense of relief wash over him. He had never felt happier in his life.

'I'm so grateful to you for giving me this chance, Mr B—'

'Newt.'

'Newt…and I'll make you proud that you did, I promise.'

'Well, it certainly looks like dear old Kenny's come up trumps again. It's him you have to thank.'

'I do…I have, yes, of course. I'm so grateful to Ken too. I've told him so, but he doesn't seem to take thanks easily.'

'That's Ken. Such prodigious talent and yet such modesty. He should have made it right to the top, but it didn't seem to matter to him. He was never madly ambitious, and his nature just wouldn't allow him to play the showbiz game. But he's the real deal. When Kenny speaks, I listen – well, most of the time! Which reminds me, he had a word in my ear just recently. He was worried that I might be…how shall I put it…well, trying to seduce you. And he was a bit cross with me, to tell you the truth.'

Neil could feel his face reddening.

'I'd like to think I can look after myself, but I guess that was sweet of him.'

'I have a reputation, and Ken knows me better than anyone. He's a very protective mentor. He made me promise to back off, the old bugger. But that doesn't mean we can't enjoy being sociable now, does it? I've had enough for today, and was thinking of popping over to The Groucho. Care to join me?'

'I'd love to,' said Neil.

Thirty

Danny was on tenterhooks all morning. He drifted in and out of meetings without any idea of what he was meant to be doing there; he found himself snapping at, and then apologising to, work colleagues; and the idea of eating made him feel sick. He drank tea constantly, and spent a lot of time walking to and from his office to the gents on the floor below. He looked at the time about every fifteen minutes.

He told himself that he had no need to worry. Hannah had been frank with him, when she could have lied to conceal what was going on, but she told him straight and her eyes had pleaded with him for understanding. He had been so close to losing his cool completely the afternoon he found her in the kitchen drinking whisky. And he had wanted to take control of the situation, let Hannah know that everything was going to be just fine, and just deal with things. Except that he couldn't. It was out of his hands, his attempt to deliver an ultimatum had only incensed Hannah, and he knew that she had to deal with this herself.

Danny had little choice but to trust that Hannah could put an end to this distressing episode in their lives. And yet his stomach churned at the thought of her seeing her one-time lover again. Yes, because part of him still wondered if their meeting might ignite some spark between them, but more so because this guy had evidently lost the plot big time. What he was doing was no less than blackmail. And for all Danny knew, he might have developed into a full-blown psycho. When he thought of that possibility, his blood ran cold. Anything could happen. What if he was carrying a weapon? What if he tried to kidnap Hannah? *For fuck's sake, what possessed me to let her go through with this?* Hannah had assured him that they were meeting in a public place and that at no time would she be alone with him, but how could he be sure?

The meeting was at one o'clock. How long would it take for Hannah to get her message across and to put an end to this nonsense? Not long. But, what if she had to listen to him raking over all the miserable details of his fractured life? Surely, she wouldn't allow herself to be snared like that.

By two o'clock, Danny was very anxious. Why hadn't she called by now? He left work early.

He speed dialled Hannah's mobile number repeatedly for half an hour, but it went straight to message each time. He left the same message each time. *'Are you all right? Call me. I love you.'*

He sat at home clutching his mobile phone, waiting. Several times he went to the fridge to get a beer, only to resist the temptation because he feared he might need to drive somewhere (where?) any time soon.

The home phone rang, causing him to jump out of his chair and almost out of his skin. He lurched across the living room floor to grab the receiver, then remembered that Hannah had said she would only call his mobile. The answer machine kicked in. *'This is an automated call from Barclaycard. Your account is now overdue. Please...'*

He pressed the delete button.

A doorbell rang, and his heart leapt. It was the same tone as their door bell, but was it too far away to be theirs? Unless...he ran to the front door. He thought he saw the shadow of something or someone through the stained glass. The police. He stood frozen to the spot for a moment. He opened the door...but there was no one there.

Danny went inside, threw his mobile phone at the sofa, and screamed out loud with frustration, slapping the sides of his face as he did so. He went to the kitchen sink and splashed himself with cold water. The running water made him want to urinate, and he ran upstairs to the bathroom.

He closed his eyes as he relieved himself, enjoying a moment's calm, and then he heard his mobile phone ring…*where the fuck is it?* He ran downstairs in a state of panic. WHERE THE FUCK IS IT?

He spotted the phone lying under a coffee table, ringing and flashing…he launched himself headlong on to the floor, reaching for his phone and grasping it…just as it stopped ringing. He looked at the caller number display. Hannah. What would she think when he didn't answer? He called back. Engaged. Of course. He waited. And waited. Then called back. Still engaged. Then he waited. And waited.

The phone rang.

'HANNAH?'

'*It's okay. I'm all right. I'm on my way home.*'

Hannah was quiet and reflective. A little sad, Danny sensed. The drama that had played out in his mind had remained a fiction, for which Danny found himself silently thanking both God and his lucky stars. Not that he believed in either. He was physically exhausted from a day's worth of worry and starvation, but Hannah was safe and that was all that mattered. He desperately wanted to know what had happened, to make sure that Hannah was really okay, that nothing untoward had gone on, and that they could move on from this at last. But he knew that Hannah needed a little time, and that if he pushed her he would do so at his peril.

'All okay, then?' he asked at last.

'I could do with a drink.'

'Sure, sure. Whisky?'

'White wine if there's any in the fridge.'

'Coming up. Look, put the telly on if you like. Relax, forget about it for a bit.'

'No, no. Just a glass of wine and some peace.'

They sat in silence for five or so minutes, Hannah with her eyes closed.

'What time are we picking Ben up?' Danny whispered at last.

'I asked Mum if she could have him for another night. He's fine, by the way. No more throwing up.'

'Ah, good. And no mention of Wayne Rooney, I hope?' Hannah smiled as she opened her eyes. Then her expression changed.

'He's in a bad way, you know...'

'Oh, I don't know. Eighteen goals in twenty-one Premiership matches this season isn't too shabby...'

'I'm talking about Ian.'

'Yes.'

'He's got no one to turn to. Wife gone, job on the line, no friends to speak of. But I think he'll make it.'

'He didn't lay the suicide number on you?'

'I didn't give him the chance. I told him there were millions of people worse off than him, and that he should have the self-respect to pick himself up and sort himself out. I gave him the number of a psychotherapist – a recommendation from Denise the counsellor, actually. Then I kissed him once, told him to enjoy the rest of his life and stop being a miserable bastard, and then I said goodbye.'

'On the lips?'

'Oh, sod off! Now, come here and give me a hug, you stupid man.'

Danny suddenly felt that the moment of his own confession had arrived.

'You remember I sang you a song at Christmas?'

'A bit random, but yes, of course I do,' said Hannah, plumping a cushion and sitting to attention. 'It was a delightful surprise.'

'Well, you know that I've always loved singing, but never really been able to bring myself to—'

'Of course. It's been a long-running saga, one of the defining narratives of your life, my darling. So, what's changed?'

'Well, not long after I started at the firm, I met Vince – the guy I went to stay with, who's really into music – well, he sings with a barbershop chorus, and he sort of introduced me to the group…that was just after I found out about, er… well, just after our problems started. When I went to stay at Vince's place, I got more and more involved…not just with the chorus, but also I started singing with a smaller group – a quartet – I know, hard to believe, but I somehow got involved with this quartet…Vince, me, and two other guys from the chorus, Neil and Henry. And so—'

'Ben really likes Vince,' said Hannah.

'Sorry, you've thrown me. Ben…oh, I see, yes, of course, he's been over to Vince's a few times. Sure, and Vince really likes Ben too. Where was I—'

'You two, plus Neil and Henry.'

'Right, right. So, ever since then I've been going to chorus practice on a Wednesday and rehearsing with the quartet whenever we get the chance.'

'So, you haven't been working late or going for a few beers with the lads every Wednesday, then,' said Hannah, starting to enjoy Danny's revelations.

'No, quite. Singing, not drinking. Well, sometimes both, but mostly singing.'

'And what's it all for? Do you sing *for* anyone or just rehearse for the sake of it?'

'Well…good point…the chorus sings at festivals, private parties, weddings, that kind of thing, but I haven't done any of that myself yet. And well, the quartet…yes, come to think of it, we did this one gig at the BBC for someone's anniversary party…'

'*Gigs? At the BBC?* I can hardly believe my ears! Is this the man I married? Whose party was it?'

'Newton Burns, the…'

'Yes, I know who he is, Danny! This is incredible…carry on, carry on…'

'Well, there's not much more, really. Oh yes, we – the quartet, that is – well, we've qualified for the finals of the British barbershop quartet championships in May. That's in Harrogate.'

'Right, I see. This is amazing.'

'And I've just remembered…are we doing anything on the third weekend in March?'

'Nothing special that I'm aware of, why?'

'Ah, well, we – the quartet again – well, we're meant to be going to Amsterdam to compete in the Holland Harmony Festival.'

Hannah hooted with laughter as she rolled around on the sofa, laying on the surprise a little too thick.

'Bloody marvellous, Danny! Were you ever going to tell me any of this?' she said at last.

'I just did.'

'I love it…just love it!' said Hannah. Part of her wanted to tell Danny that she knew a lot of what he'd just told her already, but she couldn't. She had promised Vince that she wouldn't say a word. And even though Danny had now spilled the beans of his own volition, she felt she had to keep that confidence.

'I'm so proud of you, darling!'

'And I'm proud of you. What you did today.'

'It's been a bit of a day, I'll say that much,' said Hannah, and then paused. 'But listen…I need to ask you something…'

'A-ha?'

'Well, do you think everything's sorted out between us now? I mean, *everything*?'

'Sorry, I'm not with you…'

Hannah suddenly felt nervous, her voice more serious. 'I mean…the Ben issue.'

'No issue as far as I'm concerned,' said Danny without a moment's hesitation.

A tender silence fell between them.

Eventually, Hannah spoke.

'Shall we make love?'

'I'd like that,' said Danny.

Thirty-One

One fine Saturday afternoon, following an inspirational quartet rehearsal at Ken's house, Henry decided to take a long walk by the Thames. Starting at Marlow, he planned to head east towards Cookham, where the Taylors had lived for many years. He and George had often walked that stretch together, stopping off at a quaint and ramshackle riverside pub in Bourne End, where walkers were encouraged to keep their muddy boots on, dogs and children ran amok, and the landlord extended the cheeriest of rosy-cheeked welcomes to everyone who set foot in the place.

Henry's plan was to park in Marlow, walk the five miles to the pub, then catch the branch line train from Bourne End back to Marlow to collect his car. The late winter sun was surprisingly warm, and there was a cool breeze coming off the river. Henry quickly settled into his stride and into his thoughts.

He was no nearer knowing what the next phase of his life would bring, and yet he was far from stressed about the situation. He had returned from the island with a clear head.

He wanted the quartet to improve and grow stronger in the weeks leading up to the British championships, and he longed for Harrogate in May to be their finest hour.

He wanted to conclude the divorce smoothly and without further confrontation, and he resolved to be as co-operative as he could be with Jenny. He only hoped that her legal representatives would resist the temptation to embark on a feeding frenzy; he couldn't allow that. Just so long as Jenny was reasonable, he was in the mood to be more than generous in return. And he wanted Jenny to get over the sorry episode with Jeffrey Moss and find something worthwhile to do with her life.

How could he describe his feelings towards Cat? He felt he'd been blessed by the introduction of a very special person into his life. She was a natural force for good, but so unconventional as to defy definition. Did he love her? If to love means to possess, then absolutely not. How could she ever be possessed? He didn't feel the need to describe his feelings towards Cat in conventional terms. What they had was important, and it was strong, and he knew that it would continue. He only had to hold the small grey stone in his hand to know this.

For the first twenty minutes of the walk Henry was lost in thought, barely aware of his surroundings. Then suddenly a swan reared up from the river with a great splash of water, hissing its way across Henry's path, neck extended and wings flapping. Henry came to with a jolt, deftly sidestepped the irate bird, and put on a quick burst of speed to get out of harm's way.

As he regained his stride, he looked around to see where he was and how far he had walked. Just over a mile, he reckoned. And then he spotted what looked like a familiar figure walking towards him. Jeffrey Moss. Something about the body language, even from several hundred metres' distance. Henry wondered whether there was something unmistakable about the gait of the Common Serial Philanderer, or the posture of the Lesser-Spotted Thoroughgoing Bastard. The voice-over in his head was that of Sir David Attenborough.

The fact was that Jeffrey was the last person Henry would have expected to see on a country walk. His natural habitat was the town or city, where his prey of choice – other people's wives – tends to be much more bountiful. But just then Henry noticed a female figure walking behind Jeffrey at some distance, and before long he was able to make a connection between the two. They were wearing matching wax jackets and each was eating an ice cream cone. A Golden Labrador scurried between the two of them, confirming the connection.

The couple got closer. Henry ran through the options in his mind. The immediate visceral satisfaction of a knee to the groin? The cutting one-liner, guaranteed to put him in the shit with his latest conquest? Henry decided against both.

Jeffrey was now just fifty metres away, but with his back to Henry, as he called to his lady friend, or perhaps the dog, behind him. By the time he turned around, Henry was just feet away, striding towards him with considerable purpose. Jeffrey barely had time to recognise Henry and register surprise before Henry's outstretched hand pushed Jeffrey's ice cream cone squarely into the middle of his face.

'Good afternoon, Jeffrey,' said Henry, without breaking his stride.

Henry continued at the same pace, as if nothing had happened, and though it was sorely tempting to turn around and witness the aftermath, he felt that to do so would seriously diminish the impact of this moment of high farce. Instead, he smiled all the way to the pub at Bourne End, where he sat overlooking the river with its flotilla of riverboats and barges making their way up and down stream in the mid-afternoon sunshine of what was by now a spectacularly unseasonal March day.

The air was filled with the cries of small children, the yapping of small dogs, and the smell of frying onions. These were strange times, Henry pondered, with both the economic climate and the weather climate in complete disarray. Hey ho.

Out of nowhere, Henry felt a twinge of pity for Jenny.

How could she have been so duped by Jeffrey Moss? Come to think of it, how could Henry have failed to see his true colours a lot sooner? It mattered little now. Jeffrey had been the final straw, that was all, and he was now an irrelevance. An irrelevance with a faceful of ice cream, and quite possibly a flake protruding from one nostril.

Henry was in a better place, but Jenny...how was she coping? Just then, Henry's mobile phone rang. He walked to a more isolated spot on the riverbank to answer it.

'Jenny. How are you?'

'I'm fine, Henry. You? I thought it would be a good idea if we got together for a chat...'

'Jenny, listen, if you—'

'Henry, it's all right. Things are fine. I just want to level things between us. Draw a line, so to speak. No histrionics, I promise.'

Jenny agreed to Henry's suggestion that they should meet on neutral ground, but when he mentioned the name of a cocktail bar they frequented some years ago, she thought that this was not such a good idea. Instead, she suggested they meet in the open and pleasantly rural surroundings of Virginia Water, near the Roman columns.

When Henry arrived, Jenny was sitting on a bench reading a book. This wasn't in keeping. Jenny, reading a book in public? And something about her appearance seemed different. For one thing, her hair was loose and was blowing gently in the breeze. This wasn't right. Jenny's fastidious approach to personal grooming had always required every hair to know its place, no matter what. She single-handedly kept the hairdressers, eyebrow threaders, and bikini line waxers of Ascot in business. Clearly, something was up.

Henry approached Jenny with a gentle cough, and she turned to him with the most surprising of smiles. Positively beatific. And, without saying a word, she reached out to

251

embrace him in the most overt display of affection he had seen from her in several years. Henry found himself stuck for words. Jenny was anything but.

After the opening pleasantries, Henry expected a resumption of familiar hostilities, but none were forthcoming. Jenny wanted to share something with him. His heart started beating a little faster.

'I've been away…the same as you, dar—'

Jenny stopped short of uttering the familiar term of endearment that even she could see would be over the top in the circumstances.

Henry felt suddenly panicky.

'Away? What…you mean you've been to the…my—'

'No, not to your island, dar…Henry. But I took your example, you could say. I've been away for a week by myself. A cottage by the coast in Dorset. Can you imagine, a whole week by myself?'

Henry sat down next to Jenny.

'Well, yes, hard to believe. What was the idea? What did you do with yourself?'

There was the saintly smile again.

'Going over things,' said Jenny. 'I know I've been a complete cow. A big Friesian with a fat, wet nose, bulging udders, and a moo that could scare the crows from the trees.'

'R-i-i-ght,' said Henry, feeling that they were getting into unchartered territory. Was this the sneakiest of all Jenny's sneaky ploys? What was coming next?

'I'd like to think that I've changed, Henry. I know it's only been a short time, but I want you to know that I've changed.'

Henry stood up and turned to face Jenny, narrowing his eyes against the sun as he did so.

'This is not about getting back together, Jenny – is it?'

'No…no,' said Jenny, with a soft assurance that came as a surprise. 'I think I can see things differently now. I'm not quite the cow I was, and I wanted you to know. And also, I'm sorry for everything that happened. Quite where that leaves me I'm not sure, but I want to move on peacefully now. That's all.'

Henry tried to think what best to say, but again had no words, and allowed Jenny to continue.

'I think we've both made a lot of personal progress these last few months, and the irony is that it wouldn't have happened if we hadn't…well, encountered certain difficulties. So here you are…the new you, and here I am…the new me. And I can't help thinking we might just be so good together as the new *we*. But I know it's a bit late for that, isn't it?'

There it was, Jenny's final attempt at reconciliation. Henry felt his heartstrings being seriously tugged, but there could be only one answer.

'I think so, yes,' he said.

'I'll be off, then. Good to see you, Henry,' and Jenny's voice faded on a passing breeze as she turned and walked away.

Thirty-Two

Angie had all but moved into Vince's flat full-time, and living space was now at a premium. Angie had cited, not unreasonably, Vince's health as the main beneficiary of her spending more time at the flat, and Vince had gradually acquiesced to her persistent but subtle overtures.

This was difficult for Vince to argue with, such was his gratitude towards Angie. However, it wasn't just a sense of gratitude; his feelings towards her had changed somehow. He wanted to spend more time with her, as he was enjoying her company more than ever. He found himself admiring her from a distance, not just when she was up close and personal, and this was new. Had he told her he loved her that day in the hospital?

Angie was moving between the four small rooms of Vince's flat, looking increasingly uneasy. She was searching for things, and that wasn't good.

'How the hell do you ever find stuff in here, Vince?' she said at last.

'Whatever it is I'm looking for…I usually go to where I left it, and hey presto,' said Vince without looking up from his magazine. 'A very good retrospective on Kate Bush in *Q* this month,' he continued. 'Amazing that twelve years went by between albums, and then she put out two in one year. Okay, one of them was a re-master, but still. She's practically prolific these days.'

'I doubt she has too much trouble laying her hands on a pair of eyelash curlers,' said Angie, flipping over a couple of cushions on the sofa.

'I doubt she needs them,' said Vince, realising instantly that the comment might have been unwise.

'Sorry?'

'Eyelash curlers. I mean, look at the lashes on her,' said Vince, proffering the magazine. 'And see those eyebrows. None of that plucked chicken nonsense. Good, thick Irish eyebrows.' What the hell, he thought.

Angie snatched the magazine out of Vince's hand.

'Photoshopped. She's probably got a Liam Gallagher monobrow in real life.'

Vince resisted getting into deeper water. He was enjoying the topic of conversation, discussing some of his favourite musicians, but he knew that this particular line of debate was heading for trouble. Besides, he had something else on his mind, so he steered the conversation in that direction.

'Anyway, you don't need all these curlers and straighteners and gizmos to make you look good. You're a natural beauty. You can't buy that.'

'Are you taking the piss, Vince?'

'Bollocks, am I!' said Vince, aggrieved that his attempt at a heartfelt compliment had been received with such suspicion. 'In my eyes, you are utterly beautiful from top to toe – with an extra special mention for the two big bits in the middle,' he continued.

'What are you after?'

'Your mind. Your soul. Your Double-Ds. I yearn for everything about you,' he said, overdoing it by more than a small margin.

'What are you *after*?' Angie repeated.

Vince cranked up the ham factor.

'We have unfinished business. I am an artist, and I will not be denied. I need to complete my masterwork. *Nude Reclining with the Thermostat Turned up Full.*'

'I doubt we'll need the heating on next time. Have you ever known a March as warm as this?' said Angie.

'So that's a "yes" then?'

'On the condition that you don't invite your friends round, and that you keep your own clothes on, yes.'

'Formidable!' said Vince in a mock French accent, for no good reason.

Angie had moved over to the music shelves where she was standing with her arms ominously crossed.

'Do you really need all these—'

'Whoa there…stop! That's not for negotiation.'

'What isn't?'

'You were about to ask if I really need to keep all these CDs and vinyl records, seeing as there's so little space in the flat. And the answer, perhaps unsurprisingly, is YES,' said Vince.

'But you can download everything these days. Such a space-saver, Vince.'

'But that's not the point, Ange. Just so you know, I have already transferred every single one of those CDs and records to digital format anyway.'

'Well, then. Why keep all this lot? It makes no sense at all,' said Angie, not quite getting Vince's point.

'No, no. The point is that I have them stored as MP3 files for…well, for back-up purposes, and for playing on my phone when I'm out and about. When I'm at home, I don't want to sit here listening to some crappy, gappy MP3s, do I? I want the real thing. And I want to look at the artwork, and read the liner notes. It's what it's all about, Ange.'

'Then maybe we need to approach this from a different angle,' said Angie, sitting down opposite Vince.

'Approach what from a different angle, exactly?' said Vince.

'Okay. We've been waltzing around this issue long enough. Do you want me to move in with you full-time or not?'

'Haven't we already had this conversation—'

'Yes or no?'

'Yes.'

'So, isn't it reasonable that you should make room for me?'

Vince shifted in his seat a little awkwardly.

'Well, yes. But that doesn't mean getting rid of my most precious possessions, does it? Without that lot, I wouldn't be me. And if I wasn't me, then you'd be moving in with someone else, wouldn't you?'

Angie couldn't fault Vince's logic, and so changed tack.

'Ask me what *I* want,' she said.

'Right, sure. What do you want? Apart from more space in the living room, that is,' said Vince, gesturing towards the music shelves.

'I thought you'd never ask. Well, it won't have escaped your notice that my life has taken me on a fairly colourful journey up to now. I've been a glamour model, an *au pair*, a nursery assistant, a carer, and a barmaid. And, if I go back far enough, I used to work in a bingo hall and sell potatoes door-to-door. I had my time in the sun with the glamour game, and I was happy to milk it while the going was good, but that was easy to give up when the time came, because it wasn't the real me. The real me is someone who loves to look after people. That's what I do best. I care for other people's children, I care for old folks, I care for the regulars down at The Ship…I care for you.'

'In that order? I think I've been short-changed,' said Vince.

Well done, Vince. I was hoping you'd bite on that one, thought Angie.

'It doesn't have to be in that order, if you don't want it to be. But that depends on us agreeing on priorities. The thing is, I have a contract of employment at the nursery… and at the old people's home. I even have guaranteed hours at The Ship, which means I know where I stand. With you… well, I'm not sure I know where I stand.'

Vince knew that no amount of one-liners and flip comments would do him any good now. He leant on the arm of the chair, hauled himself up, and faced Angie with his arms outstretched. She got up and held both his hands.

'This could go on for a long time, couldn't it?' said Vince, softly. 'You making all the running, me ducking and diving all the time. A merry dance.'

'Yes.'

'And that's not what you want. You want some promises, some guarantees.'

'Nothing's ever guaranteed, but promises...that would be nice.'

'You're the only girl for me.'

'Is that a promise?'

'Yes.'

'And what about our living arrangements?'

'This place was too small even for me. We need somewhere bigger,' said Vince.

Thirty-Three

Two days before they were due to set off for the Holland Harmony Festival they all received a call from Bella telling them that Ken wasn't well, and had been advised by his doctors not to make the trip. He'd had a minor stroke.

Vince, Danny, Henry and Neil were all shocked and very concerned by the news, and with Bella's consent, made plans to visit Ken at home the following day.

The news also came as a huge disappointment to the quartet. Ken had become a dear friend to them all, but as their coach and mentor he was their leader. They looked to him for guidance and expert advice on just about every aspect of quartet life, musical and otherwise. How would they get through the weekend without him?

Ken was sitting in an upright armchair in the conservatory, enjoying the early evening sun and the crossword when they arrived. He greeted them warmly, and seemed surprisingly alert and bright. Bella took orders for tea and coffee and warned them not to make a fuss as she headed for the kitchen.

After a few minutes clucking around Ken's chair, asking him how he felt, offering to peel him a banana, and generally making the fuss Bella had warned against, Ken raised an admonishing hand.

'Gentlemen! Kind-hearted though you undoubtedly are, I wish you would all calm down, take a seat, and relax. Take a deep breath, and join me in two minutes of that rather precious but outmoded commodity...silence.'

They did as they were bid, looking like four schoolboys

up before the headmaster, while Ken closed his eyes.

Bella returned in the midst of the silence.

'Oh dear,' she whispered. 'I did tell you not to make a fuss.'

She handed out mugs of tea and coffee and disappeared again.

At last Ken opened his eyes, signalling that he was ready to re-engage, but at his own pace. They waited for him to speak.

'Would you follow me to the music room, gentlemen?' Ken got up from his chair, shaking his head to decline any offers of help. 'Come with me.'

They walked through to the music room, Ken making his way to the grand piano.

'Would you indulge me, gentlemen?' Ken asked, and they all nodded, eyes wide with anticipation. 'A little Chopin, I think.'

Ken sat down, lifted the lid of the Steinway, and composed himself. Vince looked like he was about to say something, but Henry lifted a finger to his lips by way of discouragement.

Ken played for ten minutes like a man possessed, his fingers running the length of the keyboard in loud, rousing passages interlaced with softer, slower sections. He played beautifully and with consummate artistry, and as the piece reached its tumultuous ending and the sound in the room decayed to silence, the four singers stood and applauded, astonished at what they had just witnessed. Neil wiped away a tear. Henry and Danny looked at each other, mouths open in amazement.

'Fuck me,' said Vince, breaking the spell. But the way he said it was full of awe and respect, and they all understood.

'You flatter me with your response, gentlemen,' said Ken. '*Scherzo Number Two in B-flat minor, Opus Thirty-One.* I learned that piece over forty years ago, but it took me twenty years to get it right.'

'It was incredible,' said Danny.

'Perhaps not that, but certainly the product of many years' practise. Which brings me to the point. Have you been practising, gentlemen? Have you been doing the exercises I prescribed? Have you been listening to each other, really listening…working and reworking your technique? Forgive my bluntness, but I know how hard it is. Life has a habit of getting in the way, doesn't it?'

They looked at each other, and to a man felt as though they had let Ken down.

'It's been difficult to find the time some days,' said Danny.

'Yes…'

'But when we're together, it's really sounding good…I'd say we're a closer unit than ever,' said Neil.

'Mind you, it's only two weeks since you last heard us, Ken, to be fair,' Vince added.

'That's my point, Vince. These are the two most important weeks, just before a competition. How can you make certain of peaking at the right moment unless you build up to it properly? All of my coaching has been aimed at getting you to that point at just the right time. But if you haven't been putting in the hours—'

'Ken, I think we're in good shape, honestly,' said Neil. 'Give us fifteen minutes to warm up, and we'll sing you our two contest songs for Holland. Is that all right?'

'Just the ticket. Show me what you've got, gentlemen!' said Ken. 'I'll be in the conservatory. Join me when you're ready.'

'Now you've dropped us right in it,' said Vince as Ken left the music room.

'Look, Vince, are you serious about this, or just playing stupid fucking games?' said Neil.

None of them could remember seeing Neil so animated or angry, and the ferocity of his words surprised them all.

'I've been practising every day for the last two weeks, if you must know,' said Vince. 'Falsetto especially. What sort of a joker do you take me for?'

'I've done nothing else but work on my pitch,' said Henry. 'I swear I can hit the outer onion skin ninety-nine times out of a hundred.'

'I just sing the melody, what do I know?' said Danny, as much to cut through the atmosphere as anything else.

'And you're a great lead, so don't forget it,' said Neil, suddenly grabbing Danny by both shoulders.

They couldn't work out quite where Neil's leadership balls had come from, but he had certainly just grown a pair, and within minutes he had got them focused on the job in hand. He blew pitch, and they warmed up with a few scales and vowel matching exercises. Then they sang their two songs through with as much energy and artistry as they could muster.

'Let's go and do the same for Ken,' said Neil.

Minutes later, the final note of their second song had the conservatory windows rattling in their frames, with Vince posting a twenty-second long high C, Henry rumbling beautifully on the octave below, and Danny and Neil completing the chord perfectly.

'And that's barbershop!' Ken whooped, to their delight.

'Was it all right?' asked Neil, anxiously.

'More than all right, gentlemen. I have to congratulate you on a fine performance, and forgive me for questioning your preparations – you've clearly been putting the work in. Sing like that on Saturday and you'll be in with a chance of a podium finish. And did you sense it?'

'Sense what, Ken?' asked Neil.

'Why, The Fifth Voice, dear boy. You've found The Fifth Voice.'

The flight from Heathrow was more turbulent than they would have wished for, and they were delayed getting into Schiphol airport for some other reason that didn't seem to have been announced.

Vince voiced his displeasure.

'I hate flying. All the bloody fuss and nonsense – stripping off for security, being treated like cattle, the shit food, the inevitable delays…I can't stand it when people bang on about flying as if it's still some sort of treat. "We managed to get an upgrade to *business*, darling!" Two inches of extra leg room and a free gin and tonic. Big deal. Flying sucks and that's the end of it.'

'Michael Palin's job's still safe then,' said Henry, amused at Vince's rant.

'He can keep it. I'd rather sing baritone than fly around the world, even if it is on BBC expenses.'

'I wondered how long it would take before someone started on the bari jokes,' said Neil, falling for Vince's trap.

'Right, did you hear about the bari who locked himself out of the house? He couldn't find the right key…'

'I've heard them all before, Vincent.'

'You're a bari, Neil. It goes with the territory. Baris are to barbershop singing as drummers are to rock bands, or goalkeepers are to football teams. They're all a few sandwiches short of a picnic.'

'There's only one basket case in this quartet, and that's the one with the dodgy falsetto,' Neil bit back.

'Ouch!' said Danny.

And so the banter continued – through security, in the luggage collection area, and as they walked outside to the taxi rank.

'Why did you feel the need to have three Bloody Marys on the plane?' Neil asked Vince.

'I think cocktails are more in keeping with the jet-set lifestyle than those little cans of lukewarm lager. Besides, only one of them was Bloody. The other two were Virgin Marys.'

'I almost said a couple of Hail Marys while the plane was jumping around up there,' said Henry.

'I didn't know you were a Catholic, Henry,' said Vince.

'Close. Zoroastrian.'

'No way! The same as Freddie Mercury. So, what's that all about?' asked Vince, his curiosity pricked.

'We believe that the universe will undergo a cosmic renovation and time will end when good finally conquers evil,' said Henry.

'Is that it?'

'No, we also have a fundamental belief in the complete gullibility of tenors.'

Neil and Danny collapsed in a fit of laughter as Henry played the trump card, putting Vince squarely in his place just as they reached the head of the taxi queue. They bundled into a Mercedes limousine, Vince commandeering the front passenger seat before anyone else could get to it.

Neil gave the driver their hotel name and street name, and they drove in silence for a little while.

'So, are you here on business or pleasure, gentlemen?' asked the driver after about five minutes had passed.

'A bit of both, I hope,' Vince replied.

'Always good to have both, yes? No play makes Jack the dull boy, as you say. Amsterdam has everything you need. Have a look at the information in the back, please?'

Danny pulled out a handful of tourist leaflets from an elasticated pocket on the back of the driver's seat.

'You know the Bananenbar, yes?'

Danny flicked through the assortment of flyers advertising museums, water parks, canal trips, zoos and all the usual tourist attractions.

'No, not here,' he said.

'No, not there. Here we are,' the driver said, passing another leaflet over his shoulder to Danny.

'Forty-five euros at the door, you get a beer glass to fill up lots of times, and the ladies do some marvellous sexy shows. They look after you very well.'

'That takes care of three of us, then,' said Vince.

'We'll be having none of that,' said Neil, as he clipped Vince around the back of the head.

Fifteen minutes later they arrived at their downtown hotel, which was comfortable, though nothing special. Not even Vince complained. After unpacking and changing they gathered in the lobby before heading on to the streets to find an Italian restaurant recommended by their taxi driver.

Resuming his self-appointed leadership role, Neil led the way, and continued to keep Vince in check.

'I may be the youngest, Vince, but someone's got to keep order. If it were left to you, it'd be chaos and debauchery before we knew it,' he said when challenged.

Danny and Henry just smiled at each other, amused by the new double act and happy to go with the flow.

At the restaurant, they planned the following day's schedule carefully, working back from the time they were due to report at the theatre: 12.30pm ahead of their allocated performance time of 2.40pm. The banter gave way to the serious business of preparing for the competition, and that meant an early night, lots of water, and up early for a light breakfast and a final rehearsal.

At breakfast, the boys-on-tour comedy routine of the previous day was no longer in evidence, as nerves began to kick in ahead of only their second competitive outing. How they all wished Ken was there to take them through their final paces and do what he did best (though he did so many things brilliantly), and that was to inspire them.

After breakfast they rehearsed for an hour in Henry's room (he'd paid extra for a slightly larger one), then gathered up their kit bags and headed off in a taxi to the theatre. En route they passed the Amsterdam Muziektheater, and Neil mentioned that the Dutch National Ballet were performing that evening if anyone fancied it. He expected an immediate wisecrack from Vince, but none was forthcoming.

'Are you all right, Vince?' Neil asked eventually. 'You're a bit too quiet for my liking.'

'You remember our first gig at the BBC Television Centre when you were so nervous you threw up in a waste paper bin? Well that's how I'm feeling right now,' said Vince.

They completed the journey in silence.

'That's an advance on prelims,' said Danny, checking the time as they entered the theatre. 'I seem to remember they changed the stage times, and we only had half an hour to get ready before we were on. What a panic that was.'

This time there was no such panic, and having reported at the reception desk, the quartet had the best part of two hours to get changed, complete their vocal preparation, calm their nerves, and steel themselves for battle. It hadn't occurred to them until this point to ask who exactly they would be battling against.

'Who are we up against? Anyone we know, Neil?' asked Danny.

'Two other British quartets...then there's the Dutch, Danish, Germans...some good groups, but nothing like the level of competition we'll be up against in Harrogate. As Ken said, this one's all about getting some more contest experience and stage time ahead of the big one. Come on, let's get changed, and we'll head off to the rehearsal room.'

In the rehearsal room, Neil made sure that they followed Ken's preparation routine to the last detail. After a few gentle warm-up exercises, they sang through the opening bars of the two contest songs in full performance mode, focusing on unity of sound, and delivering every ounce of artistry they could muster. Then they went quiet, saving their voices and starting to get in the zone ('I hate that expression,' said Vince).

With ten minutes before they were due to be called, Neil asked the guys to gather in a huddle with their arms around each other's shoulders ('Do we really have to do this?' said Vince).

'Breathe slowly, and synchronise...let the nerves drain away, and let the energy flow. Think of Ken and the way he played for us. He was telling us how to do it. Let's sing like he played, with artistry...and feeling...and soul. And remember what he told us. *We have found The Fifth Voice.*'

Soon afterwards they were called to the backstage area, and before they knew it, Neil was leading them on to the stage in front of a noisy, colourful away crowd.

As they walked off the stage, none of them felt that they had done less than their best, and their sense of relief was such that they instinctively fell into a group hug in the wings ('Is this entirely necessary?' said Vince).

Now for the worst bit. The results wouldn't be announced until 5pm, another two hours to wait. Neil and Henry went into the auditorium to watch the remaining contestants, while Vince twisted Danny's arm to join him at the bar. They agreed to join up in the auditorium just before five.

Neil and Henry watched the rest of the competitors with growing confidence, only to be brought back down to earth by the occasional quartet who performed out of their skins. The net result was that they had absolutely no idea where they stood in the rankings.

Vince and Danny became steadily more relaxed, as they reflected on the competition and, after the third beer, life in general. There was a moment when they almost resumed the first music conversation they ever had. However, at the mention of *Sgt. Pepper*, Danny sensed danger and steered the conversation in another direction.

At 4.55pm, they were all together in the theatre stalls, as silence fell and the results were announced.

After a lot of preliminary announcements, including thanks to the organisers, theatre staff, contestants, contestants' loved ones, and too many other people to mention, the moment had arrived. The MC stepped up to the microphone.

Hearts leapt into mouths.

But they weren't there for long.

'In third place...from Maidenhead in England, we are delighted to present the bronze medal of the Holland Harmony Festival to...Neil, Henry, Danny and Vince... From The Edge!'

They were ecstatic. They had achieved the podium finish that Ken had imagined, and they couldn't wait to let him know.

After collecting their medals, and taking part in the post-contest ritual of handshakes, photographs, thanks and farewells, they ran out of the theatre to the street, nominating Neil to make the phone call.

'It's ringing,' said Neil. 'Oh, here we go...Ken! Ah, sorry...Hi Bella, how are you? We're ringing to let Ken know the news from—'

'Hello, Neil. Now listen to me, dear, because I have to tell you something...you see, Ken has had another stroke. A big one this time. He didn't suffer, dear. He didn't suffer.'

Thirty-Four

Devastated was the only word to describe how the four singers felt. They stood in the busy street outside the theatre, dumbstruck. Neil began sobbing. Danny sat down on the pavement with his head in his hands. Henry went to console Neil. Vince shouted his disbelief and defiance, punching the wall of the theatre as he did so, ripping flesh and causing his knuckles to bleed.

Why? The question had no answer.

Miserably, they went back inside to collect their kit bags, then caught a taxi back to the hotel. Nobody spoke a word.

The whole evening lay ahead of them. The return flight was not until tomorrow morning.

At the hotel, they dropped off their bags and reassembled in the lobby. Nobody wanted to spend time alone in their room, not even to freshen up.

'Drink?' said Henry at last.

Words only started flowing after the second drink.

It seemed the craziest question, and at the risk of causing ructions, Vince asked Neil if he had heard Bella correctly. Could it be that…

Neil said he understood Vince's disbelief, but he assured him of the hard reality.

'Bella was very calm and sweet on the phone. She broke the news softly. She said that he hadn't suffered. Then she said she knew Ken would be very proud, and she wished us a safe journey home.'

'Poor Bella,' said Danny.

As the doubt and disbelief subsided, they started talking about Ken.

'He was a genius,' said Neil. 'The finest musician I've ever met. And no one knew more about harmony singing. But he was much more than that. He was just the best mentor and friend, and he really, really cared. He had so much faith in me, he got me my job with Newton Burns. He took that big a risk…for me! He did more for me than my own fath—'

'Easy now,' said Henry, placing a comforting hand on Neil's shoulder, before adding his own thoughts.

'When you invited Ken to our first rehearsal, I remember thinking it wasn't such a good idea. You know, the way he goes on a bit…all very funny stuff…he often had me in stitches…but I remember thinking we'd never get anything done. How wrong was I? He was an absolute diamond,' said Henry.

'He was the funniest guy I ever met, and his stories were epic,' said Vince. 'And he knew exactly how to get what he wanted out of us. Me and my head voice, getting Neil to balance the chords every time, making Danny into a great lead, helping Henry with his lower register…I could go on.'

'What about you, Danny?' asked Neil.

'I suppose, more than anything, Ken gave me the confidence to believe I can do this stuff. When I joined you guys, I had no singing experience, certainly not in a group, and certainly not as the lead in a barbershop quartet! But I remember Ken asking me my opinions very early on, encouraging me in all sorts of ways, and, well…teaching me how to do it, I guess. He was a brilliant teacher.'

'You know what he did that was the smartest thing of all?' said Henry. 'He made us become close friends. Do you remember him telling us early on how we needed to get to know each other like brothers to really start singing well as a group? He talked about the Wilson brothers and the Everleys. That was clever.'

'More than clever, I think,' said Neil. 'I know what it's like to lose a brother. And now I know what it's like to gain a brother. Three brothers.'

'Do you think Ken knew that you'd feel that way?' asked Danny.

Neil smiled. 'I'm sure of it. He knew my situation, and though he never talked about it, he helped me sort my life out in more ways than one. He knew what he was doing all right.'

'I don't think I could have got through my marriage problems if it wasn't for singing with you guys, and that was made all the more special by Ken,' said Danny.

'That sounds familiar,' said Henry.

'It sounds to me like Ken gave us all something special. Something beyond the music, I mean,' said Vince, looking unusually thoughtful. 'I don't know how I'd have coped with my relapse without you guys – and Angie, of course – but would any of it have happened without Ken? No, it wouldn't. He gave me – all of us – something very special.'

'The Fifth Voice,' said Neil.

A moment's silence passed.

'Shall we drink to Ken?' asked Danny.

'Bloody right, and I know what we're having and no arguments,' said Vince, as he waved to catch the barman's attention. He came over to the table.

'Do you make cocktails?' Vince asked.

'Certainly, sir. What would you like?'

'Four banana daiquiris, please.'

At no point during that evening in Amsterdam did any of them question their participation in the British quartet championships, which were now only weeks away. They were as one in knowing, without needing to say it, that they were more determined than ever to acquit themselves to the best of their ability in Harrogate in May. At breakfast the following morning, they compared diaries and organised their rehearsal schedule in the run-up to the event.

Back at home, they disbanded to await news of the arrangements for Ken's funeral.

Ken had been a long-standing member of Maidenhead A Cappella, and of course, the news came as a shock to all of the club's members. On the first rehearsal night after the Holland festival, the mood was sad and subdued, but by the end of the evening the chorus was singing in fine voice to celebrate the life of one of their dearest members. James Pinter made a special announcement that Bella had requested the chorus to sing at Ken's funeral, and that she had also asked Neil if From The Edge would sing a blessing.

News of Ken's death also spread far and wide throughout the barbershop world, as Ken had been one of the leading lights of the British Association for many years, and he was well known within other barbershop associations abroad.

Gradually, the arrangements came together. Neil and Henry made a special point of offering to help Bella with anything she needed, but were careful not to intrude on what was a family matter, and kept a respectful distance. Ken's daughter Helen called Neil on one occasion to double -check that the quartet was able to sing at the service, but that was never in any doubt.

The sad day dawned, and the vicar at the little village church in Buckinghamshire had never seen so many people. Mourners overflowed into the churchyard, and were standing three deep in places. An external sound system had been hastily rigged to allow them to follow the service within, where two hundred or so people packed the pews and lined the walls. The chorus of Maidenhead A Cappella sat at the back of the church and stood to sing two songs as the coffin was carried in.

Two eulogies were given, one by Ken's son Toby, and the other by Newton Burns, whose deeply heartfelt speech was peppered with highly amusing anecdotes about Ken and the adventures they had shared together down the years. Tears and laughter were plentiful. Newton ended by referring to Ken as, 'the most talented and reluctant superstar I have ever had the privilege to know,' before introducing the quartet to sing *Irish Blessing*.

May the road rise to meet you,
May the wind be always at your back,
May the sun shine warm upon your face.
May the rain fall soft upon your fields,
And until we meet again,
May He hold you in His hand.
May God hold you in the palm of His hand.

After the service and interment the crowd gradually dispersed, and Bella, Helen and Toby thanked as many people as possible, reminding everyone that they were welcome to come back to the house to raise a glass to Ken. Bella invited James Pinter and the men of Maidenhead A Cappella to come along and sing a few of Ken's favourite songs, and then she asked if any of them had seen Neil.

James pointed to a corner of the churchyard, where Neil, Vince, Danny and Henry were standing together under the dark, gnarled branches of an ancient Yew tree. Bella approached them, and overheard Vince saying to Neil, 'It's okay, just take a minute.'

She thanked and hugged them all, leaving Neil until last, and as she embraced him she pressed a small envelope into the palm of his hand.

'From Ken,' she whispered. 'Open it here with the lads, and I'll see you back at the house.'

As Bella slipped away, they all turned to Neil. With a shaking hand, he opened the envelope, took out a small piece of paper, and read aloud.

Gentlemen, if you are reading this, then I hope you gave me a send-off to remember! I thought I would take the precaution of committing a few words to paper in case my health gets any worse. Which reminds me of the inscription on Spike Milligan's gravestone: 'I Told You I Was Ill'. But I digress, as ever. I wish you every success in your endeavours as a group, and in your lives beyond (is there a life beyond barbershop?). I have watched you develop into a fine quartet these past months, and I have come to know you all well, and to consider you as dear friends.

I know you will succeed, not just as a quartet, but as friends, fathers, sons, husbands, boyfriends, lovers. Because you found The Fifth Voice. Keep it with you wherever you go in life.

Ken

Thirty-Five

Neil was feeling the weight of the world on his shoulders. Not just the heavy sadness of Ken's passing, but a build-up of things: the considerable responsibility of his new job and the burden of expectation upon him; preparations for the impending quartet championships and a desperate desire to do well; the guilt of not having come clean with his mother on a number of matters; and the dark shadow of his father's unremitting disapproval.

The job with Yellow Braces, with eternal thanks to dear Ken, was a dream come true, and he still had to pinch himself on a daily basis to make sure it was real. If it brought with it a degree of pressure due to the high profile nature of the project, then he could live with that – no, better than that, he knew that he was thriving in that environment. He was in his element.

The quartet was also a labour of love, of course, and it was wonderful that they were making such good progress. But how bittersweet it had become with the loss of their incomparable mentor. If they were focused on excelling beforehand, the four friends were now galvanised by a new determination to achieve their ambitions, in honour of the man who gave them so much.

It was with family matters that Neil felt he had the most difficulty, and the most unfinished business.

Priority number one was to clear the decks with Margaret. He had always been completely up front with his mother, and she had always been his greatest ally, so he was feeling wretched at having cut her out of the latest developments in his life, and she had every right to feel aggrieved. He had even lied to her about his work, which was the one thing he most wanted to celebrate with her. It was a mess, and he needed to straighten things up.

It was a bright, warm Sunday morning, George was playing golf, and Neil was feeling very affectionate towards his mother. It was time to talk.

They sat on the garden terrace with coffee, pain au chocolat, and the Sunday papers. Blue tits, nuthatches and sparrows flitted here and there, and everything in the garden was rosy.

'Mama?'

'Okay darling, as it's been about ten years since you called me Mama, I'll assume that there's something wrong. What is it?' said Margaret.

'I'm just fooling around, Mother. It's my way of cosying up to you because I feel lousy about having kept you in the dark recently…'

'Oh, you sweet boy.'

'I told you the sad news about Ken, though – didn't I?'

'Yes, yes you did. I know how much he meant to you and the quartet. And he was such a wonderful chap, full of *joie de vivre*, always smiling and—'

'…talking…and telling outrageous stories…and…we all miss him so much,' said Neil.

'I remember you chastising me that time I got talking to him – yes, he did know how to tell a story. And such an intelligent man. I seem to remember taking a perverse delight in picking him up on aspects of his oratory – I could see he enjoyed the challenge! Poor Ken, what a sad loss.'

'More than you think. He was such a wonderful friend, he took such an interest in our lives as well as our singing… he believed in me so much he got me my job.'

'Your freelance work?'

'No, Mother.'

'Ah, then you must mean your position with Newton Burns at Yellow Braces?'

'What...how do you know—'

'It's okay, darling. I'm your mother. You don't think I'd allow myself to stay in the dark for too long, do you?'

'So...?'

'Well, I found Newt's business card on the floor of your bedroom while I was vacuuming, and—'

'Hang on...you called him Newt...a bit familiar isn't it, Mother?'

'Ah, well, that's just it. My surprise at finding Newt's card in your bedroom was accentuated by the fact that I knew him quite well when I was a lot younger.'

'Your ballet days? Really? Good Lord, so what did you think?'

'I was at a loss to know what to think for a moment, and I certainly didn't think you might be working with him. I guess I imagined other reasons for your acquaintance. Quite frankly, he was always avaricious when it comes to young men, and I'm afraid I started thinking along those lines.'

Neil squirmed a bit in his seat.

'So, how did you find out that I was working for him?'

'Well, I had decided to contact Henry Warrington anyway, in my desperation to find a way of healing the rift between you and your father. Call it clutching at straws, but apart from me, Henry was the only other bridge between you two that I could think of, so I called him to see if he could help. He was very sweet and kind, but I had no idea when we started talking that I'd find out about Newt and Yellow Braces.'

'Henry, the old dog. He didn't say anything to me.'

'Well, he wouldn't, would he?'

By now Neil was grinning from ear to ear. Rather than feel upset that Margaret had been digging around in his affairs, he felt relief that she knew pretty much everything already, and he admired the intrepid way in which she'd gone about things.

'I'll call you Miss Marple from now on,' he said.

'Well, I did rather feel like a private eye, I admit, but Miss Marple I can do without, thank you,' said Margaret, relieved that Neil had taken it so well.

'Have you told Father about Newt and Yellow Braces?' asked Neil, no longer smiling.

'Yes, yes I have. Are you cross with me?'

'It depends. Why did you tell him?'

'Isn't it obvious? I wanted him to see that you're getting on in the world, that you're making your mark, and that it's about time he changed his attitude towards you and started treating you like a son again. That's why.'

'How did he react?'

'I think it made a serious impression. You might not believe this, but he looked...humbled. He asked me if I thought he'd pushed you away for good...I think he wants to make up.'

'Aside from being hard to believe, doesn't that strike you as just a bit fickle, just a bit hypocritical?' said Neil, feeling peeved. 'I mean, years of snide abuse wiped away in a second upon hearing the news that his son has landed a high-profile job with a celebrity boss—'

'Be careful now, darling. I understand why you're sceptical, and you can say he's being fickle if you wish, but I believe it's genuine. And put yourself in your father's shoes...you know how stubbornly proud he is...this will be hard for him.'

'It's been pretty hard for me these last few years.'

'Yes, I know. But listen...when I told him, I saw his face change. It was like the scales fell from his eyes at that exact moment. It happens that way, sometimes. He wants to hold out the olive branch, darling, and I think you should accept it. This is the time.'

'How will I recognise this olive branch? Is he planning to broach the subject any time soon?'

'Ah, yes. Well, I wouldn't expect him to be predictable on that score. But you'll know when it happens, I'm sure,' said Margaret. 'Now, tell me more about Holland and the quartet!'

After dinner that evening, as daylight was fading, Neil took a glass of wine into the garden and sat cross-legged on the still-warm grass. He closed his eyes.

You won't believe what's been happening to me lately. I have found my first real job, which turns out to be my dream job. The quartet has won a medal in Holland, and we'll be competing in the biggest barbershop quartet contest outside of America in about five weeks from now. I have one wonderful man to thank for all of that, and he has just died. I would swap everything to have you both back.

But the most remarkable thing of all might be about to happen. I think Father and I are about to make up. Mother has played a blinder, you won't be surprised to hear.

I wonder, have you been in on this as well?

Sleep well, Bro.

Thirty-Six

It was the eve of the British quartet championships, and Vince, Danny, Neil and Henry were sitting in a park in Harrogate, bathed in glorious sunshine and surrounded by a mass of colourful spring flowers.

'We haven't really spoken much about it, but how do we think we'll do?' said Danny.

They looked at each other, no one wanting to speak first. Then Vince broke the silence.

'Well, we got bronze in Holland,' he said.

'Yes, we did well,' said Henry, 'but that was a small festival, not even their national championships. This is the big league now.'

'You're right,' said Neil. 'Honestly, we'll do really well if we make it into the top half. But that's not the point, is it? Ken never set us a target to finish here or there. We've just got to go out there, remember everything he taught us, and sing to the best of our ability. If we do Ken proud, that's all that matters.'

'Good shout,' said Vince.

The subject then turned to preparations for the following day, and their personal arrangements.

Hannah and Ben had travelled up with Danny, and were looking forward with excitement to seeing him sing in public for the very first time. Two days earlier, Hannah had revealed to Danny that she was pregnant.

They all congratulated Danny on his news, with Vince putting a consoling arm around him.

'No pressure there then, mate,' he said.

Spurred on by Danny's news, Vince decided to throw his own hat into the ring.

'Angie's looking at a couple of houses today, so she's travelling up early Saturday morning. We're buying a place together,' he said.

This was greeted by more cheers, a lot more ribbing, and a measure of disbelief.

'I'm gobsmacked,' said Neil. 'Domesticated, at last!'

'About time too, mate!' said Danny, who was especially happy for Vince. 'You're a very lucky man. I've seen the evidence at close quarters, and I know what I'm talking about!'

Neil was expecting Margaret to arrive some time tomorrow morning, also. She had taken the opportunity to visit an old friend in Pontefract, having travelled up to Yorkshire a couple of days earlier.

Henry was glad he had no such family pressures to deal with, though he secretly harboured some news of his own. Earlier in the week, he had received a letter from Cat. She must have found his current address from the booking details he had provided the last time he visited the island. The letter read:

Dear Henry,
At three o'clock on Saturday I will blow your pitch pipe to send you luck from the island.
    Remember, if your heart says fly, then fly. If your heart says sing, then sing.
Cat x

Henry couldn't recall telling Cat the exact date of the championships, but that would have been easy enough to find out. What he certainly hadn't told her, because he didn't know himself at the time, was that they were due on stage at exactly three o'clock on Saturday.

*

At the conference centre the following morning, the British barbershop community had gathered in droves. The auditorium was a thousand-seater, and the word was that it would be full. In lobbies, corridors, alcoves, and every available space, quartet singers gathered to practise or just sing for fun.

Familiar faces were everywhere. Guys from Maidenhead A Cappella, and from clubs around Britain, mingled with visiting barbershoppers from Europe, America, and a few from as far away as Australia.

Hannah said she never imagined how big and impressive the event would be, while Ben bounced up and down with excitement at her side. Danny was so happy, and as he hugged them, he felt a lump in his throat and an extra dose of butterflies in his stomach.

Vince was relieved to find that Angie had arrived safely, and she too seemed a bit taken aback by the chaos going on all around.

Hannah, Ben and Angie were introduced to the others, and then the three of them went off together to find Ben an ice cream.

Suddenly hoving into view was the considerable frame of Cliff "Tonsils" Thompson, who was wearing a yellow T-shirt bearing the slogan *"Life's a Pitch"*, red and white striped shorts, and white tennis shoes. He spoke very emotionally about Ken, and then wished them well in his usual style.

'I've had my eye on you guys ever since that first time you sang together. I knew there was something special back then, and I haven't changed my mind, fellas. You go knock 'em dead, and I'll be hollerin' for ya!'

James Pinter, himself a fine quartet singer and former gold medallist, came over to wish them luck, and told them that Ken would be watching over them.

Neil received a text message from Margaret, saying that she was on her way, was looking forward to watching the quartet, but that she probably wouldn't be able to meet up until afterwards. She signed off saying she was very proud of her youngest son.

Finally, they made their way through the throng to the performers' area and checked in. Then they headed for the changing area, and began the now familiar routine of getting ready for the stage.

In the warm-up room, they sang through the opening bars of their two contest songs a few times, and then saved their voices as much as possible.

Ten minutes before they were due to be called, they formed a huddle. For once, Vince didn't complain.

Neil spoke.

'This is it. We're ready. Breathe slowly, together. Let the nerves go. Remember Ken's last words to us. *I know you will succeed, because you have found The Fifth Voice.* Let's go, guys.'

Neil led them on to the stage in front of a packed house, and the audience went wild.

It took about fifteen minutes to leave the performers' area, during which time Neil received a call from Margaret. She sounded delighted by their performance and she said she was waiting at the front of house.

Neil spotted his mother in the crowd, and rushed towards her. Just as he reached her, she stepped aside, and there stood his father. He had tears in his eyes. He held out his arms, and they embraced. Neither of them said a word.

After the preliminary announcements, the auditorium fell silent as the MC prepared to deliver the results.

First the award for best senior quartet.

Then the award for best junior quartet.

Then the award for best novice quartet.

'From Maidenhead A Cappella...Neil, Henry, Danny and Vince...From The Edge!'

To their enormous surprise and delight, they had won the prize for best rookies. Just twelve months together and they were the best new quartet in Britain.

It took Vince about a minute to suggest that it was altogether possible that they were the *only* new quartet in Britain, in which case they had won from a starting line-up of one. The others laughed, but they were all so proud.

Then they watched the presentation to the third placed quartet, who were called to the stage to receive their bronze medals and make a brief acceptance speech.

Then came the award for second place – the silver medal quartet.

And the big surprise.

'In second place...your silver medal quartet...from Maidenhead A Cappella...Neil, Henry, Danny and Vince... From The Edge!'

They couldn't believe their ears. They leapt out of their seats, jumped up and down, and hugged each other in wild celebration.

In a blur, they somehow made their way to the stage to receive their medals, and they bowed to the audience, who were cheering them all the way.

Danny spotted Ben in Hannah's arms, waving a blue-and-white scarf.

Vince pointed to a cardboard sign being held up by none other than Cliff "Tonsils" Thompson. It read *I Knew It, Fellas!*.

Then, amid the mayhem, Neil stepped up to the microphone. He cleared his throat as the room fell silent.

'Thank you all so much. We're stunned by this. Twelve months ago, we didn't even exist. Danny hadn't even sung in public before, let alone sing lead in a quartet. And now here we are, British silver medallists...'

Neil looked into the audience and saw Bella's smiling face. Fighting back tears, he continued.

'…and we owe it all to one person…a much loved person who, as you all know, was taken from us recently. He was our inspiration, and we miss him dearly. This is for Ken…our Fifth Voice.'

Epilogue

After the celebrations, and as they returned to everyday life, the question "what next?" hung in the air. They had achieved so much, and exceeded their own expectations by a long way. And each of them had big responsibilities and challenges in their private lives that needed attending to.

And yet, they couldn't just leave it there. They were bound together by a special chemistry. They all agreed that the quartet had to continue, and they felt that Ken was looking on in approval.

Neil and George put the past behind them, and were able to rebuild their relationship. Margaret was content in the knowledge that it's what Robert would have wanted.

Henry's divorce from Jenny was completed without a hitch, and they remained friends. Henry continued to visit the island, where he and Cat became even better friends.

Danny and Hannah presented Ben with a baby sister, who had no choice but to become an Evertonian.

Vince and Angie announced their engagement, and the quartet sang at the celebration party – probably for much longer than the other guests would have wanted. For the time being, Vince's wheelchair remained unused.